MUIR'S BLOOD

By Charles Larson

MUIR'S BLOOD

CHARLES LARSON

PUBLISHED FOR THE CRIME CLUB BY
DOUBLEDAY & COMPANY, INC.
GARDEN CITY, NEW YORK
1976

All of the characters in this book
are fictitious, and any resemblance
to actual persons, living or dead,
is purely coincidental.

ISBN 0-385-12033-8
Library of Congress Catalog Card Number 76–18357
Copyright © 1976 by Charles Larson
All Rights Reserved
Printed in the United States of America
First Edition

For Pearl and Frank, my sister and my brother in everything but the minor matter of blood.

PROLOGUE

Toward noon the showers stopped and the washed day grew chilly and brilliant. A yellow Dodge full of college men and women splashed past Muir and was gone before he could ask anyone where the hospital was. He leaned against a splintered bench, determined not to vomit. On an old lawn under an oak tree a California child, swathed from head to foot against the breeze, stared at him out of feverish eyes.

"Hospital," Muir said, and threw up again.

The child began to run. Thoroughly ashamed of himself, Muir tried to kick leaves over the mess he'd made. He was a thin-chested, shy man, nearly bald, forty-two years old. He believed he knew where the trouble lay. He'd been abusing his ulcer, drinking and fretting, and here was the retributive result. Muir had a strong Scottish sense of debt and payment, although the tit demanded for this particular tat alarmed him. Everything between his throat and his lower belly was alive with pain; he already had befouled himself; the stench was dreadful.

On the campus to his left, church bells pealed joyously. A bicyclist in a plastic raincoat wobbled by. "Help," Muir said.

The bicyclist stopped, bracing her foot in a puddle, aghast.

"Please," Muir went on. "When I was in school here, years ago, I remember a hospital on this—"

"A what?"

"Where's the hospital?"

"Moved. It's around the corner now. Just down there."

"I'll never make it," Muir said. "Can you—"

But the cyclist had pushed off. From time to time she cast a look of absorbed disbelief over her shoulder at Muir, who continued to wave dispiritedly at her. He understood her attitude even while he deplored it. It had been sunny in Hollywood when he'd set out, so he'd come away without a cap or topcoat or even adequate shoes. Now, in his malodorous extremity, he stood before God and man in a patched pair of bell-bottoms and a grayish blood-spotted sweat shirt marked STOLEN FROM NFB PRODUCTIONS, and he knew in his heart that he wouldn't have given anyone who looked like that the time of day, much less aid and comfort.

He picked up his overnight bag wearily. The wind off the San Gabriels penetrated his sweat shirt and smelled of snow. *Just down there* might have been in China for all the faith he had in his strength now. Hiccuping, he held his stomach between his forearms and slid one foot after the other up the root-buckled sidewalk. His left leg ached.

And for a subliminal second he was ten again, surrounded by flames, hearing his own skin hiss and crackle. He caught at a hedge for support. My God, how many years had it been since he'd thought of all that? Outside of nightmares? They'd lived on El Centro then, in a flat Spanish bungalow surrounded by avocado trees and jasmine. He'd concentrate on the jasmine . . .

Doggedly he slid his right foot forward. His left.

His left leg squirmed and ached . . .

"Grab him!" someone shouted, and "Grab him, grab him!" they all kept yelling. "He's caught fire!"

Well, naturally, the first question everyone asked once he'd been put out was what in Christ's name he's been doing, but Muir told so many muddled stories through his facial bandages that even his brother Emmett, who'd lit him, began to breathe again.

"It was Emmett, wasn't it," his father said to Muir at the end of his sixth week in bed.

Most of the bandages were gone by that time. Muir's hair had grown back in spotty clumps; his forehead and cheeks were a tender piglet pink, but the specialists were optimistic; there'd be no scarring to speak of, they prophesied. His left leg alone gave them concern. Male nurses worked on it daily, stretching it with weights, oils, and massage. "Emmett," he muttered vaguely. "Was Emmett there?"

The old man, a motion picture studio barber who resembled Grover Cleveland, sat with his thumbs in his vest pockets, one heavy calf across the other knee, waggling his polished shoe. "Come on now, Chettie," he said. "I found the cigar stubs. You were all out back, puffing away—you, Spencer, Emmett—everybody but the baby. Eh?"

"My leg aches," Muir said.

"Did he mean to kill you or was he just horsing around?"

"Who?"

"I'm waiting, Chester," said his father.

"I can't remember what happened," Muir said. "Everything went black."

"Bullshit," said his father.

"I was playing with some matches—"

"Lighting cigars."

"No—just—"

"Who suggested this party? Emmett?"

"No—"

"Was Emmett there?"

"No."

"Which of your brothers was there?"

"I was alone."

"They've both admitted they were in on it. Spencer put the flames out."

"I can't remember."

And so it went, thrust and parry, shift and shore-up, until the old man gave in and went home with another of his migraines. Muir learned later that he'd won more than a skirmish. Spencer brought him a circus chameleon on a delicate chain one Saturday, reporting at the same time that he'd overheard the old man asking a doctor if the pain could have affected his son's mind. While the doctor said he wasn't prepared to go quite that far, he did advise the old man to postpone his probe and to let shock, the merciful sedative, take its course.

"Shock," Muir's father jeered. "Shock didn't shut him up, guilt did. I told him I'd whip him bloody if I caught him smoking again. That's what he's afraid of. He wants to protect his damned behind."

Well, yes. His skin was valuable to him. But godlike judgments normally rest on misapprehensions, and so did this one. What Muir feared far worse than a few licks of the strap was the disclosure that he'd called his mother a bitch.

He'd never meant it; that ought to go without saying. Muir, more than any of the boys except Robert, the baby, loved his mother. He doted on her soft sweet voice and her long hair. He hung around when she was cooking. He drowsed in her bed and daydreamed of the old man's removal by death.

On the other hand, Emmett at thirteen loathed this same paragon clear down to his finger tips, which was a line he'd appropriated from a Bette Davis movie. He chewed on a cigar in the weeds behind the garage and called Muir a pansy, a nut who was queer for his own mama. Muir disgusted him, he said.

"Yeah?" Muir screamed. "Yeah?"

Spencer, the oldest, half-sick from the effects of his panatella, told them both to cut the crap and smoke up like men.

"You want to know who the nut is?" Muir screamed. "You're the nut, you balled-up son-of-a-bitch, you don't even know enough to come in out of the rain!"

The sudden silence should have warned him, but he was off and

I

The cottage sat at the dead end of Genesee, about Sunset, wrapped like a French hotel in perfumed vines. No one remembered how old it was; it may have been a farmhouse in Hollywood before *The Squaw Man* was shot, when rabbits plunged past the orange trees, and Los Angeles was half a dusty day's buggy ride away. Successive owners had altered a wall here, added a room there, extended a patio, tiled a balcony, dug a pool, until it all seemed, now, as unique and as beautiful as a fingerprint. "Coffee?" asked its mistress.

"Black," Blixen said, "please."

He had strolled into the shaded garden through the Dutch kitchen doors in an illogical attempt to spot the nightingale they'd heard singing all through luncheon.

"He won't be there," Irene had warned him. "Nightingales are invisible. You might as well expect to surprise the tooth fairy."

She was right, of course. There was no sound at all in the garden beyond the buzz of a displaced cicada, and even he fell silent as soon as Irene came drifting down the walk.

"Here," she said. "It isn't quite black. I added a little brandy."

"You spoil me."

"It's just the cheap stuff."

"Even so."

"You're looking," Irene said, "at your watch again."

Embarrassed, Blixen dropped his hand. "Was I, by God. It must be some kind of an occupational twitch. I don't think anything gets through to the brain. I'm never aware of it."

"Is your company shooting today?"

"Never on Saturdays, if we can help it. No. I couldn't be freer. It's a twitch."

Smiling and pale, Irene raised her cup, sipped, and sat on a weathered bench by a wild rose bush. She was a dark, long-limbed woman, ageless, perhaps forty, with ravaged eyes in a serene face. Blixen had seen the eyes at a TV Academy seminar, been haunted by them, and had introduced himself. Her name, she said, was Irene Nicholas. She was newly arrived from New York, an actor's agent. She confessed that she had no business whatsoever at the seminar. She wasn't a member of the Academy; a friend had lent her his card and it had been either that or *Stagg at Bay*, not much of a choice.

Blixen explained that *he* produced *Stagg at Bay*.

"Ah," Irene had said. "Well, you're not home watching it either, so there you are."

"Valid point," Blixen admitted.

"I really don't like private-eye programs much," Irene said, "though I do think you have a smasher of a star."

"Smith, or the girl?"

"Oh, Smith. You were lucky to find Murphy Smith. You don't pay him nearly enough."

Blixen had turned to regard her reflectively.

"He's left Griswold-Decker, you know," Irene went on. "He felt he was lost in so large an agency."

"And—you represent him now," Blixen ventured.

Her smile was sparkling. "Yes."

"I see."

"How nice it is that we met like this," Irene said. "I always like to have the ice broken before the formal meetings start."

Inside the auditorium, someone had begun rapping a gavel against a water pitcher and crossly requesting everyone to take his seat, and Irene had gotten halfway down the side aisle before Blixen could untrack himself. She sat at the end of an empty row and patted the place beside her. "Join me."

"Thank you," Blixen said. "*Formal* meetings? To discuss what?"

She seemed surprised. "Well—salary—justice. Reality."

"Ten thousand dollars an episode isn't just?"

"Well, is it? For the star of a series consistently first in its time slot?"

"And consistently thirtieth on the Nielsen list?"

"Oh, you'll be renewed."

"I can't tell you how how relieved the studio will be to hear it. Especially after losing three other series at mid-season."

She grinned at him. "It's true. I have spies at the network. Everyone over there adores Murf. Everyone wants him to be happy."

"And—how much do you imagine that would take?"

"To make Murf happy?" She peered at the stage, at the despondent panel there, the choleric chairman. "Oh, I'd think at least twice what he's getting now." She glanced at Blixen, who was regarding her with his chin in his hand. "By the way, I made an appointment to see your lawyer day after tomorrow—a Mr. Schreiber? Will you be there?"

"I'm afraid I wasn't invited."

"Well, it's not important, it'll just be a preliminary get-together," Irene said, "to clear away some of the underbrush." She smiled, put a gloved finger to her lips, cast a warning glance toward the podium, and sank back to listen.

Three days later, Blixen called Schreiber to ask how the meeting had gone, and Schreiber told him complacently that they were making progress.

"What the hell are you talking about, progress?" Blixen had exploded. "That contract still has two years to run! It's not negotiable."

"None of the important clauses are, no," Schreiber had said. "Certainly not."

"Wade—" Blixen had snapped, and then stopped. "All right, never mind. What's her number?"

But when he phoned, she said that she was just on her way to buy a lute from a man who sold guitars in the anteroom of a former massage parlor on Western Avenue, which made for a certain amount of merry confusion when the fleet was in, and she suggested that Blixen meet her there. She said that she'd invite Blixen to her own office, but unfortunately she shared it with a crazed accountant who was up to his neck in income tax returns and everything was bedlam.

Blixen looked for a moment at the telephone mouthpiece, and then said fine, he'd meet her at the guitar shop.

She was there before him, already testing the lute, her dark hair spread forward across her slender shoulders. She smiled and played Bach for him in a limpid Bream transcription, while the shop's owner was obliged to deal smartly with a sailor from San Pedro who had a discount card from the massage parlor. After that, Blixen had asked her what she was doing Saturday and she had said: "Nothing, come have a swim."

Bemused, Blixen said: "All right. What time?"

"Oh—noon? One o'clock? Here's the address."

She had scribbled something on a notepad, torn off the top sheet, and given it to him. He must still have looked a little addled because she had cocked her head and said: "Tell me something. If you were a grown woman, would you play those transparent games? Would you frown doubtfully and flip through an engagement calendar and then say you were sorry but Saturday was taken—when it wasn't?"

"No," Blixen said.

"I'm a grown woman," Irene said.

In the cloistered stillness the garden was as placid as a brush painting. The tip of an open sandal extended past the hem of Irene's ground-length robe; a loose silver chain spanned her waist, its free ends falling like spilled mercury into her shadowed lap. She turned to offer a remark to Blixen, but saw his expression and lifted her eyebrow instead. "What?" she asked.

"If I believed in time warps," Blixen said, "I'd swear this was Cornwall. It's a medieval afternoon."

"It comes of eating out of iron pots and hearing nightingales," Irene said.

"With a woman who plays the lute."

"It must have been a very still time then, too, don't you think? No radios, and none of that strange hum the freeways make . . . Can you believe we're in the heart of town? The trees muffle everything."

"How did you find the place?" Blixen asked.

"Oh, I didn't," Irene replied. "My husband stumbled across it before I came out from New York. It's really his house."

The cicada had grown used to their stationary voices; it commenced to tick now in a pink silk tree.

"I think I've startled you," Irene said.

"That's why I never play poker in Vegas," Blixen said. "I jump when I'm caught off-guard."

"Why were you caught off-guard?"

"I'm not sure. Too great a dependence on symbols? I've never seen you wear a ring."

"We're separated."

"Well, I'm pleased to hear that, at least."

"Yes, you wouldn't get along at all, the two of you. He's very good fixing engines and speaking at Chamber of Commerce luncheons. He's a Chrysler-Plymouth dealer. Romance to Curtis was always a can of beer and making love on the back seat. His friends keep saying he'll drop dead in his fat lady's arms doing that, but he won't. He's got a heart like a stallion. Nothing else like a stallion. Just the heart."

"How do you know she's fat?"

"Oh, I've met her. She's his secretary. She followed him when he bought the dealership out here. Great jovial Austrian girl with a laugh like Helen Traubel's. The odd thing is that I was glad to see them move in together. I can't imagine what I'm being bitchy about. When I finally realized he was serious, when I saw him leaving, I was so relieved I nearly fainted. I remember thinking that this must be what an LSD trip was like. I'd had to mother him for fifteen years. I hadn't realized how tired I was."

"Is the agency new?"

"Yes—I started it in New York, five years ago, when I thought the marriage had begun to crack. I love it."

"You're a lucky woman."

"You're the first man who's ever said so. If they've known Curtis, they want me to go back to him. They think we had a hell of a marriage. They can't understand what happened. The others—the ones I meet at the parties my friends throw—always want me to be something else. Listener—adjunct—mother—child—something."

"You're threatening them by being yourself," Blixen said. "It's the sign of the maverick. People have been jailed for it."

The sun emerged from a mottled cloud; a breeze sent the roses quivering past Irene's cheek. "Nils," she began, and stopped.

"Yes?"

But she hadn't yet gotten a grip on whatever question she'd thought to ask. "Never mind," she said.

"Are you cold? Shall we go inside?"

She took a breath. "Nils—why did you come here today?"

"Because I enjoy your company," Blixen said. "You offered me an opportunity to know you better, and I wanted to do that."

"Are you surprised that we haven't talked about Murf's contract yet?"

"We'll get to it sooner or later. It's important to both of us."

"As important as—getting to know each other?"

"Ah." Blixen tugged at the tip of his nose. "I see. I think I see. You wonder if doing business with an attractive woman is basically a sexual encounter to me."

"Is it?"

"No," Blixen said.

Irene rose, moved down a line of cracked flagstones to the pool's edge, where the sun floated like a bitten peach in the ruffled water. Almost to herself, she said: "What a complicated person you are."

"Comp—? You can't mean it."

"Don't you think you are?"

"About as much as a Mickey Mouse watch."

She pushed her hair away from her eyes, a curiously young and distracted gesture. "Then maybe it's me . . . To tell the truth—"

Inside the house, a phone began to ring, mindless, measured, strident. The cicada in the pink silk tree broke off, but took up his refrain again in a tentative way when the phone went right on ringing.

At last Irene said: "There simply cannot be a ruder sound on earth than that . . . How do you feel about telephones?"

"I place them second only to automobiles as man's heaviest cross," Blixen said.

"Does anyone know you're here?"

"Schreiber does. But he's gone sailing."

"Then it's Curtis," said Irene. She swiveled her lovely head. "Hang up, Curtis," she said.

The phone stopped obediently.

Confounded, Irene glanced back at Blixen.

"Maybe you've never been direct enough with Curtis," Blixen suggested.

"Can that be?" She folded her arms under her breasts. "Now I'm cold," she said. She shivered, though she made no move to return to the house. Miles above them a plane slid through the brassy sky, slow and soundless as a meteor.

"Irene?" Blixen murmured, but she wouldn't look away from the floating sun. A pulse pounded in her throat; her cheek against the backs of his fingers was cool and soft; she inclined her head to catch his hand against her shoulder.

When he kissed her closed eyes, she whispered: "My God, how lovely it is not to be twenty again."

"If you can understand that, you *are* a grown woman."

"I told you."

Her mouth accepted his; her arms rested like a dancer's across his back.

"Nils . . ." she said.

"Yes."

"I still intend to negotiate a fair contract for Murphy."

"He has a fair contract."

"Not compared to the new one you'll write for him."

"He'll have to live with the one he signed."

"We'll see," she said.

II

They lay lazily across the sun-streaked bed, hand in hand, like two slain sailors on a battered beach. The wide old room was cool and fragrant, open to the day on three windowed sides. "There," Irene whispered. "Listen. Hear him?"

"Hear what?"

"The nightingale. He's been singing like that for half an hour."

"You realize it's the wrong time of year for nightingales—the wrong time of day—the wrong continent."

"Yes."

"All I could hear was you," Blixen said.

Her mouth curled against his cheek. "How friendly an act that is. Don't you think so? How *sane*. How breathtaking—"

The downstairs phone burst into life.

"God in heaven," Irene groaned.

"Isn't it in the kitchen?" Blixen asked. "How can we hear it way up here?"

"I suppose we left the doors open—" She lifted herself on her elbows. "Curtis, hang *up!*" she said.

But the bell continued to clang and jangle.

"Just ignore it," Irene said.

Eyes closed, Blixen counted: "Thirteen—fourteen—fifteen—"

"Well," Irene said, "he's not going to quit and that's all there is to that." Grumpily, she maneuvered on her feet, hands, and bottom to the end of the bed.

"Do you have to go all the way downstairs?" Blixen asked. "Aren't there a couple of wires up here I could rip out?"

"There's a silent extension in the bathroom." She padded across the room. "If this turns out to be some dithering person who wants me to subscribe to the *Times,* I'll get her name and I'll track her down and kill her." She snapped the bathroom light on; a dozen tanned Irenes stood reflected in the opposing mirrors, left hands on naked left hips. "Hello!"

Smiling, Blixen contemplated the multiple images, remembering the jealous grip of the long legs, the joy . . .

"Well—" Something had jolted her. "Yes, he is here, but he can't come to the phone right now. He's too excited to talk."

Blixen shot upright.

"Oh, of course I'm kidding," Irene told the telephone. "We girls have to do something to while the tedious hours away. Actually this is his answering service. Is there a message?" She drew her head back. "Socrates?"

"Hold it," Blixen said.

"Hold it," Irene told the telephone and covered the mouthpiece. "It's either a gag or a drunk," she muttered to Blixen. "Nobody's named Socrates."

"My production manager is," Blixen said. He thrust his feet back and forth beneath the bed.

"What are you doing?" Irene asked.

"I'm looking for my shoes."

"What for?"

"Oh, Christ, I don't know," Blixen said, but he persisted until he'd found them and slipped them on, and then he strode into the bathroom.

"You look so virile and sheepish," Irene said. "Like the lead in a Danish blue movie. It's the shoes."

Blixen turned his back on the mirrors and accepted the telephone from her. "Hello, Socrates. Nils."

"I'm very confused," Kapralos said. He sounded distant and dreadfully sad, his voice draped in perpetual black, like his gaunt body. "She said—"

"How did you get this number?" Blixen asked.

"Well. I called your place and there was no answer, so I eventually thought of phoning Wade Schreiber and his secretary had it. The number. I've been trying to track you down all afternoon."

"If it's a production problem, I don't want to hear about it."

"Well, it is and it isn't," Kapralos said. "Or rather, one is and one—"

"Give me the non-production one first."

"Chet's dead."

Irene, brushing her hair at the door, shot Blixen a queer, inquisitive look, and he realized that he must have made a subconscious response of some sort, a tic or a grunt. She lay the flat of the brush against her throat, her eyes dark and still.

"Are you there?" Kapralos asked.

"Chet, you say," Blixen repeated.

"Chet Muir. I'm out here with Wanda now. She teaches a quilting class on Saturdays but luckily they had her number."

"Who did?"

"Children's Hospital in San Urbano."

"I don't know where San Urbano is—"

"Foothill Freeway," Kapralos said. "Pasadena, Arcadia, San Urbano."

"Right, of course," Blixen said. "All those colleges."

"That's it," Kapralos said. "Anyway, she tried to contact some of the family, but they were scattered to the four winds, so she called me. But Chettie was dead when we got here. That was around—oh, two, two-thirty—"

"I just can't seem to zero in on this," Blixen said. "I suppose it was his heart?"

"They don't know," Kapralos said. "Wanda wants to talk to you, Nils. Here's Wanda. Hang on."

Blixen transferred the phone to his left ear, lowered the top of the toilet seat, and sat down. Irene had vanished; soon he could hear the click of hangers in the bedroom closet, the slippery whisper of silk.

"Hi, Nils," Wanda Muir said. Her low voice was raw and exhausted. The picture it evoked was of a bludgeoned woman, back bent, straight brown hair hiding the high-cheek-boned face, ice-cold hand gripping the telephone too hard.

"Sweetheart, I'm so terribly, terribly sorry," Blixen said.

"Can you believe this?"

"Not yet."

"They didn't even call me until he was dead. He came in here to ask for help and they told him to get *out!*"

"Go ahead and cry . . ."

"Everybody else tells me not to."

"Screw everybody else," Blixen said.

Crying, Wanda said: "And, Nils, I think they've robbed him!"

"Now, now, now," Kapralos kept saying in the background.

"He cashed his check Friday," Wanda said. "Four hundred and fourteen dollars, and there isn't a cent left."

"Are you sure he had the money with him?"

"Sure he had it, I know he had it. We went out Friday night and I saw it."

"Was he wearing the same suit today?"

"No, he just looked like hell. He had a sweat shirt on—these terrible pants—"

"Could he have left the money in the other suit then?"

There was a moment's silence. "The other suit," Wanda said vaguely. "The Friday suit. Well, he *could* have . . ."

"Where's your daughter?" Blixen asked. "Could your daughter check this out for you?"

"No, she went to the public library," Wanda said. "Gail's keeping an eye on her. I *hope*." The frayed voice shook. "I left a note, I *told* Gail to—to—"

"Who's Gail?"

"Gail. My sister-in-law. Robert's wife. They live next door."

"Oh, certainly . . ."

"It's been an absolute nightmare," Wanda said. "I couldn't reach *anybody*. Robert's gone, Emmett's gone, Spencer's on location, the old man's in the hospital—"

"Again?"

"Yes, they took him away this afternoon. Who in the world would have dreamed that Chet would have died before his dad? Now we'll have to tiptoe around about that. Nobody'll want to upset him. Nils, I just—I could just—"

"Kill all of them for putting this whole mess on your shoulders," Blixen said.

"I must be crazy—"

"You must be normal."

"How can it be normal," Wanda asked, "to want to stand here and yell and cry and scream every dirty word I ever thought of? They'd throw me in the booby hatch." But she sounded a little less driven.

"Anyhow," Blixen said, "after you've yelled and cried and screamed a while, you go on home and look through the Friday suit —will you do that?"

"Oh, for crying out loud," Wanda moaned. "I'll bet it's gone. The cleaner comes three times a week. And that's the suit I want Chettie buried in, Nils—"

"Does he come on Saturdays?"

"Saturdays, Tuesdays, and Thursdays."

"And what's the name of the company?"

"Company," Wanda repeated. "Uh—it's the big one there on Fountain—"

"LoSordo's?"

"LoSordo's," Wanda said.

"What about an undertaker?"

"Oh, I don't care—"

"Klein Brothers?"

"All right, but there's a problem—"

"Don't worry about the suit. I'll get the suit and take it out to the mortuary myself—"

"No, it's worse than that. They won't be able to pick up the body—"

"Why not?"

"Well, the authorities won't release it," Wanda said. "They want to do an autopsy first. I asked them not to—I can't stand the thought of them cutting him up like that—but they insisted—"

"Normal procedure," Blixen assured her. "Nothing to worry about." And yet for the first time, the hair on the nape of his neck stirred.

"It was his ulcer," Wanda said. "I begged him and begged him to get it taken care of, I said, Chettie, your dad's had cancer for three years, maybe you can inherit a weakness for that, but oh no—"

"Do you know where they took him?"

"Well, it was an L.A. County truck—"

"Downtown, then. I'll look into it and get back to you as soon as I know anything. Is Socrates there?"

"He's coming. Just a second."

"You sound better, Wanda."

"You're lucky you can't see me. I look like something Jack the Ripper just abandoned. Here. Good-by, Nils."

"Good-by, sweetheart."

"Yes, Nils," Kapralos said.

"I don't want her left alone," Blixen said.

"No, no."

"If the daughter isn't home when you get there—what's the daughter's name?"

"Jennifer."

"If Jennifer isn't home, ask a neighbor to come in. . . . Can you contact the rest of Chet's family?"

"Yes, I'll do that," Kapralos said.

"We'll shut down production for the funeral—whenever it is—probably Tuesday."

"Yes," Kapralos said cautiously, "well, you know we're a day behind on that particular episode already—"

"Then we'll be two days behind," Blixen said.

"Check," Kapralos said.

"All right—is that all?"

"Do you want to skip the second little problem?"

"What second little—" Blixen began, and then remembered and groaned. "Yes. Skip it."

"I don't think we can," Kapralos said.

"Make an effort," Blixen said. "I'll see—"

"Leo canceled our Monday location," Kapralos interrupted rapidly. "We're back inside for the rest of the picture."

The silence lengthened.

"Hello?" Kapralos said.

"Leo did what?" Blixen murmured. Leo was Leo Newmarket, dapper, handsome, small, acid-tongued, a private pilot, a championship swimmer, vice-president in charge of physical production for the studio.

"Canceled—"

"For what reason?"

"Cost. I told him you were particularly keen on the trestle—using the trestle—because of the view—but he said by the time you got a crew in and out of that ravine, it'd cost another thirty-five thousand dollars and he wasn't going to stand for that. He said he tried to phone you this morning but he couldn't locate you."

"What's Leo's number?" Blixen asked in a tone of terrible calm.

"Leo's not home," Kapralos replied. "He's with Mr. Todd."

"Thank you," Blixen said.

"Uh," Kapralos said, "what do you want me to do about—"

"Have you rescinded the Monday location call?"

"Not yet. I wanted to talk—"

"Let it go."

"Let it go," Kapralos repeated.

"Let it go," Blixen said. "We're shooting in the ravine. We're shooting the trestle."

"Right," Kapralos said. "See, the trouble is that I'm more or less in the middle here—and—"

"Don't worry about it," Blixen said. "I'll handle it."

"Good," Kapralos said. "Okay. Good-by, Nils."

"Good-by."

He depressed the telephone bar and sat for a moment with the cool telephone earpiece aginst his cheek, his eyes closed, thinking about Chet, and then he dialed Arthur Todd's number. Irene glanced into the room and smiled a little when he smiled automatically at her, and then disappeared.

"Mr. Todd's residence," the telephone said.

"Hello, Pauline," Blixen said. "Nils Blixen. Is Arthur there?"

"Oh, hi," Pauline said. "Yes, sir, I think so. Hang on. Lemme look."

Something clicked, the extension on the patio probably, and Todd's fog-horn voice said: "Okay, I've got it, hang up," and then: "Hello? Nils?"

"Hello, Arthur."

"Well, well, well," Todd boomed. "Speak of the goddamn devil. We were just talkin' about you, boy."

"Is that a fact."

"If the head of the studio says it's a fact, it's a fact," Todd said. "No matter what it is." The big voice was at once tentative and hearty, the voice of a man whose mouth was one wide grin but whose eyes were cautious and preoccupied. Blixen could imagine the corpulent old body stretched like a beached whale in a canvas lounge. There would be a Tom Collins in one liver-spotted hand, a blue yachting cap jammed over the white hair . . . "You'll never guess who I got sittin' right across from me here," Todd said.

"Gerald Ford," Blixen said.

"Jesus Christ, that's eerie," Todd said. "It's wrong, but it's eerie. No, Leo's here. Were your ears burnin'?"

"Something was," Blixen said.

"What?"

"Socrates called."

"Ah," Todd said.

"Tell Leo we're going to go ahead at the trestle."

"Uh—" Todd said. "Trestle. Well, wait a minute—"

"Put him on," Blixen said. "I'll tell him."

"Yeah," Todd said, and crushed a hand over the mouthpiece and ordered someone in a muffled growl to take the phone.

"Nils?" Leo Newmarket said.

"Hello, Leo."

"Kapralos must have found you."

"He found me," Blixen said.

Leo's flat faint tone was calm, detached, a vice-president's tone. "Any problems?"

"None that I can see," Blixen said. "The story hangs on the trestle —there's no story without it—so of course we'll have to go ahead."

"Oh no, you won't," Leo said. "Go ahead—with what? The trestle?"

"The trestle."

"Oh no, you won't."

"Oh yes, we will."

"Oh no, you won't!"

"Leo," Blixen said, "I can keep this up as long as you can."

"Oh no, you can't!" shouted Leo.

"He's thinkin' about the view," Todd rumbled in the background. "He don't want to lose the view—"

"View, view!" Leo shouted. "Who wants views? That's what's *wrecking* TV! And just how do you expect to transport a crew up there?"

"All I'll need—" Blixen began.

"You'll need a camera—"

"Hand-held Arriflex."

"No dialogue at this trestle?"

"We'll loop it."

Leo laughed wildly.

"Leo," Blixen said, "they can be in and out in two hours. Master. Close on Stagg. Reverse to the girl. Quick insert of the bomb. You never see the train. Never see—"

"Yes, two hours there," Leo shouted, "and I doubt that, but let's say two hours, but first what? An hour to climb in, an hour back, two more hours on the road from the studio, two hours back, *six* hours, and you haven't shot one foot of film! Add *your* two hours and you've got a full day! Do you have any idea of what that's going to cost? With *luck,* thirty-five thousand! And thirty-five thousand is one seventh of your entire budget! You can't—"

"Oh, Leo, for Christ's sake," Blixen said wearily.

"Yes, for Christ's sake, for Christ's sake!" Leo cried. "All right, I'm sorry, but that's the name of the game, *budget!* You know it. I know it—"

"*I* know it," Arthur Todd said.

"Arthur knows it," bellowed Leo.

"There's more," Blixen said. "I'm also going to have to suspend production on Tuesday."

In the lengthening silence, Blixen heard Todd say: "What'd he tell you?" and then: "Here, gimme the phone," and then: "What'd you tell him?"

"I said I was going to have to shut down on Tuesday."

"Listen, I want you to stop toying with this man," Todd said. "You're teasing a man who never did have a sense of humor. He's sitting over there as white as a sheet."

"Can't be helped," Blixen said. "Tell him we'll resume on Wednesday."

"I think you're serious," Todd said.

"Certainly I'm serious."

"You can't be," Todd said. "Overhead goes on just the same, whether you're shooting or not. Salaries have to be paid just the same. You're already a day behind—you say you want to spend an extra thirty-five thousand on a trestle—and now you want to add another thirty, thirty-five in idle money. It's out of the question. If you're having script problems, forget the script. Tell 'em to ad lib it. Nobody knows the difference anyway—"

"It's not the script," Blixen said. "Chet Muir died today. They'll have the funeral Tuesday."

"Who's Chet Muir?" Todd asked.

Blixen closed his eyes and massaged his tired neck. "That's the old Great-White-Father image, Art. He's your head cutter."

"Oh, *Muir!*" Todd said.

"What about him?" Leo asked in the background.

"Died today," Todd said.

"Muir? How?"

"How?" Todd asked Blixen.

"They're not sure," Blixen said. "They're performing an autopsy now."

"Was it drugs?" Todd asked.

"They don't know, Arthur," Blixen said.

"How old was he?"

"Early forties."

"And it wasn't an accident?"

"No."

"I'll bet you four hundred dollars to a nickel he was mixed up in some kind of hanky-panky," Todd said.

"Watch that soft heart of yours, Arthur," Blixen said. "I hate to see a strong man break down."

"Well, damn it," Todd snapped, "this is the wrong time for headlines."

"When's the right time?"

"The second the network's picked up your series for the new season."

"Don't encourage him," Leo said in the background. "One more new season and he'll bankrupt us."

"Where you goin'?" Todd asked.

Leo mumbled something and Todd said: "All right, but use the one upstairs, the main one don't flush," and then muttered: "I don't like that man's color," into the phone.

"Tell him I've cut the next show down to six speaking parts and four interiors. He'll recover."

"It isn't just him," Todd said. "The boys have been on his neck again."

"What boys? The Board?"

"The Board, the Chairman. I guess they've got a point. The Motion Picture Division's making money. The Record Division makes money. The *Book* Division makes money, for God's sake. TV's dragging the whole operation down. The Chairman wants to dump it."

"He wanted to dump it last year."

"I think he means it this time," Todd said. "It's that dirty phrase *deficit financing*. He can't understand why we spend a quarter of a million dollars on an hour episode and then license it to a network for two hundred and six thousand. I said I couldn't understand it either. It's hard to argue with a man when he's right."

"He's not right," Blixen said. "*Stagg*'ll make money if it goes into a third season. Foreign sales—domestic syndication—"

"If."

"That's why I'm spending the money, Arthur."

"Explain that to the Chairman."

"I will."

"You'll have to. On the fifteenth."

Blixen frowned. "What happens on the fifteenth?"

"Armageddon," Todd replied. "Secret pre-stockholder-meeting meeting. At Catalina, can you believe that? It'll be bloody, boy. I want you there. Particularly if somebody gets the idea that *Stagg*'s border line."

"I can't pull a renewal out of my hat, Arthur."

"All I want you to do is radiate hope."

"How about a little cautious optimism?"

There was a moment's heavy breathing. Then: "Just between you and me and the gatepost," Todd said, "what do you think its chances are?"

"Right now? Fifty-fifty."

"Based on what?"

"Certain gut feelings. Certain things I've heard. Certain facts I know about Pablo."

"Throw the last one out," Todd said. "Nobody can figure network presidents."

"You're probably right."

"*What* facts?" Todd asked.

"I know Pablo's very high on the show—"

"Because of Murf. He likes Murf."

"Whatever."

"No, don't dismiss that," Todd said. "I've seen Pablo hold onto border-line shows year in and year out because he had a warm spot in his heart for the star. On the other hand, this is a man who'd cancel the Second Coming if he ever heard anything funny about Jesus."

"I thought nobody could figure network presidents?"

"Nobody but me. That's why I get the big money."

"Of course."

"So—is Murf all right?"

"How do you mean?"

"Well—is he happy?"

Blixen glanced toward the empty doorway. "Yes, I think so."

"Got all his marbles?"

"More or less."

"I mean," Todd persisted, "he's not about to run for Congress or start molestin' little girls or nothin' like that, is he?"

"No way."

"Well, you keep him healthy and out of the headlines until the twentieth, and I think we got a chance."

"Why the twentieth?"

"Network locks in next year's schedules on the twentieth."

"In the meantime," Blixen said, "I'm going to shoot the trestle Monday and stop production for the funeral Tuesday. I take it you have no objection."

After a moment Todd said: "You're a real gambler, ain't you. I like that. I don't understand it, but I like it."

"Where's the gamble? The picture has to have an ending—"

"You could rewrite the ending, shoot on Tuesday, save us all a bundle, be a big hero—"

"No heroes if the series is dropped, Arthur."

"No," Todd agreed reluctantly, "no heroes. But a little co-operation now might salvage you a little something later. Like—backing for a new series?"

"It might."

"By the same token," Todd continued, "a cancellation coming on the heels of this last big deficit—well, that'd be all she wrote, boy. The end of the TV operation. The end of NFB Productions. The end of both of us. Believe me."

"I believe you, Arthur."

"And you still want your goddamn trestle?"

"Still want my goddamn trestle."

"You've got it," Todd said, "numbskull."

III

After the phone clicked in his ear, Blixen continued to sit lumpishly on the toilet top until Irene touched his shoulder. He raised his eyes. She'd put on a light lemon-yellow shirt and a pair of faded denim pants and she was holding a torn piece of note paper for him to read. Blankly he contemplated the unfamiliar telephone number scribbled there.

"Klein's Mortuary," she said.

"Ah."

"I can dial it for you if you like."

Blixen shook his head. "The coroner's holding the body. I'll have to drop by there first."

He trailed her into the bedroom, passionless and pensive, remembering the oddest things about Muir. His cheap dentures. His brief insubordinations . . .

"It's strange," Irene said, "but I never think of myself as curious until I overhear one end of a telephone conversation like that."

Rousing himself, Blixen said: "I'm sorry. The first part was bad news about a man I work with. A cutter named Muir."

"And he lived in San Urbano?"

"No, Hollywood. I have no idea what he was doing in San Urbano. Apparently, though, he felt sick and went into a hospital and they turned him away."

"Oh, dear . . ."

"I'll have to see if I can find out what happened."

"Were you close?"

Blixen buckled his belt, extended his arms backward for the shirt she held. "That's almost the worst part of it," he said, "we weren't. I didn't like him much. I don't think anyone did. He was very arrogant about his work and his work wasn't very good." Blixen knotted his tie, saw that he had botched the job, and yanked it apart again. He recalled with a sense of exasperation how square and even the ends of Muir's ties always had been, as if he had put them on in the same inexact way every other man did and then had chopped them off with a scissors. "Chettie annoyed people," he said.

"Why?"

"I'm not sure. There was something underhanded about him.

There'd always be one or two horrible cuts in his first assembly. Bones to throw the producer. Do you understand?"

Irene nodded. "Mistakes for you to find. So that you'd leave the rest of the film alone. Children do that."

"Well, that's what Chettie was, a great big, balding child." The old floor creaked when Blixen moved away; Irene walked beside him into the musty hall and down the shallow stairs. "Maybe that's what put me off about him."

"Don't you like children?"

"Not the ones I frighten."

Grinning, Irene said: "What?"

"I don't know *why* I frighten them," Blixen went on. "I set them on my knee and laugh like hell, but it doesn't do any good."

"Poor old Frankenstein monster . . ."

"You don't think it could be these pegs coming out of my neck?"

"Never. Who'd notice, if you didn't keep drawing everyone's attention to them?"

"That's true."

"Anyway—you frightened Chettie—is that it?"

"Everyone he set up as a father image frightened Chettie," Blixen said. "Especially his real father."

"Was he a frightening man? The father?"

"Oh, not very. At least not to an outsider." They dawdled through the cool well of the living room, through the pools of sunlight that shone on the bare beautiful floor and the leather sofa, the edge of a white area rug, a piano bench, a kaleidoscopically colored crystal ashtray. They searched for objects to delay them, like schoolbound children poking into mud puddles.

"Tell me about the father."

"Um—big man . . . Stout. The kind of uncle you'd pick to play Santa Claus. Or he used to be. All the air's gone out of him now. He's been sick for several years. He was born in Hollywood, are you ready for that?"

"When?"

"Nineteen four."

"*Was* there a Hollywood in nineteen four?"

"Oh, absolutely," Blixen said. "It was ten years old by that time. A man named Wilcox bought a hundred and twenty acres out here to retire on. His wife picked the name."

"Pretty. Hollywood."

"Yes. Anyway, the old man was born on a farm near Las Palmas and Sunset. He was seven when the first studio was opened. He started shining shoes outside the old Paramount lot and he's been part of the industry ever since."

"Not as a shoe shiner?"

"Barber. Someone—I forget who—DeMille, Lasky, Zukor—someone—helped him through school. He loved the business. He married a secretary at Fox, and he saw to it that all four of his boys got studio jobs."

"Like an old Catholic," Irene said, "dedicating his sons to the priesthood."

"Very much like that."

"Are they all cutters?"

"No, Chettie's the only one he put into editing. Spencer's a stunt man, Emmett composes and conducts, and Robert's an assistant director."

Irene stopped short, eyebrows arched. "He *put* Chettie into editing?"

"That's what Chet told me."

"And Chet didn't *object?*"

"I don't think he cared much. He needed a job—his dad had connections—"

Irene stared at him, and then shook her head and preceded him through the entry hall toward the front door.

"See what comes of fearing your father?" Blixen said.

"Ghastly," Irene said.

"The old man even chose Chettie's wife for him—in a way."

"Good grief."

"Very pretty girl. She was a contract player at Universal for a while after the war—"

"Would I know her?" Irene asked. "I watch the late late shows . . ."

"Well, maybe you would then," Blixen said. "Wanda Mills?"

"Oh, *certainly!* Slender, doomed sort of child?"

"That's Wanda."

"Well, how did—"

"Well," Blixen said, "Chet was going with an older woman at the time and the old man objected."

"Why?"

"I suppose it violated some private image he had of the perfect marriage."

"The perfect *movie* marriage."

"Probably. At any rate, he asked Emmett if Emmett knew any eligible younger women, and Emmett knew Wanda, so—" Blixen shrugged.

Aghast, Irene said, "But—didn't Wanda have anything to say about this?"

"Well, Chettie had all his hair in those days—"

"What has *hair* got to do with it! Did they love each other?"

"Now who's talking about movie marriages?"

"What?"

"Did you love Curtis?"

She raised her finger and then thought about it and closed her mouth. She pulled the door open and walked beside him down a winding path to a honeysuckle-covered gate. "Okay," she said, "but it all sounds awfully Asiatic to me. Whether they lived happily ever after or not."

"They didn't," Blixen said.

"There, you see?"

"I think Chet was jealous," Blixen mused. He stood looking over the top of the gate at a mustard-colored dog who had stopped to wet magisterially on his tire. "I remember our first year's wrap party. We'd had a hard season and we hadn't gotten our pickup yet. Everyone was a little tense, a little depressed. . . . Anyway, Wanda went with one of the gaffers to get more ice and when they got back, Chet threw a glass of white wine in her face."

"Sweet," Irene said.

"He was drunk."

"Sober enough, though, to pick the woman instead of the man to insult. He sounds like a coward along with everything else."

"Not a physical one," Blixen said. "He loved to fight when he'd been drinking. I saw Chettie deck his brother Robert once in the men's room at Chasen's."

"Are you serious? *Deck* him?"

"Blood all over everything—"

"Well—what was the fight about?"

"I have no idea. It happened just as I walked in. Chet was gone by the time I got Robert cleaned up, and Robert wouldn't talk about it."

Irene shuddered. "Are you sure this man died in a hospital? He sounds like a perfect candidate for murder, doesn't he?"

High above them, a rising wind sent the dead brown palm fronds clashing against each other like curved old swords. "Doesn't he," Blixen murmured. And then again: "Doesn't he . . ."

He turned and smiled and kissed her hand and her hair and her mouth. "Well. I'll call you tomorrow."

"Not tomorrow. I'm going to Disneyland."

"All right, Monday."

"You won't want to postpone the meeting?"

Blixen shook his head and then paused halfway across the street to frown back curiously. "What meeting?"

Her eyes were amused. "Didn't Wade tell you. Eleven o'clock.

Your office. To discuss whether Murf stays or leaves. But if you think—"

"No, no," Blixen said. He watched the dog trot heavily off down the street. "No, we'll have to get it settled." He waved, smiling. "I'll see you . . ."

"Yes. Good-by . . ."

"Good-by . . ."

IV

Now and then it seemed to Blixen that Hollywood had grown camera-wise too soon. It posed for everyone, like an aging child-star on Academy night—chin lifted, lips apart—but the old face was so blank and pleased and familiar that it bored the eye. The eye preferred Century City and Beverly Hills, the tall glassy buildings, the tanned girls with poodles in their arms. During the day, tourists still clotted the forecourt of the Chinese and took movies of the Brown Derby on Vine. But sometime before six, a soft, regressive change would begin. One by one the disappointed visitors would slip away and the long small-town night would begin to rewrap the tacky butterfly in its old cocoon.

This was the time and the town Blixen always had preferred. The truncated Spanish duplexes on El Centro and De Longpre and Fountain and Gower. The stubborn Nebraskans watering the lawns that wouldn't grow. Kids on one skate with their shirttails out. Dogs barking and the bells of ice-cream trucks. Muir's Hollywood . . .

Spellbound, thinking of Muir, trying to relate Muir's death to tragedy as well as shock, Blixen nearly missed LoSordo's.

It wasn't altogether his fault. He had had an eye set for the Alhambra, but when he circled the block and came back again on Fountain, he saw that LoSordo's was the Taj Mahal now, placed behind a greenish reflecting pool and puffing steam from its presses through stubby minarets. The trucks parked in the lot had *LoSordo's Laundry and Dry Cleaning* written across their white sides in an orientalish script, and there was a big Nordic girl in a green sari behind the customer counter.

"*Plus ça change,*" Blixen thought, and must have said it aloud, or partly aloud, because the girl in the sari smiled at him and said: "Oh, hi," and then, "What?"

"What happened to your Spanish décor?" Blixen asked.

"Were we Spanish once?" the girl said. "I'm new."

"You were the Alhambra in 1950," Blixen said.

"Oh, wow, well, I'm sure newer than *that*," the girl replied and laughed. She swept long straight yellow hair away from her nose with both hands. "Let's see, do you have something to pick up?"

"A suit. It may not be ready yet."

"When did you bring it in?"

"Your driver took it this morning."

"Oh! Well, no, then, it won't be ready until Tuesday. I'm sorry."

"I wonder," Blixen said, "if there's any way we can expedite that? An emergency's come up."

Her face was doubtful. "Well—"

"Are you open on Sundays?"

"Every day except Christmas—"

"Can I pay extra and pick it up tomorrow then? Or Monday at the latest? It's needed for a funeral."

"Oh, gee," the girl said. "Wow, I'm sorry." She chewed her lip in distress. "Listen, I'll tell you, let me call the driver on that route. Maybe he can—" She reached for a microphone on an extension arm next to the wall telephone. "Where would—"

"Muir—McKinley Drive."

She ran the tip of a finger down a typewritten list pinned to a bulletin board, pulled the microphone closer and muttered: "Twenty-two?" into it. She gave Blixen a pretty, apologetic grimace. "If he's back there, he'll answer. The day shift isn't supposed to leave until six, but they, you know, sneak off . . ." She pushed the gold bands on her forearm further toward her elbow and twisted to peek nervously at the curtain beyond the racks of clothes waiting to be called for. "Twenty-two, please?" she said into the microphone, and then relaxed when a small potbellied man in shirt sleeves and a black plastic bow tie came hurrying up the aisle. "Hoy," said the potbellied man in a rattled baritone.

"Hoy," said the girl. "Mr. Crouch, we need some help. Uh—this is Mr. Muir—?"

"Blixen," Blixen said.

"Blixen," the girl repeated vaguely. "Anyway—"

But Blixen, hypnotized by the funereal face and the bald head and the earnest nervous eyes before him, said: "Excuse me—I'm sorry—but I'm almost certain we've met. . . . Haven't we?"

"No," said Mr. Crouch.

"Everybody thinks that," said the girl. "It's because he looks like a movie star."

"All right, Marge," said Mr. Crouch.

Blixen frowned.

"D.M.," Marge said.

"D . . ."

"*Stagecoach.*"

"Donald Meek!" Blixen shouted. "Of *course!* Donald *Meek!*"

Mr. Crouch gave a skittish cough and said in Donald Meek's broken jittery tones: "I don't see it myself," and smiled shyly.

"Isn't that cute?" said Marge. "Do it again, Bert."

"I'll do you again," said Mr. Crouch, and blushed a startled crimson.

"My girlfriend used to say I looked just like Cybill Shepherd," Marge said.

"You look just like yourself," said Mr. Crouch sententiously. "A good, strong, healthy, young American lady."

"Gee, thanks."

"It's better than looking like W.H."

"W.H.," Marge repeated. "Are you an actor who later went into interior decorating?"

"No, I'm not William Haines," Mr. Crouch said.

"Are you a director's father?"

"No, I'm not Walter Huston."

"Can anybody hop in there?" Blixen asked.

"Join the party," Marge said.

Blixen pondered. "Are you a small-eyed Warner Brothers flatfoot?"

"No," said Mr. Crouch slowly, "I'm—not—" He scowled horribly at the ceiling.

"If he can't think of the one you're thinking of," Marge said, "you get to ask him a question. Ask him if he's alive."

"Oh, I can think of it, all right," said Mr. Crouch. "That's the trouble. That's who I am. Warren Hymer."

"Warren *Hymer!*" Marge exclaimed.

"Warren Hymer," Blixen agreed fondly. "Dear, dumb Warren."

"You're very good at this," Mr. Crouch said.

"Comes of all those misspent Saturday matinees at the Hollywood theater on Sandy Boulevard in Portland, Oregon."

"Remember the newsreels?" Mr. Crouch asked.

"Ah, sweet heaven, the newsreels," said Blixen. "The Westerns. The Charlie Chans. The Hardy Family . . ."

"Uh—sir?" said the girl. "Did you want to ask him about—?"

"Oh!" Blixen said. "Yes." He cleared his throat. "Mr. Crouch—I wonder if you remember picking up a suit at 1220 McKinley Drive this morning—"

"Gray single-breasted twill?"

"I have no idea. I wouldn't be surprised."

"Yes, I did," said Mr. Crouch. "Never saw so much interest in one garment."

"This gentleman wants to wear it to a funeral," Marge said.

"Well—not really," Blixen said. "I should have explained. I'm here on Mrs. Muir's account . . ." He hesitated over the words. "There's been a tragedy, I'm afraid. Her husband passed away this afternoon."

Mr. Crouch, whose long vicar's face had taken on an aspect of benign piety at the first mention of funerals, started to sigh: "Well, it's —" and then stopped. "You mean—her father," he said. "Father-in-law, the—her husband's—"

"No," Blixen replied, "her husband. Chet."

Presently Mr. Crouch said: "*Young* Mr. Muir?"

"I'm afraid so."

"The father's been bad for years—"

"I know."

Absently Mr. Crouch looked out the broad dirty front window, his eyes gentle and jarred. "Well, for heaven's sake," he murmured. "You expect some kind of logic, sense—something—justice—and—of course there isn't any. God's not a sportsman, after all, is he. There that old man's been trying to die for I don't know how long—"

"At least two years."

"The two of us talk about the old days. They're all on my route. Him. His four sons." Mr. Crouch expelled his breath quietly. "Well. Was it heart?"

"There'll have to be an autopsy."

"You met him, Marge," Mr. Crouch said. "He came in once or twice. Thin chap, offered you the Rolaids. *Nice* fellow. Well, it's his poor wife I'm sorry for. He's out of it now."

"Was that the W.M. you pulled on me?" Marge asked.

"Wanda Mills," Crouch nodded. "Lovely little girl, always wearing felt hats and screaming at vampires."

"Mr. Crouch," Blixen said, "a moment ago you said something about never seeing so much interest in one garment—"

"Never did," replied Mr. Crouch. "First the brother and then you . . ." He broke off, brow furrowed. "Now that's funny. *He* didn't say anything about a death—"

"Who?" Blixen asked.

"The brother. Do you know all the brothers? This was Emmett."

"Emmett came by?"

"Called," said Mr. Crouch. "About—twenty minutes ago. He didn't say who it was, but I knew that voice. I never used to be able to tell the difference between Chester and Spencer, but I always knew Emmett and I knew the father."

"What did he want to do, pick it up? The suit?"

"No, sir, he wanted to know if we'd gone through the pockets."

"Ah!" Blixen said. "Of course. And had you?"

"Yes, sir. We do that in the truck, the boy and me."

"And did you find the money?"

Mr. Crouch, who had been scratching his tall forehead, hesitated, and then leaned forward a little.

"The four hundred dollars," Blixen said.

"Oh-oh," said the girl.

"All right, you just hold your horses, missy," Mr. Crouch said.

"I didn't say one word. He's your problem, not mine."

"Isn't that what Emmett was interested in?" Blixen asked.

"Why, no," said Mr. Crouch.

"I *knew* this was going to happen," the girl said.

Face dark, Mr. Crouch thrust a hand toward heaven. "*Though I speak with the tongues of men and of angels,*" he said deeply, "*and have not charity, I am become as sounding brass, or a tinkling cymbal!*"

"Oh, bushwa," said the girl.

"Mr. Crouch," Blixen said, "what was it Emmett was after if not the—"

"In the first place," bellowed Mr. Crouch, "I picked up that suit myself, what do you think about that? He didn't lay a hand on that suit until I brought it back to the truck! All right?"

"Sure, fine," Marge said.

"All right," said Mr. Crouch. He filled his lungs through his nose, glaring around and trembling and straightening his plastic bow tie. "I'll tell you how I remember that," he said to Blixen. "I usually drive, but I let the boy drive today, to see if he knew the route. The Muirs weren't home, so I went around back, and the suit was in the garage. So I brought the suit *back* to the truck, and I marked the ticket, and we went through the pockets together. No money."

"No money," Blixen repeated. "Well—but what did—"

"I thought they took your driver's license away from you in this state if you were convicted of a felony," Marge said.

"The trouble with you," shouted Mr. Crouch, "is that you don't think at all. How do you suppose he could have gotten a job as a driver-trainee without a license?" He got a glance at Blixen. "He's got a license. He's a good boy. I recommended him for the position. He's been with us since last December and there hasn't been one complaint about him. This is a boy who just needs a chance. I've known this boy all my life."

"This is also a boy," Marge said, "who pistol-whipped a bartender and two women customers because they only had twenty-seven dollars between them. Among them?"

"Shame on you," cried Mr. Crouch.

"Shame on *me!*"

"Why don't you tell him the whole story!" Turning to Blixen, Mr. Crouch continued passionately: "His mother and sisters were on welfare, starving! *Yes,* he went into the bar, he admitted that—"

"He was caught in there, for crying out loud, he had to admit it," Marge said.

"What a pity it is," said Mr. Crouch in a shaken voice, "that you don't have a little compassion in place of all that tan. You'd be a prettier girl for it."

"Well, excuse me for living," Marge said.

"Uh—Mr. Crouch," Blixen began, "in another area, what was it that Emmet—"

"I don't like Kenneth, I don't trust him, I don't want him around me," Marge said sullenly. "I'm sorry."

"You ought to be sorry," said Mr. Crouch.

"Yes," Blixen said, and slapped the counter lightly with his open hands. "So. We can have the suit by Monday, then—?"

Mr. Crouch squinted at him.

"For the funeral."

"For the *funeral,*" Mr. Crouch repeated. "Right. I'll tell them. Yes, it'll be ready."

"Around noon?"

"By noon, yes."

"Thank you . . ."

"Had we ought to have your number," Marge asked, "just in case?"

"Maybe you should," Blixen said, and gave her the number at the apartment as well as the studio.

"You be sure to tell Miz Muir I'm just sick about this," said Mr. Crouch.

"Yes, I will."

"And if you see the brother—"

Blixen halted at the door.

"No, never mind," said Mr. Crouch. "There's no reason to bother you with—"

"But it's no bother at all," Blixen said. "What's the message?"

"That I looked through the suit again," said Mr. Crouch, "personally, and I couldn't find any sign of the paper he was worried about."

After a moment Blixen said: "Did he say what sort—"

"Well, I gathered it was some kind of music notation. He's a composer. Emmett."

"Emmett," Blixen repeated pensively. "Right."

"I hope he hasn't lost something important."

"What would something important of Emmett's be doing in Chet's suit?"

"Um," said Mr. Crouch. "Well, with brothers, who knows?"

Blixen studied him for a time, and then nodded and pushed the door open. The damp vivid twilight had deepened. "Who knows, indeed," he said. . . .

V

The Hall of Justice on North Broadway was cavernous and echoing, corseted in marble, a place of pain, vacant information booths, and desperate Spanish graffiti. It was past seven when Blixen reached the first floor autopsy room, and the chilly corridor was empty except for an adolescent girl slumped near a sand ashtray, gripping a slick red purse in her crossed arms and swaying from foot to foot like a tethered elephant.

Astonished, Blixen hesitated with his hand on the icy doorknob.

The child was thirteen or fourteen. Her bones were long and delicate, her feet enormous. Or perhaps it was the frightful, fashionable shoes. Her blue skirt was short, her white sweater loose; she wore a tiny limp blue ribbon at the top of her head. She regarded him out of stunned, mistrustful eyes.

Damn these neck pegs, Blixen thought. He released the doorknob and said in the kindest voice he was capable of: "Excuse me. It's rude to stare, but I think we know each other. Aren't you Jennifer Muir?"

She'd been told all her life not to speak to strangers. She crouched like a cat behind her fine blond eyelashes.

"I'm Nils Blixen," Blixen said.

It rang a distant, barely audible bell; she rested her chin on the purse's golden clasp. "Oh."

"You don't remember me."

"In a way."

"You came to a studio party two years ago. Somebody played a Lawrence Welk record and you danced a polka with your uncle Robert."

"Please, not while I'm eating," said the girl.

"Times change, don't they," Blixen said.

She nodded, too polite to wince at the platitude.

Presently Blixen said: "Well, this is a surprise. . . . I—suppose your mother brought you down—"

Another nod.

"Is she inside?"

"Yes."

"Alone?"

The clear blue eyes rose briefly, dropped again. "Women who look like my mother are seldom alone," Jennifer said. "A man from the studio's with her."

"Mr. Kapralos?"

"I don't know."

"Thin kind of a—"

"Yes. And Uncle Emmett."

"Spencer? Robert?"

"Spencer's in Las Vegas, and Robert's in San Diego," Jennifer said. "Gail's around someplace. She went upstairs with a cop."

"With—" Blixen blinked. "Why?"

"She didn't say." The little chin dug down against the pointed purse clasp. "Maybe they think she killed him."

A breeze washed their ankles. In the dead distance, a metal door boomed and someone shouted and laughed. Blixen waited until the blue eyes sought his again. "Killed him," he repeated.

"What's the matter?"

"Why should you think your dad had been killed?"

She shrugged. "We're all here. Talking to the cops."

"Well—maybe your mother wanted to see Chet again—or—"

"No. The sheriff called her at the hospital and asked her to come down. At least that's what she told me when she picked me up at Gail's."

Blixen smoothed the hair over the crown of his head contemplatively. "I see . . . So—"

But the girl, surprisingly, had started to hum. It was a faint, throaty sound, toneless and harsh. When Blixen looked up, she gyrated away from him and went stumbling down the hall, humming against the red purse, blind as a mole.

"Jennifer—"

"No. Don't—"

She was crying; she struck her knee on one of the sand-weighted ashtrays and turned like a dunce into a corner, wracked with anguish. Blixen moved in quick, diffident pursuit, touched her shoulder, tried to take her elbow, but each time she spun further away. "Don't—!"

"Jennifer, I'm sorry," Blixen said. "I shouldn't have—"

"I'm not crying for *him!*"

"It doesn't—"

"I'm *not!*"

"All right, all right . . ."

"Hypocrites!"

"Who?"

"Everybody!" Her hands hung onto the purse helplessly and broke Blixen's heart. "I don't see why adults always have to be so bloody *dumb!*"

"Neither do I."

"You wait. They'll all be moaning and groaning." Her voice climbed to affected heights. "'Oh, sweet Chettie, perfect Chettie.' I know that bunch. 'Perfect husband, perfect son, perfect brother, perfect father.'" She ground her forehead against the wall. "What's *wrong* with people? They ought to take everybody over twenty out and SHOOT 'EM!"

"Twenty? What happened to thirty? I thought thirty was the—"

"Twenty."

"But wouldn't that cast a certain pall over your own nineteenth birthday?"

"No way in the world I'll ever reach nineteen."

"Don't bet on it."

"Don't *you* bet on it."

"If the oil slicks don't get you, the smog will," Blixen said. "Is that it?"

"Something like that," Jennifer said. She measured him, sniffling, suspicious. "Do you think that's funny?"

"No, I don't."

"Maybe there wouldn't be any oil slicks and smog if the people your age hadn't been laughing so hard."

"Maybe not."

She watched him for a moment more, and then opened her purse and dug in it until she'd found a tattered Kleenex tissue. "I'm not trying to be rude," she muttered. "I'm trying to be honest."

"I understand."

"It's hard."

"I know it is."

She rubbed the tissue around each eye and across her nose, staring down the hall. Presently she said: "You try to do what people expect, and that doesn't work. Mom wanted me to go all to pieces when she told me Chet was dead."

"You call him 'Chet'?"

"Chet."

"Yes . . ."

"And I couldn't. I pretended. I thought about a turtle I'd had that died and finally I got up a couple of tears. I don't know whether I fooled her or not." Jennifer unfolded the Kleenex and crumpled it and smoothed it again. "Did you like my father?"

"Sometimes," Blixen said.

"Did you? Why?"

"We shared the same politics, he was a good company man, a fast worker—"

"I guess I should have known him at work," Jennifer said.

"Or shared the same politics."

"Or shared something . . ." She shivered and hunched her shoulders.

"Cold?"

"No."

"There's a vending machine around the corner. Can I buy you a cup of coffee?"

"No. Nothing."

But she trailed him anyway, lost in thought, when he went to find the machine. He leaned over, jingling the coins in his pocket, reading the labeled slots. "How about a bag of peanuts? Candy bar?"

"Well—"

"Butterfinger?"

"Okay."

He bought them each a Butterfinger and they stood facing each other stoically in the glacial shadows, munching.

"Someday they're going to be selling pot in those things," Jennifer said.

"I suppose so."

"My boy friend says it's inevitable."

"I think he's right."

She put her head on one side, a blond wren on the alert for a worm. "How come that doesn't set your adult teeth on edge?"

"If they can sell poison, why shouldn't they sell pleasure?"

"Poi—? Oh, cigarettes?" She nodded, and examined the candy in her hand. "I guess chocolate's poison, too, for some people."

"I believe it is."

"I wonder how poison and pleasure got all mixed up like that?"

"It's a shame, isn't it."

She nibbled at the bar. "Have you ever smoked pot?" she asked.

"Yes."

"Did you like it?"

Blixen considered. "I think I liked the fact that it was forbidden. It seems very mild to me. I prefer beer, I think."

"So do I," Jennifer said. "It's just that pot's easier to get. For kids." She crumpled the candy wrapper, tossed it into a trash can nearby, and started to whistle between her teeth. When she saw that Blixen was grinning at her, she flushed and said: "Quit it."

"I'm sorry."

"I'm not *just* trying to shock you. I'm trying to carry on a conversation, too."

"I know."

"I could curl your hair if I really wanted to shock you."

"I have no doubt of it," Blixen said.

"This is the weirdest talk I ever had with a grownup," Jennifer said. "You don't follow the rules."

"Like your dad did?"

She threw him a piercing look and nodded.

"Well," Blixon said, "maybe the rules are important to a parent. Sometimes I think it must be as hard to be a parent as it is to be a child."

"Do you have kids?"

"No."

"That's too bad. The nuts of the world unite and beget kids by the million, while the good guys just lie there." She grinned swiftly at him, half defiant, half flirtatious. "Why don't you do something about that?"

"Thank you," Blixen said.

Her ears and the tip of her nose bloomed pink; she scowled back at the bend of the corridor. "My *mother* isn't a nut, though," she said.

"No?"

"Not exactly. Do you know what she is?"

"What?"

"Painfully weak."

"Ah."

"She knows that women aren't made of sugar and spice and everything nice but she doesn't want anyone else to know. She pretends all the time."

"Maybe it's the actress in her," Blixen said. "What is it she pretends?"

"Everything. Love." Jennifer opened and shut her purse. "Tears . . ." She lowered the purse and lifted her head. "I take it back. Maybe she *is* a nut."

"Here's a little secret for you," Blixen said. "At thirteen everybody's parents are nuts."

"Now don't get pompous and spoil it all," Jennifer said.

"Sorry."

"She's either a nut or she's a liar," Jennifer said. "How else could she have cried over him like that? I would have thought she'd have been glad to get rid of him. Am I shocking you yet?"

"Surprising me," Blixen said.

"Why? Didn't you know they hated each other?"

"Jennifer," Blixen began, "sometimes—"

"Tell me another secret," Jennifer said. "Do some women really like to be beaten up?"

"If I wore glasses," Blixen said, "this is where I'd put them on and look owlish."

"Do they?"

"So I understand."

"Well, he's lucky he never tried it on me," Jennifer said. Her voice was low and savage, her eyes hooded. "I wouldn't have stayed around there five minutes." She shook her hair back over her shoulders. "I used to lie in bed and listen to them at night—when he'd come home drunk and try to find something to fight with her about. . . . He'd tell her to bring him a glass of water, or a cigarette—fetch the bone like a nice doggie—and if she was too slow or sleepy, he'd whap her."

"Jennifer . . ." Blixen murmured.

She grinned. "Now you sound just like Kenny. So sad."

"Who's Kenny?"

"Oh, another good guy. You'd like him. He tries to be honest, too. Chet hated him."

"Boy friend?"

"Yes. I should have trusted him. I wouldn't have fretted so much."

"Fretted about what?"

"Chet." The fresh, cruel, unforgiving face had gone ivory-white in the shadows. "Kenny always said that Chet's karma would have to catch up to him. Somebody'd kill him, he said. Someday."

A blur of voices drifted down the hall. "Jennifer?" one of them called. "Jennifer? Jennifer?"

"There they are," Jennifer said, and started briskly back toward the bend of the corridor. When she perceived at last that Blixen wasn't beside her, she switched in mid-stride and went skipping backward, her purse banging against her knees. "Well?" she asked. "Aren't you coming?"

Gravely Blixen looked up, and then tossed his candy wrapper in the trash basket and smiled and started after her. "Yes, of course," he said. "Go ahead . . ."

VI

There were four of them grouped together outside the autopsy room door like shipwrecked survivors on an atoll, three men and a woman, dazed and intimate. The woman, dressed in tan slacks and a thin green golfing jacket, extended her slender arms to the running girl and said: "Well, Skeezix, we thought you were lost—what happened to you?"

"I was kidnaped," Jennifer said. She touched her mother's pale cheek. "Are you all right?"

Nodding, the woman held out a hand to Blixen. "Hi, kidnaper."

"Hi, sweetheart."

"He bought me a candy bar," Jennifer said.

"That's remarkably generous for a producer," Wanda said.

"Last of the really big spenders," said the large man beside her.

"Nils, you know my brother-in-law—Emmett? Nils Blixen . . ."

"I know his music."

"Then you know me," Emmett said. His grip was hearty and firm. He stood like a balding bear on his short legs, ragged and long-nosed. His smile was sad, his beard nicotine-stained.

"And this," Wanda said, "is Sergeant—uh—?"

"Fries," the sergeant said. "How are you." He was in plain-clothes, young and red-haired, with the thick neck of a weight-lifter.

Kapralos, behind them all, appeared frailer than ever, a matchstick of a man. "Nils, I called you again," he said morosely, "but you'd gone."

"Called—?"

"When Sergeant—I'm sorry—" Wanda said.

"Fries."

"When Sergeant Fries called us."

"We've run into some complications," Kapralos said.

"Baby," Wanda began.

"No, I'm not hungry," Jennifer said, "and no, I don't want to go buy a magazine, and no, I don't want to wait in the car." Her face was bloodless, drawn, shockingly mature. "And please don't call me 'baby.'"

Wanda shook her head a little, and then put her arm through her daughter's and faced Blixen. "All right," she said. "It doesn't make any sense, but it happened, so I guess we're all just going to have to accept it." She braced herself. "Apparently Chettie found some poison somewhere," she said. "The autopsy showed that Chettie poisoned himself."

Blixen, aware that his jaw was dangling, snapped his mouth shut. "*Chettie?*" he said.

"I know—"

"*Suicide?*"

"I know, I know," Wanda said, "it doesn't make any sense—"

Sergeant Fries was lighting a pencil-thin black cigar for Emmett. He watched Blixen over the flame in his cupped hand. "Doesn't that seem consistent with this man's character to you, Mr. Blixen?"

"Last person in the world I would have thought—"

"Why it's absolutely the dumbest thing I ever heard of in my life," Jennifer cried.

"Sure," Wanda said, "suicide *is* dumb, and cruel, but that doesn't—"

Jennifer whirled on Sergeant Fries. "How do they know it was suicide?"

"What else could it have been, darling?" Wanda asked. "He couldn't have taken it by accident—"

"Why not?" Blixen asked Fries. "What sort of poison was it?"

"Oxalic acid," Fries replied.

"He hadn't eaten any breakfast or any lunch," Kapralos said, "so they think it worked pretty fast—"

"How fast?"

"Immmediate severe stomach cramps," Fries said. "Death within an hour, hour and a half, or sooner, with his ulcers. There was an indication that he'd taken some kind of an analgesic, too. Probably Alka-Seltzer . . ."

"You remember how he loved that, Nils," Wanda said.

"Yes . . ."

"He was dead by twelve thirty-five, according to the hospital records," Fries continued. "Which means that he ingested the poison sometime between eleven and twelve."

"I see . . ."

"You still seem a little skeptical, Mr. Blixen," Fries said.

Blixen, who had been watching Wanda, said: "No, no . . ." and then, more slowly: "It's—just such a temper tantrum, suicide . . . Isn't it."

"And what? Mr. Muir wasn't the type to throw temper tantrums?"

"Oh, you didn't know Mr. Muir," Emmett put in.

Blixen took a deep breath. "No, I think what I mean is that Chettie wasn't the type to hurt himself—if he could help it. He had a strong sense of survival. If someone crossed him, he wouldn't kick and scream and turn blue. He'd lash out."

Fries had opened a notebook, found a ball-point pen in an inside jacket pocket. "Do you agree with that analysis, Mrs. Muir?"

"Yes, I think so," Wanda said blankly. "In general."

"Although he could brood with the best of them when he put his mind to it," Emmett said. "He could be a very vindictive man."

"Really?" Fries said. "In what way?"

"Chettie kept his mouth shut, but he made you pay your debts."

"For instance—?"

"Well . . ." Emmett considered. "*Well*, I remember a time when we were kids. My dad was very old-fashioned about some things, hyper-orthodox—still is. Children were to be seen and not heard. Children went to Sunday school. Children were allowed a ceremonial glass of whiskey on their twenty-first birthdays, never before. Anyway, he found out somehow that we were smoking. Spencer and Chettie and me. Or he suspected it. So he said he wanted to be fair. He wanted to warn us, he said. Not against the nicotine. Against him. He said if he ever got proof of it—if he ever caught one of us with smoke on his breath or a cigarette in his mouth, he'd whip us until we bled."

"Just trying to scare you," Wanda said.

"He scared us all right," Emmett said. "Because he meant it, and we knew he meant it." Inhaling, Emmett stretched his heavy shoulders. "It didn't stop us from smoking, naturally. We'd steal the old man's cigars and go out in the weeds behind the garage . . ." He glanced at Wanda. "Didn't Chettie ever tell you about this—?"

"About the fire? Yes, but he didn't mention cigars. He said you were all playing with matches." To Blixen, she explained: "Chettie's sweater caught fire. It was terrible. He was in the hospital for weeks."

"Did he tell you who lit him?" Emmett asked.

"*Lit* him! No . . ."

"Fantastic," Emmett said. "After all that time—"

Wanda's face was bewildered. "Em, I don't understand. What do you mean, *lit* him?"

"I lit him," Emmett said. "I threw a match at him and it caught in his sweater. He went up like—like—"

"Oh, Em . . . !"

"Well—what did you do it *for*?" Jennifer asked.

"No reason. Or if I had a reason, I've forgotten. Emmett stared at the floor for a time, smoking his cigar, swaying back and forth. "The point is that Chettie never told the old man on me. Never."

"He didn't want to get you into trouble," Wanda said.

"He didn't want to let me off the hook."

"What hook?"

"He didn't want to kill the goose that laid the golden egg."

"What are you talking about?"

"Blackmail," Emmett said.

VII

For a moment the only sound in the corridor came from the whisper of Fries's ball-point across his lined notebook paper.

"Got all that?" Emmett asked at last.

"Yes, sir," Fries said.

"Very hard story for me to tell," Emmett said. "Harder than I thought it was going to be when I started out. Maybe I'm still afraid of the old man."

"How long did this blackmail continue?" Blixen asked.

"Oh, years," Emmett said absently. And then: "I can't remember when it actually stopped. I just woke up one day to the fact that he hadn't asked for anything for a while. I guess he'd decided that enough was enough."

"And how old were you at this time, Mr. Muir?" Fries inquired.

"Well—I was out of college. . . . Twenty-one or twenty-two."

"I just can't imagine Chettie *doing* anything like—"

"Oh, Mother," Jennifer moaned.

"No, I can't—"

"Mother, stop it!" The blue ribbon had lost its bow; it straggled off toward one temple like a bedraggled New Year's streamer. "It's *exactly* what he'd do! It's so *exactly* like him!"

"Like him how, young lady?" Fries asked.

"Well—to *threaten* people, and get his own way!"

"Jennifer, for heaven's sake—"

"It *is!* It *was!*"

"Who else did he threaten?" Fries asked.

"Skeezix, please—"

"Let her answer, Mrs. Muir."

But the storm had passed; the eyes were clouded; the chin pressed against the clasp of the purse.

"Young lady?" Fries said.

"Oh, I didn't mean anybody specific," Jennifer said. "Just—" She folded her short upper lip between her teeth and walked slowly away from them, head down, chin against her purse.

"Sergeant," Blixen said, "I wonder if we couldn't postpone this questioning for a while? These people have had a mean day—"

"Yes, sir," Fries said. He brushed a hand through his coarse red hair and squinted at his notebook past the wavering smoke of Emmett's cigar. "How about you, Mr. Blixen? Did you ever hear him threaten anyone?"

"Hear him?" The memory of Robert's body pinwheeling across the room to slam into the wall at Chasen's pricked his mind.

Fries lifted his eyes. "Hear him—see him . . ."

At last Blixen said: "No. Not at work."

"Socially, then?" Fries asked.

Blixen swiveled his head to gaze at the other.

"Our information," Fries said softly, "is that you walked in on it."

"Walked in on what?" Emmett demanded.

"Em, I want to go home," Wanda said.

"Just a minute," Emmett responded. "What information? Walked in on what?"

"A fight," Blixen said. "Between Chet and Robert. At Chasen's."

"When?"

"December, last Christmas."

"Well, what's that got to do with anything?" Wanda asked.

"Good question," Fries said. His eyes remained fastened on Blixen's. "Mr. Blixen? What's that got to do with anything!"

"If you're trying to tie Robert into Chet's—"

"Oh, for God's sake," Wanda said, "that's ridiculous, ridiculous! Chettie killed himself!" She swung accusingly to Fries. "You keep saying that!"

"No, ma'am," Fries said. "*You* keep saying it." He paused. "Mr. Blixen?"

Wanda's face was a slapped-white; her eyes were huge. Blixen shifted his glance to the plain-clothesman. "Where did you hear about the quarrel?"

"Through channels," Fries replied.

"Wouldn't channels tell you?"

The corners of Fries's mouth twitched. "Channels didn't know. You tell me."

"I don't know either."

"You did walk in on it?"

"Yes."

"Didn't hear any words exchanged?"

"No."

"Didn't ask what was happening?"

"It was obvious what was happening. They were in a battle royal. I broke it up."

"Anyone else in the rest room at the time?"

"No."

"How did Robert explain this situation?"

"He didn't. He said something about Chet being drunk. That's all."

"*Was* Chet drunk?"

"He'd been drinking," Blixen said.

Fries jotted a word down. "You knew about the fight, naturally, Mrs. Muir . . ."

"Oh—of course." Wanda pressed shaky fingers against one temple. "Everyone who was there knew about it . . ."

"How did your husband explain it to you?"

"I can't—what did he say? He never did explain it, really. He said Robert had been snotty to him—"

"Snotty?"

"Listen, it's not my story! Why don't you ask *Robert?*"

"Yes, ma'am, we're going to," Fries said imperturbably, "as soon as we can locate him."

"He's in San Diego . . ."

"Yes, ma'am," Fries said.

"Tell me something," Emmett put in. "Why am I beginning to get this gut feeling that you people have already made your minds up here?"

"About what, Mr. Muir?" Fries asked.

"That Chettie was murdered and that Robert's involved in some way."

Beside Blixen, Wanda jumped, literally jumped; he could feel the snap of her leg like an electric shock against his knee.

Fries, watching her, said: "Are you all right, Mrs. Muir? Would you like a sedative? Like to lie down?"

Wanda shook her head.

Stiffly Emmett said: "You're one hundred per cent wrong, you know, Sergeant, one hundred and eighty degrees off target. My brother Robert could no more—" He stopped and rubbed the back of his hand across the beard below his chin, choppily, against the grain. "Well, it's out of the question," he said.

"I feel crazy again," Wanda said. "Everything goes along fine for an hour or two and then bang—somebody . . . Sergeant, what are you trying to *say?* That Robert *mailed* Chettie the poison from San Diego, or that he sneaked back here somehow and—"

"About what time does the mail usually arrive on Saturdays, Mrs. Muir?" Fries asked.

"*Oh,* for—!"

"Around two in the afternoon," Emmett said.

Fries lifted his eyes.

"We all live on the same street," Emmett said. "McKinley Drive. My dad built five houses on a cul-de-sac."

"And you all—?"

"We couldn't beat the prices," Emmett said. "They were free."

"Very generous."

"He wanted his chicks with him. Especially after our mother died."

"Rare for a family to be so close," Fries said.

Emmett tapped the fragile ash off his thin black cigar without looking up. "Isn't it," he said.

"Are you married, Mr. Muir?" Fries asked.

Emmett shook his head silently.

"When was the last time you saw your brother alive?"

"Last night. We all had dinner together—at Lawry's, on La Cienega."

"Now—when you say 'all'—"

"Chettie, Wanda, Gail, and myself."

"And where was the rest of the family?"

"Spencer was in Vegas, my dad was home in bed, Jennifer—"

"Jennifer went to a movie," Wanda said. "And Robert was in San Diego."

"Yes."

Angrily Wanda said: "I don't know why you get that *look* on your face! The studio sent him! He was checking out locations! Wasn't he, Nils!"

For a moment Blixen was thrown so thoroughly off balance that he could do little more than gape at her. Her own tired face, thrust toward Fries, was a study in vindictive triumph; it was clear that she'd been hoarding her decisive information slyly, actress-like, one eye on the curtain. Soon she would sweep away to delighted gusts of applause. "Nils?" she repeated.

While the silence lengthened, she peered at him, puzzled. Fries was waiting politely.

"Locations?" Blixen said.

"Yes! Locations! For the next episode!"

"Wanda," Blixen began.

"He went," Wanda said furiously, "to San Diego to scout *locations!* He told us *all* he was going! He told Gail!"

"Right," Blixen said.

"Did you send him, Mr. Blixen?" Fries asked.

"I'm sorry, no," Blixen said.

Straightening, Wanda said: "Why, you did, too. He told us you did."

"Socrates?" Blixen murmured.

"No," Kapralos said.

"Now, you'll have to help me out a little here, Mr. Kapralos," Fries said. "Is this an order that would normally come from your office?"

"Always come out of my office," Kapralos said.

"You'd arrange the transportation, meals, whatever? For whoever was hunting the location?"

"Yes. Everything."

"And you made no such arrangements for Robert Muir—"

"No such arrangements."

"Could he have decided to look around on his own—to—"

"He could have decided anything. But he'd better not put in a requisition for it. We wouldn't shoot in San Diego. He knew that."

"Sergeant," Wanda said, "when you offered to let me lie down a while ago, did you mean it?"

"Certainly."

"Where would I have to go?"

"There's a cot in the autopsy—"

"Yes. That's what I thought. Never mind."

She was much calmer, although her skin had taken on a paperish glint that was disturbing.

"All right," Blixen said abruptly, "I think you've had your quota of casual questions, Sergeant. My lawyer really wouldn't approve of this. So why don't we wrap it up—"

"Of course," Fries said. "Did your husband say anything about meeting someone in San Urbano, Mrs. Muir?"

"Come on," Emmett said and took her arm. "The producer's right. The producer's always right—"

"No, he didn't," Wanda said. She drew her elbow out of Emmett's grip like a willful, exhausted child; a pulse throbbed in her throat when she raised her chin to look at Fries.

"No indication at all of—"

"Robert's name was never mentioned."

"I wasn't speaking of Robert necessarily, Mrs. Muir."

"Weren't you?"

Fries fell silent, doodling on the notepaper. Past the bend of his arm, Blixen could see a Pinocchio's head taking shape, a nose elongating itself in bambooish sections. "So," Fries said, "Chet simply made up his mind one day, out of a clear blue sky—"

"It wasn't out of a clear blue sky. He'd planned to go for several days, three or four days—"

"Planned to go to San Urbano—"

"Yes."

"Why?"

Discouraged, Wanda said: "Oh, you'll never understand. It doesn't make any sense unless you know Chettie."

"I'll never understand if you don't tell me," Fries said. He waited, pen poised.

Wanda glanced at Emmett, and then sighed and said: "He thought it renewed him."

Fries studied her unblinkingly.

"See?" Wanda said.

Fries tapped his pen against the notebook cover for a moment. "Renewed him," he repeated. "Do you mean renewed him—spiritually? Or—"

"Em, is that what I mean? I think it is."

Nodding, Emmett said: "Spiritually—mentally—even physically, in a way . . ."

"You knew about this, too, Mr. Muir?"

"Oh, sure, it was a routine with Chettie. He'd get discouraged—or worried—sick—and he'd make his little pilgrimage. He'd hop on the bus, ride out to San Urbano, walk around the campus, talk to some of his old professors, stay at the College Inn . . ."

"For how long?"

"Never more than a couple of days. Was it, Wanda?"

"A weekend, usually . . ."

"You said he'd take the bus—"

"Yes."

"Why?"

"I don't know—part of the routine—"

"It rested him," Wanda explained. "He hated to drive. He was the best passenger I ever saw—and one of the worst drivers."

"RTD bus?" Fries asked. "City bus?"

"I guess so," Emmett said.

"No, no, no," Wanda said. "One of those orange and silver things. San Gabriel Valley Transit."

"Valley Transit," Fries repeated, writing.

"They have a terminal on Vine," Wanda said. "Chettie'd walk over there and board the ten forty-five bus and get out to the San Urbano terminal at ten minutes to twelve. He loved it."

"And that's the last you'd hear of him until—"

"Last I'd see him," Wanda said. "Until Monday. But we'd talk on the phone. He'd call home, or I'd call the College Inn. We always talked."

"What time was it when he left the house this morning?"

"This—" She stopped blankly. "My God, was it only this morning?"

Emmett touched her elbow.

"I'm okay, Em," she said. She wet her dry lips. "It was—around—ten-fifteen—a little after . . ."

"And what was his attitude?"

"Normal."

"Bovine," Jennifer said.

They turned to her like fans at a tennis match, in comical unison.

"Bovine?" Emmett inquired.

"Bovine, bovine, don't you know what bovine means?"

"I know what bovine means," Emmett said. "What do *you* mean?"

"Oh, skip it," Jennifer said wearily.

"Do you mean he was—complacent?" Fries asked. "Or—"

"I mean he was bovine! He was like a great big dumb cow!"

"Jenny—"

"All right, Mother!" Jennifer shouted. "You loved him! I didn't love him! We're two different people! All right?"

"You make yourself ugly when you talk to your mother like that, Jen," Emmett said quietly.

"Tough. I'm ugly." She bent in despair over the purse.

"In other words, Jennifer," Fries persisted, "your father seemed fairly happy when he left the house—self-satisfied—"

"Yes." Her voice was muffled, suicidal.

"No sign of nausea? Stomach ache?"

"No."

"Did he tell you he was going to San Urbano?"

"Not then. He'd mentioned it a couple of nights before."

"Did he say what he was going to do out there?"

No answer.

"Jennifer?"

"He didn't *say* anything—"

"But what?"

"But I thought to myself, boy, when you look like that, you're sure out to screw somebody." She spun to Wanda. "And don't say, 'Oh, Jennifer!'"

Wanda's dark eyes were haunted. "I won't say, 'Oh, Jennifer.' I won't say anything. I don't know what to say to you any more."

"Fine."

"So you had the impression that he might have been planning to meet someone in San Urbano?" Fries asked.

Confused, Jennifer pressed her cheek against the purse.

"Don't let me put words in your mouth," Fries said.

"Oh, never," Emmett muttered.

"Well, it couldn't have been anybody important," Jennifer said.

"Why not?"

"He looked terrible. He had a sweat shirt and a pair of old pants on—"

"Was he carrying a suitcase?"

"Little overnight bag . . . I said, 'Hey, you look like a bum, they won't even let you into the hotel,' and he said, 'Well, if you and your mother would get off your fat asses and do a little laundry around here, this wouldn't happen.' And then he told me to be sure and put his gray suit out for the cleaner."

"And did you?"

"Yes."

"Right," Fries said. "Now. Just for the record, Miss Muir—where were you between—oh—eleven and twelve? Roughly?"

"Jennifer," Blixen said, "obviously there's no way I can shut this man up short of gagging him with a court order, but I can at least point out to you that you're under no obligation whatsoever to answer him. Just for the record."

"Don't care to answer that one, Miss Muir?" Fries asked.

"She was at the public library," Wanda said.

"I was at the public library," Jennifer repeated.

"Thank you." Fries wrote, turned a page. "Mrs. Muir?"

"Where was *I*?"

"If you don't mind."

"I teach a quilting class from eleven to one at the East Hollywood Recreation Center on Sunset. I dropped Jen off at about—what?—ten-thirty?"

"I guess so."

"And I got to my classroom at quarter to eleven or so and I was there when the hospital called sometime after one."

"And—Mr. Muir?"

"Yes," Emmett said. "What?"

Smiling, Fries said: "I might as well try to place all the members of the family. Where were you between eleven and twelve?"

"I was home."

"The whole time?"

"Yes, the whole time. I work at home."

"Alone?"

"I suppose you want some corroboration."

"Please."

"I haven't any."

"None?"

"My cat . . ."

Fries smiled again. "Thank you—"

Blixen, who had been studying Jennifer thoughtfully, said: "Jennifer—excuse me—"

She glanced around warily.

"It's nothing important," Blixen said. "But—a moment ago, you mentioned putting Chet's gray suit out for the cleaner—"

"Yes—"

"I just wondered," Blixen said, "whether you happened to go through the pockets first."

She opened her mouth, closed it again. "Why?"

"Never mind," Wanda put in suddenly. "I don't know where my head's been, Nils. I went through them myself. This is about the four hundred dollars?"

"That's right."

"The pockets were empty. Jen brought the suit down just before we left and I turned everything inside out. Nothing."

"What four hundred dollars?" Emmett asked.

"His salary. He cashed his pay check Friday. It's gone."

"He had the money at dinner—"

"I know."

"Did you search the house?"

"I will. I haven't been back yet. I just picked Gail and Jen up—and you . . ."

"Well, I don't know how you can be so casual about it, Wanda. Four hundred—"

"I'm not *casual* about it! I'll search the *house*, Em!" She realized, evidently, how harsh her voice had become, so she laughed and said: "All right?" but her eyes, Blixen noticed, continued to dance electrically. Her free hand sought her daughter's, clasped it tight.

"Well, it's your money," Emmett said. "I just want to make sure you get everything that's coming to you."

"Don't worry about me," Wanda said. She enlaced Jennifer's fingers in her own. "Us. We'll be just dandy. Won't we."

"That's the old Muir fight," someone said behind them, and Blixen turned to see a square-rigged, heavy young woman approaching on slow slippered feet. Her short hair was thin and styleless, her bosom maternal. "Or the old Wanda optimism. Or something." She was wearing a flowered skirt with a long uneven hem; the sleeves of her mannish gray sweater had been neatly patched. "Hi," she said to Blixen. "I'm Gail."

"Hi."

"Robert's wife."

"Yes, I remember."

"Where have you been?" Emmett asked.

"Don't ask," Gail said. "Golgotha, calvary. Do you know what I need?"

"Double scotch on the rocks," Emmett said.

"Double scotch on the rocks."

Wanda glanced at Fries. "Can we go now?"

"Of course."

"Gail," Wanda said, "something funny's come up about Robert. The studio didn't send him out to look for locations—"

Gail faced Blixen. "Is that a fact?"

"Yes, it is."

"Ah, dear Jesus," Gail said.

"I think you ought to call him," Wanda said, "find out what the heck's going on—"

"I can't."

"What do you mean, you can't? You know where he's staying—"

"He's not there. The San Diego police went over. The hotel said he'd never signed in."

In the silence, they could all hear the click-click of Fries's pen point snicking in and out, in and out.

"That's what we've been doing," Gail said, "calling every hotel and motel in the San Diego area."

Tears swam in her nearsighted eyes.

"Nothing," she said.

VIII

Outside, the mild winter weather had turned sullen. A coastal wind brushed papers down the dark street and chilled their noses while they buttoned their coats in the shallow stone entrance way. None of them knew what to say to Gail, how to lighten her gloom. Kapralos complained of a headache; Jennifer declared that the candy bar had sickened her. Emmett sniffed the sharp air and said he smelled rain. Wanda clutched her head and cried: "Oh, my hair!" which started a stampede to the parking lot that left them all puffing and heated and giggling lamely at their own sheeplike skittishness. But at least it loosened their tongues.

"Nils, come home with us," Wanda suggested. "Have you eaten?"

"I've got some macaroni salad," Gail said. "Cold cuts—"

"I'll put a frozen pie in the oven," Wanda said.

"You'll lie down is what you'll do," Emmett said.

"Oh, Em, for God's sake, I'm not made of porcelain—"

"Sugar and spice and everything nice," Jennifer muttered. "That's what little girls are made of."

Wanda was smiling tiredly. "Nils?"

He hesitated.

"Please, Mr. Blixen," Gail said, and when he looked at her, he saw her thickish lips repeat the word mutely. *Please.*

"Well—all right—"

"Now how'll we work this transportation?" Emmett asked.

"Let's see, do you have a car?" Gail asked Blixen. "All right, why don't I go with you, then, and give the rest of them a little more room?"

"I can take one," Kapralos said.

Emmett put his arm around Jennifer's teen-age waist and urged her toward Kapralos' sports car. "Listen, you go with Mr. Kapralos, babe, and I'll drive your mom's car home, okay?" Wanda already had begun to slip behind the wheel of her Buick, and Emmett called: "No, move over, sweetheart, I'm driving . . ." and Wanda slid onto the passenger side and let her head fall against the back of the seat.

Emmett hauled open Kapralos' passenger door. "Get in. Watch your skirt."

Slowly Jennifer sat down. Emmett waited until she lifted her feet into the car and then he slammed the door. "Be careful, man," he called to Kapralos, "you've got a precious cargo here," and Kapralos grunted something although his reply was lost in the roar of the engine.

Blixen was standing beside his Colt, searching for his keys, when Emmett charged by.

"Everything all right?" Emmett asked. "Do you know how to get out to the place?"

"Gail knows."

"Who? Gail! Certainly. Okay—"

"By the way, Mr. Muir—"

"Yes . . ."

"I have a message for you."

Distracted, Emmett hesitated with his hand on the Buick's door.

"From the laundry," Blixen said.

Emmett swayed in the dim light, blinking. "What laundry?"

"LoSordo's. Mr. Crouch."

"I don't know any Mr. Crouch—"

"The driver?" Blixen said. "Donald Meek?"

"Oh! Is that his name? Crouch?"

"He asked me to tell you that he can't find the paper you mentioned. He said he looked through the suit again personally. No luck."

For a second or two, Emmett continued to blink in the same mystified way, then he raised his hand to his beard, smoothing it, chopping it. "Is that a fact."

"That's what he told me."

"Mr. Blixen," Emmett said, "I haven't the faintest idea in the world of what you're talking about."

"Didn't you call LoSordo's earlier today?"

"No . . ."

"Talk to Crouch?"

"No . . . What was I supposed to have said?"

Inside the Buick, Wanda leaned across the wheel to look up at the two men in the lot. "Em?"

"Yes, just a second . . ."

"Forget it," Blixen said slowly. "It isn't important."

"Well, if somebody's using my name—"

"They didn't give a name," Blixen said. "Crouch thought he recognized your voice. Apparently he was wrong . . ." He forced a smile. "Doesn't matter . . . Go ahead . . ."

Emmett shrugged and piled into the car like a steamer trunk falling downstairs.

The wind tugged at Blixen's coattails; mist freckled his face.

"Don't get wet!" Emmett shouted. "We'll see you!"

Blixen watched the red taillights bob across the lot.

Kapralos honked and glowered as he passed.

"Come on!" Gail yelled. "Can you make it?"

"Just a matter of pre-planning," Blixen said. "Like packing a knapsack."

He collapsed backward into the Colt.

"You *did* it!"

"Oh yes."

"This is a darling little car."

Her voice was as bright and metallic as a girl's on a first date. Her knees were pressed together, her back was straight. Her hands gripped the bag in her lap convulsively.

"Are you warm enough?" Blixen inquired.

"Lovely, thank you."

"I'm sorry you had to go through such a wringer back there. I don't expect the man who interrogated you bothered to mention that you were entitled to counsel."

"He didn't—but it wouldn't have mattered anyway. Robert and I don't have a lawyer." She swallowed noisily, gazing straight ahead at the suck and flap of the windshield wipers. "I don't count at this point anyhow. Wanda's the one on the rack. I don't see how she stands it. Really. If anything ever happened to Robert, I'd be out of my mind. Stark, screaming crackers. But then we're different women. With different marriages."

"Weren't Wanda and Chet happy?"

The question, he saw at once, was too blunt. She needed to talk—about marriage, about Robert, about Wanda and Chet—but she needed to approach these thorny things in a mannerly circumspect way. "Well, I wouldn't know about that," she said vaguely. "After all, who could ever gauge another person's marriage? Who'd dare try?"

"True."

The wipers flapped; the tires sang; Blixen waited.

"Why do you ask?" she asked.

"No particular reason. I'd heard rumors."

"At the studio?"

"From Jennifer."

"Ah," Gail said. "Jennifer." She settled more deeply into the seat, pulled her long dress down. "Jennifer's had a rough time of it," she said finally. "Chet never should have had a daughter."

"Why not?"

"He didn't know how to cope with a girl," Gail said. "I think he was afraid of most women."

They slid to a stop at a flooded intersection; hail bounced in popcorn waves off the Colt's hood and rolled like candy on the drowned sidewalks. A potato-shaped old man under a black umbrella stood on the curb at right angles to them, scowling stubbornly at the green light.

"Chet," Gail said, "was just too—" She held her open palm out, switched it back and fourth. "Crafty. Do you know what I mean?"

"I think so."

"A girl needs someone straightforward to grow up with. Someone like Robert. Someone she can trust and take care of."

"Someone who can take care of her, you mean," Blixen said.

"What? Take care of her. Yes. What did I say?"

"Someone she can take care of."

"No, no," Gail laughed. "My God."

Blixen's signal turned green. The potato-shaped old man glared at the red light facing him and set out past Blixen's bumper.

"Look at that," Gail said. "Well, there you are. That's what poor Jen had to deal with. A father figure she had to watch every minute."

"Was he strict with her?"

"Well, now, strict doesn't matter, strict's all right—as long as it's consistent. But Chet was so—what?—*roundabout*. She'd ask him if she could see an R-rated movie with a girl friend's mother, and Chet would grin and nod—and then make her pay for it for a month."

"How?"

"Well, in this particular case, by pretending that it had all been a very subtle test on his part—that she'd failed him in some critical way by not turning the invitation down at the last moment. A *good* girl would have turned it down, you understand—not even asked her father. God alone knows what kind of a man she'll choose for a husband."

"Have you met any of her boy friends?"

"I don't think she has any."

"She has one, at least," Blixen said. "Named Ken."

"Ken I don't know," Gail said. "Ken? He might be a fantasy. Thirteen's a marvelous age for fantasizing."

"How did Wanda react to all of this?"

"To—?"

"To Chet's attitude toward his daughter."

"Do you know what I think?" Gail asked. "I think Wanda was biding her time."

Blixen glanced at her.

"That really is an answer to your question, believe it or not," Gail said. "I think she was just waiting until old man Muir died—"

"Before what?" Blixen asked.

"Asking Chet for a divorce."

"I see," Blixen said slowly. "Because of—?"

"Oh, because of a lot of things. Because of Jennifer. Because of—oh, a lot of things." Gail's reflection was masklike on the rainy window. The wipers slapped back and forth, whispering and hypnotic. "Wanda and I talk in the mornings, you know. We have a couple of cups of coffee and we talk about—oh, you know—life, sex, one thing and another."

"Yes."

"I don't think Wanda had a very good marriage."

"Really?"

"Not like mine. Of course, mine's pretty corny. Maybe I don't mean corny. Serene. Oh—Robert and I fight—but we've never gone to bed mad at each other."

"I envy you."

"Maybe you shouldn't. We aren't exactly Antony and Cleopatra. Sometimes I think we're more like Ma and Pa Kettle." She hesitated, trying not to smile, hands quiet in her lap. "I used to listen to Wanda, and I'd wonder sometimes if we were both from the same planet. Sex means a lot to Wanda."

"Doesn't it to everybody?"

Shrugging, Gail said: "I don't know. Maybe it's me." She stared out the window, at the black, shiny night. "Maybe it's what we're brought up to expect."

"I don't follow you."

"Well, look at Wanda. She'll be a beautiful woman until she dies, she's always been beautiful, she *expects* men to pant over her. Like poor Em. Or maybe it's lucky Em now."

"They were very close at one time, I understand," Blixen said.

"Yes, they were," Gail said. Her voice was soft. "Yes . . ."

"Still are, perhaps?"

But she was staring out the window, and wouldn't answer him.

Presently Blixen said: "I—notice that Emmett's the one she seems to turn to when—"

"Well, it's his shape, I think." A sudden grin transformed her plain face. "Doesn't he look like a koala? A little?"

"Well—"

"Maybe another man wouldn't see it. Or wouldn't react to it. I like him."

"I like him, too," Blixen said.

"They're all so different, the brothers," Gail went on. "Em's so kind of sentimental and slow, and Spence—" She hesitated. "I forget. Do you know Spencer?"

"Spencer's done a couple of stunts for me," Blixen answered. "Automobile crashes, bike spills . . ."

"Then you know what a gambler he is, how crazy he can act—"

Musingly Blixen said: "How did Spence and Chettie get along, Gail?"

"You mean when they weren't fighting?"

"They fought a lot, then . . ."

"Oh, they had their tiffs."

"Over what?"

"Spence's gambling, mostly."

"Chettie objected to that?"

"Yes, you bet he did."

"Why?"

Gail frowned. "Well, you have to realize that Chettie was a very moral man inside. Unfortunately he was also a sneak. You never knew when Chettie was going to sort of rise up and denounce you in front of the whole congregation for some peccadillo or other. I never trusted Chettie as far as I could throw him."

"They *were* different."

"The brothers? Totally. And it was all the old man's doing. He formed 'em, he whipped, 'em, he twisted 'em—"

"What did he do to Robert?"

"Well, Robert was lucky," Gail said. "See, Robert's nearly eleven years younger than Chet. He's *fourteen* years younger than Spencer. I think Robert was really an autumn accident. His mom never was well after he was born. She died when he was just a baby. Two or three. He doesn't even remember her. So the old man never really had time to muck him up." She pressed her palms to her cheeks. "Of course, Robert's got his flaws . . . He doesn't talk to me enough. He watches too much TV. He's terribly vain—"

"*Robert?*"

"Listen, you ought to see all the bottles of hair restorer that man's got in the medicine chest—"

"Why doesn't he wear a wig?"

"Too *vain* to wear a wig," Gail said. "He storms around and pours this smelly stuff on his head and says by God, he's going to grow hair or know the reason why! I wouldn't care if he was 100 per cent skin from top to bottom. I wouldn't care if he had *scales*. What does bald matter, when he's the kindest, sweetest—" She stopped, looking out at the driving rain between her palms. "And he loves me," she said.

"Then you're a lucky woman," Blixen said.

"I'm the luckiest woman who ever lived," Gail replied. The blunt fingers pressed against the sallow skin. "We went to school together, same class. We're exactly the same age." She glanced back at Blixen. "Would you have guessed that?"

"Is it a secret?"

"Most people think I'm older than Robert."

"I don't suppose I ever thought about it one way or another."

"Same age," Gail repeated. "I've always seemed older. I was *born* older. My dresses were always too long. I was a little old woman at six and a half. But Robert must have liked that. We were both quiet. We didn't scare each other. He'd help me with my arithmetic and I'd give him my tuna-fish sandwiches."

"Very handsome arrangement on both sides."

"Yes, very."

"The old man must like you, too."

"Whatever in this wide world makes you think that?"

"You're part of the family," Blixen pointed out.

"Not through any help of his," Gail said. "Damned old bastard." She squared her shoulders irritably. "Oh, I'm sorry he's sick, but, I mean, my God. He did everything he could think of to break us up. He had some chippie in the MGM make-up department all picked out for Robert."

"At least Robert stood up to him. That's more than Chet was able to do."

"*I* stood up to him," Gail snapped. She dropped her hands to her lap and sat up straighter, furious at some memory. "I told him Robert and I loved each other and we were going to get married whether he liked it or not, and we'd both be much obliged to him if he'd just piss off." She gave a throaty chuckle. "I think I added 'please.'"

"And he did?"

"He did. Or rather, he didn't do anything and Robert and I marched away to Tijuana and had the job done there."

"But the old man seems to have accepted it . . ."

"Oh, who knows? I guess so. It doesn't matter anyway. Robert matters. Nothing else. And nobody's going to hurt him. *Nobody.*"

"Do you think somebody's trying to?"

"You should have been in on the grilling those cops put me through. You bet they're trying. I don't cry much, but they made me so mad I couldn't help it." She gazed at her hands. "They think they've got motive—"

"The argument at Chasen's?"

"That crazy argument . . ."

"Do you know what it was about?"

"Robert wouldn't tell me . . . And now they're sniffing around for opportunity. I could see their little eyes light up the minute they found out that Robert hadn't checked into his hotel."

"Yes, how about that?"

"Oh, lord, I don't know." Her face seemed to sag. "He went someplace else, I suppose."

"But you said you'd called every other hotel in—"

"We couldn't possibly call *all* of them. Or he may have gone on down to Chula Vista or National City or someplace. A thousand things could have happened. The point is I'm not going to let these dummies or anybody else crucify my husband just because—" She broke off. "The point is he didn't do it," she said.

"Why not?"

Distraught, she exclaimed: "Well, you know him! You've worked with him! I'm surprised at you."

"Are you capable of murder?"

"Me! God, yes."

"Is Wanda? Emmett?"

"Well—"

"Spencer?"

"Yes . . ."

"All of them?"

"Yes! I *said* yes . . ."

"And so am I," Blixen said. "Now—what makes Robert different?"

Gail continued to stare at him for a moment, her mouth open, and then she switched abruptly away. "Boy," she said, "what a great comfort you turned out to be."

"Comfort's a very tricky business," Blixen said. "I don't think whistling in the dark can sustain it. I think it has to be built on reason."

"Love's reason enough for me," Gail muttered.

"Was it reason enough for the police?"

"That's the only four letter word they never heard of."

"Neither have defense attorneys."

"I really don't know what you're talking about," Gail said.

"Still talking about reason," Blixen replied. "I've seen your husband get mad. So have you."

"All right, what about it?"

"What happens?"

"Oh, come on—"

"Tell me."

"What *happens*? He gets *mad!*"

"Right away?"

"You're damn right, right away! He goes stomping around, hollering—"

"How long have you been married, Gail?"

"How—? Twelve years—"

"What's the longest you've ever seen Robert hold a grudge?"

"About a minute and a half—" She was goggling at him now, beginning to understand, biting off her answers. She had hunkered around until she was perched on one leg, facing him.

"So if he wanted to get even with Chet after the fight in Chasen's—"

Excitedly Gail said: "He'd find a chair and come out and whop him over the head with it!"

"Or shoot him in the chest or gut him with a butcher knife," Blixen said, "or do almost anything at all except wait two months to poison him. Right?"

"Well, for pete's sake," Gail breathed. Her eyes were glowing.

"Now how do you feel?" Blixen asked.

Rapturously, she hooked a hand around his neck and planted a kiss on his cheek. "Anyway, poison's a woman's trick, isn't it?" she asked.

"Ask Neill Cream and Dr. Crippen . . ."

"Well, it isn't *Robert's* kind of trick—"

"It wouldn't seem to be."

"But how do we convince the dumb police of that?"

"Maybe we won't have to," Blixen said. "District Attorneys are very much aware that a man's innocent until he's proven guilty. Their jobs depend on being aware of it. If Robert has any kind of an alibi for this morning, he won't be charged."

"He'll have an alibi," Gail said, "even if I have to furnish it myself." She grinned: "I'm kidding. I'll find out where he was. He may not want to tell me, but I'll find out."

"Why wouldn't he want to tell you?"

"Well, examine it," Gail said. "Man says his studio's sending him down to San Diego for a couple of days. But he's lying. Why?"

"I'll bite. Why?"

"Because he wants to do something else—something secret—something he's ashamed of. The police think, sure, he's murdering his brother. But what does his wife think?"

"That he's lolling around with another woman . . ."

"Right on," Gail said. Her grin had grown forced, sullen. "Well, we'll see what little Mr. Innocence has to say about *that*."

"Now don't jump to—"

"I won't, I won't." Her big hands lay still in her lap, palms up, fingers curled like a child's. "Don't worry, I know the routine." She stared at the rain sluicing down the side window. "Man's innocent until he's proven guilty, okay?"

"Okay."

She was still for a moment, studying the rain and her own faint reflection on the black glass. "But a man's human, too," she went on. "I mean, who'd blame him?" Her reflection jiggled beside her like a dry ghost in the wet night, strong-jawed, ugly and lost. "I mean, *look* at me," she whispered.

IX

At eight o'clock on a Saturday night in Southern California in the rain, a madman (Blixen reflected) could shoot a cannon down Hollywood Boulevard without drawing blood. Rain traumatized Southern Californians. It hit them in the face and made them squint. It lay in dimpled lakes on their flat lawns. Rivers of it roared against the grilled mouths of their huge inadequate sewers and sometimes swept drunken men to their deaths. So the smart money stayed home, or ran for cover, angry and anxious, wondering why it had ever left Indiana in the first place . . .

"It's the next street," Gail called over the clatter. "Next corner!"

"Right," Blixen said.

"Isn't this terrible? Maybe it's the end of the world!"

"Why, this is just a pretty shower," Blixen said, "although I'd feel better if the animals would stop lining up, two by two."

Pointing, Gail said: "There's the house! The white one."

"Is that yours?"

"Wanda's. We're the big brick thing on the right."

"We must be the first. Everything's dark—"

"Here they are," Gail said, and waved when the Buick honked and passed them, spraying water like a fireboat.

Blixen pulled in ahead of a nondescript gray sedan. "Sit tight. There's an umbrella here somewhere—"

"We'll have to wait until she unlocks the door anyway," Gail said. "We all double-lock everything. Ever since the robbery."

"What robbery?"

"She was robbed," Gail said. "Wanda."

"Really? When?"

"Oh, it must have been a couple of months ago. Well—just before Christmas. They didn't get anything valuable—just a purse—"

The Buick lumbered up the driveway beside the white ranch house and rocked to a stop, taillights flaring, while Wanda activated the automatic garage-door opener and then leaped out, even before the huge door had swung all the way up, to run wildly back to the Colt at the curb.

Appalled, Gail threw the door open. "Wanda, are you *crazy?* Get in here! You'll drown! What are you—"

"Did you see him?"

"Who?"

"Robert!"

"*Robert*—!"

"On the boulevard," Wanda gasped. "At the signal. We *passed* him. He's right behind us." She wigwagged her arms. "There he is!"

Gail had swung around to stare out the rear window. Now, as she scrambled into the street, Blixen grasped her arm. Her face was ashen but composed. "I'm perfectly all right, let go . . ." She jerked her forearm out of his grip and ran back through the frenzied rain toward the station wagon that was nosing into the driveway beside the red brick house.

The umbrella, of course, had worked its way under the seat like a barb into flesh, and since Blixen had to get into the gutter even to spot it, he was sodden by the time he'd yanked it out and cursed it open. Wanda, he saw, had gained her front steps, and was huddled under the overhang, looking for her key. He slammed the Colt's door shut and splashed off past the nondescript gray sedan. There were two men in the sedan, one behind the wheel and one in the back, and as he passed, Blixen realized with a start that he recognized the one in the rear, that it was Fries, red hair, notebook, and all.

He nearly tapped on the window. He bent down, but Fries, who must have seen him, pretended that he had not, so Blixen drew his hand back and continued on, feeling peevish and disturbed.

Gail, short hair plastered to her skull, had slipped into the station wagon beside her husband and appeared to be remonstrating volubly when Blixen sloshed up. This time he did tap, and Robert, after turning a frightened face to him, reached back and unlocked the rear door so that Blixen could pile in. "Nils . . ." he said.

"Welcome home."

"Well," Gail said, "at least he wasn't hurt and lying in some ditch someplace." Her voice trembled; she was on the brink of tears. "He didn't know about Chettie."

"Did she get it right?" Robert asked Blixen. "Poison?"

"Yes, oxalic acid."

Robert whistled and dried the corner of his mouth on the heel of his hand. He was balding and long-nosed, like his brothers, though far younger, still the baby of the family at thirty-one. He was a capable assistant director, not as forceful as he might have been, but conscientious and diplomatic.

"Guess where he was," Gail said shakily. "Tijuana."

"Every bloody time I lie, this is what happens," Robert said.

"So when are you going to learn your lesson?" Gail asked.

"Robert," Blixen said, "when the police get to you—"

"When the what?"

"Oh, Robert, wake *up!*" Gail cried. "Chettie's been killed!"

"Well—I didn't kill him," Robert said. He gaped at Blixen. "Do they think I killed him?"

"They'll certainly want to know about the brawl you got into at Chasen's."

"Ah, Nils, that didn't amount to a hill of beans! You were there—"

"I thought it looked pretty rough—"

"We were *kidding*—"

"You weren't *kidding!*" Gail said. "Now quit it!"

"What was the fight about, Robert?"

"The fight," Robert muttered. "I don't even remember—"

"You'd *better* remember," Gail warned.

Robert glanced at her, and then rested his hands on the top of the steering wheel and stared past them at the wash of the rain. "Okay, how did it start," he said. "He was drunk—he'd spilled something on his tie—he wanted mine . . . I told him no—and he hit me . . ."

Gail closed her mouth and stared at Blixen and then looked back at Robert. "Well, that's the dopiest—"

"It's true."

"I didn't say it wasn't true. It's so dumb, it's probably got to be true. Nils? What do you think?"

Pensively Blixen said: "Where did you stay in Tijuana, Robert?"

"I drove down to Rosarita, but the hotel was full so I slept on the beach."

"Alone?"

"Of course alone."

"Talk to anybody down there?"

"Well—the desk clerk. It was crowded. I don't know if he'd remember me."

"How about women?" Gail asked.

"How about what women?"

Raising her eyes, Gail said: "Did you see any women?"

"Not to talk to," Robert said.

"To do anything else to?"

"No," Robert said.

"Look," Gail said, "you're going to need an alibi. Now, I'll ask you again. Who were you with?"

"I was alone."

"Okay, it's your funeral," Gail said. But her relief proclaimed itself in every line of her square body.

"You know, this is wild," Robert said. "I take a couple of days off and all of a sudden I'm Cain."

"I still don't see why you wanted to feed me all that baloney about San Diego," Gail said.

"I wanted to be alone—"

"Why didn't you just *tell* me you wanted to be alone?"

"I don't know. Maybe I'm crazy."

"Maybe you are," Gail said. "But I guess I'll keep you anyway." She lifted her fingers to a lock of his thinning hair but stopped when he stiffened. "Your hair needs combing," she said.

"So does yours," Robert said. "Who's this?"

Blixen followed his gaze. "Oh, Socrates and Jennifer." The tiny sports car wheeled into Wanda's drive.

"Well, we're all here then," Gail said in a bright artificial voice. "I was beginning to worry about those two." She patted Robert's knee.

"I think Wanda wants to keep busy. She's having a pot-luck dinner. Have you eaten?"

"Not yet—"

"Come on—"

"You go ahead," Robert told her. "I'll put the car away."

"Wait a second," Blixen said to Gail, and ducked into the rain, fighting the umbrella. The tattoo on the taut black silk was deafening; water flooded into his shoes as he waded around to the front passenger door. The wind tore the door out of his hand when he opened it, and Gail tumbled toward him, laughing and scared.

"I tell you it's the end of the *world*—!"

Blixen slammed the door shut and rapped on the steamy window, whereupon Robert gave them a brisk toot and headed on up the drive toward his open garage door. Out of the corner of his eye Blixen could see a raincoat flapping beside the gray nondescript sedan at the curb. Fries had emerged.

"Nils, hurry up!" Gail hollered.

"Here, take the umbrella!" Blixen called to her. "Have you got it?"

"Well, what—"

"I want to talk to Robert—"

"I'll come with you—"

"No, go on, go on!" He beamed reassuringly and urged her away. She moved a suspicious foot or two sideways, like a puppy, and stopped.

"Go on!"

But she had noticed Fries, now, who was cutting sloppily across the lawn, bearing toward Robert's garage, and she threw Blixen a look of scorn and betrayal and broke into a knock-kneed lope back up the drive again.

With a groan, Blixen started after her.

Robert by this time had berthed his hulking car and slid out on the passenger side: Blixen could see him moving carefully along a cabinet of some sort braced against the wall.

"Robert!" Gail yelled, but Fries, running hard, cut diagonally in front of her and said: "Mr. Robert Muir?" and Robert whirled and threw an open can of yellow paint at him and then sprinted, white-faced, around the station wagon and through the service door in the rear. Fries managed to duck away from the paint can, but went sprawling when Gail—perhaps accidentally, probably deliberately—tripped him. She kept screaming in a thin, breathless, school-girlish way, and tried to kick Fries's wrist before he could draw his hand out of his raincoat pocket. He succeeded finally in freeing the hand—which held a whistle instead of a gun—and blew the whistle, but

Gail continued to scream and kick him, this time in the back, until Blixen was able to wrap his long arms around her and literally lift her away.

"Wernstedt?" Fries kept yelling. "Wernstedt!"

"Stop it!" Blixen snapped into Gail's ear.

"They'll kill him!"

"They won't kill him! They've caught him. Be still!"

She wriggled around to stare into his eyes. "Caught—"

"Listen!"

Fries had gone limping into the garage to turn the overhead light on. "Bring him back here, Charlie!"

"They were hiding in the yard!" Gail said.

"Yes."

"They must have been there for hours!"

"It looks like it."

"Robert?" Gail screamed.

But he was safe—wet and panting, but unharmed. A uniformed L.A. patrolman had him in a hammerlock; he came stumbling into the garage, head bent and face beet-red. "Are you Robert Muir?" Fries asked.

"You'd be in a hell of a fix if I said no, wouldn't you?"

"Are you Robert Muir?"

"Yes!"

"Sheriff's office. You're under arrest. You have the right to remain silent. You have the right to counsel. If you can't afford counsel, it'll be supplied. Do you understand?"

"Don't give the bastards the time of day, Robert!" Gail screamed.

"He's got counsel," Blixen told Fries. "Wade Schreiber. Where are you taking him?"

"Hall of Justice. This is still a county case."

"Nils," Robert said, "I can't—"

"No charge," Blixen said. "NFB Productions retains Schreiber."

Robert stared at him. "I don't know what to say, Nils."

"I'll bet you don't," Fries said. "I'm damned if I'd know what to say in your place."

"I don't think we need any smart comments from you, Sergeant," Blixen said.

"You're going to get 'em whether you need 'em or not," Fries said. "Connie?"

"Yoh," said a plain-clothesman behind him, the driver of the non-descript gray sedan.

Fries snapped his fingers and held his hand out and the plain-clothesman put a battered half-gallon can into it.

Robert straightened slowly.

"We went through the garage before you got here, Mr. Muir," Fries said. "Through those cabinets." He balanced the battered can on his palm. "Is this what you were looking for?"

Staring, Blixen read the label. DILL'S RUST AND SCALE CLEANER, it said. And below that, POISON, KEEP AWAY FROM CHILDREN. And below that:

OXALIC ACID . . .

X

He was suspended in a muscle-aching limbo, neither asleep nor awake, when the phone rang. He had neglected to close his bedroom's blackout curtains the night before, and a low red morning sun vibrated between the bars on his balcony. His throat ached. He had kicked his bottom sheet loose in the night and he was wrapped up in that like a silkworm halfway to his hips. It was six minutes past six, according to the clock on his bedside table; he had gotten to sleep at four-fifteen.

The phone was too heavy for his hand, but at least he had stopped the ringing. He put his ear by the receiver and grunted, "What," into the pillow.

"Who is this!" someone snapped.

"There are only two people on this teeming earth," Blixen said, "who would dial an unlisted number in the dead of night and then ask a voice as familiar as mine who it was. You're either my secretary, or you're Arthur. Am I right?"

"Jesus, you're crabby when you first wake up," Todd said.

"I knew it," Blixen said.

"Do you take the *Times*?" Todd asked. "I forget."

"I take the *Times*."

"Have you seen it?"

"No."

"You're in it."

"Am I," Blixen said, and turned heavily onto his back. "I kind of thought I might be."

"But you didn't kind of think I might like to know about it first?"

"I told you Chet had died—"

"But you didn't tell—"

"Arthur, may I go to the bathroom before we get into a big discussion here?"

"There again," Todd said, "you seem to give me a choice, but you really don't. You'll go no matter what I say."

"I'll call you back," Blixen said.

"No, you won't," Todd said. "I'll hang on."

Blixen shook his head a little and sat up, squinting at the sun, and then he plodded into the bathroom, where he relieved himself and washed his hands and face and grew progressively madder when he thought about being waked up at six minutes past six on a Sunday morning. He considered shaving, but dropped the idea and picked up the phone instead and prowled out to the balcony. The day was fresh and bright, pleasantly chilly. Hollywood smelled of cold pavements and honeysuckle. "Arthur," he said, "do you realize what time it is?"

"Oh, there you are," Todd said. "You bet your bottom dollar I know what time it is. Do you know why?"

"Why?"

"Because I got called at five-thirty," Todd said, "when the Chairman in New York heard about the murder on his eight o'clock news broadcast."

"Ah."

"He was certainly upset," Todd continued. "He asked me if I'd heard from the network this morning, and I said no. He thinks they'll dump us."

"He's wrong."

"Don't be too bloody sure."

"I'm sure because I talked to Pablo last night."

"To—!"

"I called him from the Hall of Justice," Blixen said. "I explained what had happened. I told him that Chettie had been murdered and that the police suspected Robert. I said that I disagreed with that, and that the studio would stand behind Robert 100 per cent until the whole mess was cleared up. I talked about a man being innocent until proven guilty, and I said that I knew the network would support our position to the death."

"Why, you lunatic," Todd said. "Don't you understand—"

"Pablo said naturally they'd support us," Blixen went on, "because after all, that's what *Stagg* was about, wasn't it? Justice?"

"Pablo said what?" Todd asked.

"Pablo said—"

"Was he sober?" Todd broke in.

"As a nun."

"Then where's the catch? He knows how the affiliates are bound to react when they see those headlines!"

"He claims he can handle the affiliates. Just as long as one of the stars didn't do the murder."

"I knew there was a catch!" Todd shouted.

Wearily Blixen said: "Arthur—" and then, "Oh, forget it."

"You don't know actors like I do," Todd said.

"Arthur," Blixen said, "listen—ordinarily there is nothing I would enjoy more than standing here on my cold balcony in my ripped pajamas arguing with you about actors, but I think I am just too tired for it this morning. I didn't get home until three-thirty—"

"Where were you?"

"Downtown. I told you that. Arranging bail for Robert—"

"Do they allow bail on a capital charge—?"

"They didn't charge him with murder," Blixon said. "Schreiber finally got the thing reduced to resisting an officer."

"Are you sure?" Todd asked. "Because the paper calls him Muir's killer."

"The paper'd better not, unless the paper wants a suit on its hands."

"Wait a minute. Oh."

"Alleged killer?"

"It was continued on page fourteen," Todd said. "It's funny. They make out a hell of a case against him on page three."

"There *is* a hell of a case against him," Blixon admitted. "He had motive. He may have had opportunity. He certainly had access to the kind of poison the murderer used—"

"Maybe he's guilty."

"Maybe."

"Well—then what are you defending him for?"

"Because I think everything's moving too fast," Blixen said. "I think everybody ought to sit down and ponder awhile. So did the District Attorney in the end."

"Do you know the best thing that could happen?" Todd asked. "If it turned out to be suicide."

"It wasn't suicide."

"It might have been. Quit fighting it."

"I'm not fighting it. I'm just telling you that nothing about that death was consistent with suicide. He wasn't terribly ill, there weren't any money problems, he didn't leave a note—"

"A hundred things might have depressed him," Todd insisted. "The paper says he always went out to San Urbano when he was depressed.

"Well," Blixen said, "that's not strictly accurate. As I understand it, he went out there to renew himself spiritually. And—maybe this time—to meet somebody . . ."

"To meet who? The killer?"

"I don't know, Art. It was an impression his daughter had."

"Man or woman?"

Blixen hesitated. "She wasn't sure . . ."

"Stagg would have been sure," Todd grumbled.

"Yes he would."

"And there you stand without a thought in your head—"

"Well—that's not strictly accurate either. As a matter of fact, if I were Fries, I know at least three people I'd keep an eye on—"

"Who's Fries?"

"Sheriff's detective in charge of the case."

"Um. Which three?"

"I don't want to go into that yet."

"Now don't start talking like a mystery novel—!"

"The names wouldn't mean anything to you, Art. Members of the family."

"I don't know," Todd said unhappily, "I just wish you'd leave the thing alone. I keep getting the feeling that there's this volcano over my head and you're up there pitching bombs down it."

"I'm just going to ask a couple of questions, Arthur."

"Like what?"

"They wouldn't mean anything to you—"

"How can you tell?" Todd demanded. "You always underestimate me."

"All right, then," Blixen said. "First of all, I'd like to find out where the missing note is—if, indeed, it even exists—and what it said, and why Emmett Muir denied calling the laundry about it."

"What laundry?"

"Second," Blixen continued, "I think it's vital for us to trace Chettie's four hundred dollars. Third—is the Kenneth who pistol-whipped two women and a bartender the same Kenny who told Jennifer that Chettie's karma would have to catch up to him someday? Fourth—"

"Nils-Frederik," Todd said.

"Yes."

"Bug off. I'll talk to you tomorrow."

"Good-by, Arthur."

Thoughtfully Blixen hung up the phone and pondered motives and opportunities and liars and lovers and volcanos and bombs while the red sun rose and turned yellow and the city began to wake. . . .

XI

By nine, he had showered and shaved and was enough awake to make himself some coffee, which helped. He phoned Ronald, the doorman, and asked him to bring the Colt around, and then he consulted the Yellow Pages and dialed LoSordo's Laundry and Dry Cleaning.

"Good morning, LoSordo's," Marge said.

Startled, Blixen said: "Well, for crying out loud. Is this you?"

"What?" Marge said.

"I'm sorry," Blixen laughed, "I didn't expect to hear your voice. What do you do, work every day in the week? This is Nils Blixen."

"Oh, *hi,*" Marge said. "No, I'm off Fridays and half a day on Tuesday. Hey, we lost your number! Don't hang up until I get it. My goodness, I read about the *murder!* Isn't that awful?"

"Awful . . . I don't suppose Mr. Crouch is there—?"

"Not today," Marge said. "But I know he wants to talk to you. You'd have thought I lost the number on purpose. I said, 'Bert, listen, I don't have to take that kind of talk from anybody.' He wanted to call you yesterday."

"Oh?"

"He found the note."

Blixen, pouring himself a cup of coffee dregs, put the pot down and sat back on his breakfast bench.

"Well, *he* didn't find it," Marge said. "The presser found it. Guess where it was."

"I can't imagine."

"In the watch pocket. All folded up. I didn't think anybody put anything in watch pockets any more—even watches. But there it was."

"Well, well, well," Blixen murmured. "And—what did it say?"

"We don't know."

"Why not?"

"It's music—a staff with eight or nine squiggles on it. We tried to whistle it, but we all got something different. I think it's an army trumpet call, but Mr. Crouch says it's Beethoven."

"Where's the note now?"

"Well, it's property," Marge said, "so I guess it must be with the suit. They put whatever they find like that in a little plastic envelope, and then they pin it to the jacket . . ."

"I'd like to see it," Blixen said. "Is the suit ready?"

"Uh—yes, it is."

"I'll be right over."

"Okay—when?"

"Ten minutes," Blixen said, and added an absent good-by and hung up. He sat tapping a fingernail against his coffee cup while he reread the *Times* account of the murder and then he lifted the phone and dialed again.

"Hello," a deep male voice said.

"Oh, I beg your pardon," Blixen said. "Wrong number."

"Quite all right," said the voice.

Blixen depressed the receiver bar with one finger, fished a card out of his pocket, and redialed carefully.

"Hello," said the deep male voice.

"Well, what's wrong here?" Blixen said. "I'm terribly sorry. I'm trying to get five-three-five nine-one-two-four—"

"Yes," said the voice, "this is five-three-five nine-one-two-four. Who did you want?"

"Uh—Mrs. Nicholas?"

"Hang on."

Blixen stared at the receiver and then put it back to his ear when Irene said: "Yes . . ."

"Hello—Irene?"

"Yes . . ."

"Nils Blixen . . ."

"Oh, hello! I think we must be on the same wave length or something. I was just about to call *you*."

"You were?"

"I've been reading about your poor cutter. How shocked you must have been! I mean, that it was murder. And then to have his own brother guilty. . . . I understand the brother worked for you, too . . ."

"Yes, but Robert isn't necessarily guilty—"

"Oh? Hasn't he been arrested?"

"Not for murder," Blixen said. "The paper got a little ahead of itself."

"Then who gave Muir the poison?"

"We don't know yet."

"Better call on Saul Stagg . . ."

"I wish we could."

Her voice softened. "Oh, Nils, I don't mean to joke about it. I know how dreadful this must be for everyone at the studio. Is that why you phoned? Have you changed your mind about the meeting tomorrow?"

"No, no," Blixen said. "No. As a matter of fact—" He hesitated. "Well—I've arranged to meet Wade Schreiber in San Urbano at noon—and—I thought you might like to come along. For the ride," he added awkwardly. "For lunch."

"Oh, Nils, I'd love to, but—"

"I remember you mentioned something about Disneyland. Still—I thought—"

"*Damn* it!" Irene said. "You know, if it was *anyone* but Curtis, I'd cancel like a shot, but he's been after me and after me—"

"*Curtis?*"

"Curtis. Yes. My husband, Curtis—"

"You're going to *Disneyland?* With *Curtis?*"

"Well—yes—"

"Who answered the phone just now?" Blixen demanded.

"Curtis did."

"This is unbelievable," Blixen said. "You don't even *like* Curtis. You told me that."

"Nils," Irene said, "I don't have to justify my actions to you—inexplicable as they may seem. *Or* my words. Now if—"

"Oh yes, you do!"

"Why?"

"*Why!*" But his position was untenable and he knew it. "*Why!*"

"Do you know what I think," Irene said in a tone of serene reason, "I think you're overwrought. You've begun to sound like a French farce. This is my husband you're being indignant about. I'll see you tomorrow, when we're both calmer. I'm awfully sorry about your editor. Are you there?"

"Yes," Blixen said.

"Good-by, Nils," Irene said.

"Good-by," Blixen said.

But she'd already hung up.

XII

Nothing could counteract his inner sense of ruin—not the brook-fresh, surprising morning, not the crystalline air, not the woman walking her duck on a leash past the old Columbia Studios on Gower, not even Marge in a new sky-blue sari and a ruby in her nose.

"It's fake," Marge said of the ruby. "It's got a little gummed sticker on the inside, but the trouble is if I sweat too much, it falls off."

"Story of this town," Blixen muttered. "Sham, all sham."

"Yeah, right," Marge said, and turned and called "Mr. CROUCH?" in a stentorian bellow.

When his head stopped ringing, Blixen said: "I thought he was home this morning."

"I phoned him," Marge replied. "He just lives a couple of blocks away. He's as excited as I am. Neither one of us ever knew a victim before."

"Hoy," said Mr. Crouch, rolling through the curtains. He was wearing an ancient brindle-colored jacket, billowy bermuda shorts, and open sandals, and he looked flushed and sheepish and somehow wrong, like a priest in leotards. Mr. Crouch was built, it seemed to Blixen, for snow-white shirts and black plastic bow ties.

"Hoy," Blixen said.

"Did you give it to him?" Mr. Crouch asked Marge.

"Huh-uh, not yet."

"This," said Mr. Crouch, "is the craziest thing I ever heard of."

"The note?" Blixen asked.

"Well, that, too. But I meant the murder. I couldn't believe my eyes when I opened the paper this morning. Who'd poison a man like Mr. Muir? You told us it was heart."

"I said they weren't sure."

"How's Mrs. Muir? Have you seen her?"

"Yes, she's bearing up."

"Poor thing. Like the *Daughter of the Red Death* . . ."

"Like what?" Marge asked

"You don't remember that?"

"No . . ."

"*You* do," Mr. Crouch said to Blixen.

"I don't think so . . ."

"*Daughter of the Red Death?*"

"Clue me in," Blixen said.

"B.K.," Mr. Crouch said, and then: "Wait a minute. I'm wrong. Wanda Mills never starred with Karloff. Uh—well. She was married to this monster from outer space, but she didn't know it because he was in human form."

"Wow," Marge said.

"I must have missed that one," Blixen said.

"Brutally bad picture," said Mr. Crouch. "She was good, though. She finally turned on him."

"On the *monster?*" Marge cried. "What happened?"

"Well," Mr. Crouch said and stopped.

"I'm going to look for this on TV," Marge said. "What happened?"

But Mr. Crouch's eyes had become fixed on some horizon beyond her shoulder.

"Bert?" she said.

"Get the note," said Mr. Crouch.

"Yes, but what—"

"It's with the suit. Hurry up. Please."

Irritably Marge steamed away. Mr. Crouch glanced at Blixen, who had folded his arms and was studying the tips of his shoes.

"How about this weather?" Mr. Crouch said. "Say, here's a pair of initials for you. R.A."

After a time Blixen said: "Were you left behind when the troops pulled out?"

"No," Mr. Crouch said, "I'm not Renee Adoree."

"Were you better known by your nickname?"

Mr. Crouch rested his nose on the tip of a forefinger and closed his eyes. "Give me a second," he said.

"Here you go," Marge growled, and brought the gray twill suit to the counter and handed the envelope to Blixen, still a little huffy.

The multi-folded rectangle of paper inside had been torn off a lined music tablet. The notes on the two treble staffs had been scrawled in pencil:

"Da-da da," Blixen muttered. "Da, da, da, da . . ."

"No, I'm not Roscoe Arbuckle!" Mr. Crouch shouted.

"Well?" Marge said.

"The two parts are in different hands," Blixen said. "I wonder why . . ."

Marge divided her long hair over her nose and grimaced at Blixen. "Yes, but what *is* it?"

"I'm no good at this," Blixen confessed. "I can't hear written notes. I'm like a blind man feeling a canvas . . ."

"Look," Marge said, and touched the paper with one silvery fingernail. "Its a trumpet call—retreat or something."

"Ignore her," said Mr. Crouch. "It's not a trumpet call. Trust me."

"Why trust you?" Marge snapped. "You're the one who tried to tell me that 'God Bless America' was England's national anthem."

"I meant 'America,'" said Mr. Crouch.

"That's even dumber," Marge said.

"Could Emmett have written it himself?" speculated Blixen. "He's a composer."

"Um . . ." Mr. Crouch said.

"Well, if he did, he stole it from a trumpet call," Marge said.

"Maybe that's why he won't acknowledge it," Blixen mused. Mr. Crouch looked blank, and Blixen added: "I had a little talk with him last night."

"About this?"

Blixen nodded. "He denies phoning here."

Mr. Crouch wrinkled his large forehead and Marge peered from him to Blixen in confusion and said: "He *does?* Why?"

Blixen folded the note without answering and replaced it in the envelope. At last he said, "Mr. Crouch—"

"Bert."

"Bert. How sure are you that it was Emmett you were talking to?"

"Well—I thought I was positive . . ." Mr. Crouch pursed his Donald Meek lips, cradled his elbows, and blinked down at the floor. He gave a sharp nod. "I'm positive."

"It was Emmett?"

"Emmett—absolutely. I talk to the man twice a week. I know his voice when I hear it."

"Did you talk to him, Marge?" Blixen asked.

"Yes . . ."

"What did he say?"

"He asked to speak to Bert. So I—"

"Wait now. Did he say 'Bert'? Or did he say 'The man on the route,' or—"

"He said 'Mr. Crouch.'"

"'Mr. Crouch . . .'"

"He knows my name," Mr. Crouch said. "They all know my name."

"Hey," Marge said, "is that a clue?"

Blixen studied the envelope on both sides before handing it back to Marge. "I wonder. . . . Can you pin it on again?"

"Don't you want it?"

"I think I'll let the undertaker discover it. See what happens."

"He'll probably call Mrs. Muir," said Mr. Crouch.

"Probably."

"She won't know what's going on."

Half to himself, Blixen said: "Won't she?"

"Well, I don't see how . . ."

"Funeral still on Tuesday?" asked Marge.

"As far as I know."

"How did the old man react to all this, by the way?" Mr. Crouch inquired.

"I don't think anybody's told him yet. I'm not sure he'd understand if they did."

"Ah, why don't they show some mercy?" Mr. Crouch groaned. "Pull the tubes out and let him die."

"Because life's sacred," Marge said.

"Bert," Blixen said, under the prodding of another thought, "when I was here last, you mentioned that you often had difficulty spotting the difference between Emmett and Spencer on the phone—"

"No, between Spencer and *Chet*," Mr. Crouch said. "Emmett I always recognized. . . . Why?"

Blixen tweaked his nose and lifted his shoulder. "I don't know. . . . I guess I'm just trying to touch all the bases. Even the ones that aren't there."

"Spencer isn't home anyway," added Mr. Crouch. "I think Columbia sent him over to Vegas."

"Oh, wow, *sent* him?" Marge said. "There's a tough assignment."

"It is for this fellow."

"Spencer's got a little gambling problem," Blixen said.

"Not so little either," said Mr. Crouch.

Intrigued, Marge said: "Now how the heck would you know that?"

"Oh, I get around."

"People tend to gossip with their laundrymen, do they, Bert?" Blixen asked slowly.

"Laundrymen and butchers."

"You'll have to write your memoirs someday."

"I wouldn't dare."

After a time, Blixen said: "Ever hear anything about Chet and his wife?"

Mr. Crouch pulled his tentlike shorts up a little and straightened. "Well—"

"How did they get along? As far as you could see?"

"Tell him about the blood on her nightgown," Marge said.

But Mr. Crouch's cornered face already had begun to assume the truculent blush of a man who had signed more bond pledges than he could redeem. "What blood?"

"The time she came to the door with the black eye and the split lip. When—"

"He doesn't want to hear about that—"

"Sure he does. Tell him."

"Tell me," Blixen said.

Unhappily Mr. Crouch said: "That's it. She came to the door with a black eye—"

"And a split lip," Marge said.

"Lip was a little puffy—"

"When did all this take place?" Blixen asked.

"Quite a while ago—"

"Right at Christmas," Marge said. "'Twas the season to be jolly. Don't you remember?"

"No."

"Oh, you do, too."

"Listen," Mr. Crouch said cheerlessly to Blixen, "all of this has to be off the record—"

"Of course."

"I'm sorry we got into it. She claimed she fell down."

"But you doubt that?"

"Well—"

"Sure she fell down," Marge said. "The same way those poor guys do who get in the ring with Muhammad Ali."

"So the daughter wasn't fantasizing after all . . ." Blixen reflected.

"Fantasizing? About what? What did she say?"

Blixen gave Marge a thoughtful glance. "Oh, much the same thing. The beatings happened so often, as a matter of fact, that she began to wonder if her mother enjoyed them."

"Oh, come on."

"'There are more things in heaven and earth, Horatio,'" said Mr. Crouch glumly, "'than are dreamt of in your philosophy.'"

"Yeah, maybe," Marge said. "And maybe not."

"The girl told me something else interesting," Blixen went on. "She said she had a boy friend." He paused. "Named Ken."

Mr. Crouch raised his bruised eyes.

"Yeah," Marge said, "well, what's that got to do with anything?"

"Either of you know anything about it?"

Marge frowned. "She didn't mean our Ken, did she?"

"Did she, Bert?" Blixen asked.

"*Our* Ken!" Marge repeated incredulously.

Exhaling, Mr. Crouch said: "All right, why would that be so crazy?"

"Why would it be so *crazy!*" Marge yelled. "Bert, that little kid can't be more than fourteen—!"

"Neither was Juliet."

"But Juliet was in love with Romeo, not the L.A. Slasher—"

"He's not the L.A. Slasher—"

"It wouldn't surprise me!"

"Oh, hold your tongue!" Mr. Crouch barked at her. "It's none of your business anyway! They're not hurting you. They're just a couple of little kids in love—"

"They're one little kid and a degenerate is what they are!"

Pivoting, Mr. Crouch leveled a forefinger like a pistol at Marge's nose. "Do you know what *you* are?" he exploded. "Shall I tell you what you are?"

"Tell me—"

"You're a pretty bigot!"

Marge looked confused. "Oh no I'm not," she said.

"You go around here," Mr. Crouch roared, "twitching your behind for Israel and weeping for the Indians and reading Jane Fonda, but let somebody serve their sentence and come out and try to earn a decent living and you're down on him like a ton of bricks! Why can't you show a little compassion?"

"How much compassion did that rotten kid show to the people he hit over the head?"

"He paid for that!"

"Which gives him the right, I suppose, to start on somebody fresh!"

"Has he hurt *you?*"

"There's four hundred dollars missing, isn't there?"

"I *told* you we went through the pockets together! Or do you think we shared the loot?"

"No—"

"Why don't you suspect *me?* I was the first one to pick up the suit." Mr. Crouch appealed to Blixen. "Wouldn't that make more sense?"

Weighing his words, Blixen said: "Yes, sir, it would. Much more."

Startled, Mr. Crouch stopped waving his hands. He peered over his shoulder again at Blixen and cleared his throat. "Oh," he said. "So you thought of that."

"Now *that's* insulting," Marge said.

"Why?" said Mr. Crouch, shaken but stout. "If I were the police, I'd be the first one I'd grill."

"Actually," Blixen said, "there seems to be some doubt now as to whether the money was ever in the suit at all Saturday morning. Mrs. Muir claims that she went through the pockets herself after the daughter brought the suit down."

"Then that's it," said Mr. Crouch, "isn't it? She wouldn't rob herself—"

"Wait a minute," Marge said. "After the *daughter* brought it down?"

Blixen nodded.

"Well—what's to prevent the *daughter* from having taken it?"

"Nothing," Blixen said.

Stiffening, Mr. Crouch said: "Nothing except ethics. Upbringing. An allowance big enough to choke a horse—"

Marge glanced at him and then walked to the misted front window and wiped the steam away and looked out through the first two O's in *LoSordo's*. "Taken it," she said, "and given it to our boy—"

"So we're back," said Mr. Crouch, "to Mack the Knife."

"I don't know. Are we?"

"Back to the jailbird. Funny how that always happens."

"I don't think it's funny," Marge said. "I think it's understandable, but I don't think it's funny." She pressed her thumb against the ruby in her nostril. "He was a pimp, too, Mr. Blixen."

His face pale, Mr. Crouch said, "No. He wasn't."

"Oh yes, he was. I've seen his record."

"Not true."

"His sister was a whore, and she gave him the money."

"To give to their mother."

They were both addressing Blixen now, in the swift urgent high tones of attorneys at the bench.

"The mother's from the old country, Lithuania," Mr. Crouch continued into Blixen's face, "she wouldn't have understood, they told her the girl was going to school, that Kenny was working."

"I see . . ."

"They lived next door. They never had a nickel, never complained. My wife and I wanted to adopt him. He'd come over when he was a little boy—three, four years old—and help me weed the yard—"

"There are no bad weeds, there are only bad gardeners," Marge chanted. "God must have loved the weeds, for he made so many of them."

"Keep it up, keep it up," said Mr. Crouch.

"The gospel according to S.T. . . ."

"Who's S.T.?" Blixen asked.

"Nobody, she's just being snooty," said Mr. Crouch.

"S.T. in B.T. as F.F. with M.R.," Marge said.

"Oh," Blixen said, "*that* S.T."

"The trouble is that Spencer Tracy's dead and Ken isn't Mickey

Rooney and *Boy's Town* wasn't a documentary, it was fiction."
Marge looked at Mr. Crouch. "Why didn't you consider the parents?
You knew how Mr. Muir must have felt."

"How do *you* know how he felt? Or might have felt? He never
met Kenneth—"

"Ah," Blixen interrupted. "Well, now—"

"Never laid eyes on him!"

"Well, the girl," Blixen said, "disagrees, you know."

Caught in mid-gesture, Mr. Crouch lowered his hand slowly to
the top of his bald head. "No, I didn't know," he said.

"Her statement to me," Blixen said, "was that Chet hated Ken,
but that Ken didn't care because he felt that Chet's karma was
bound to catch up to him someday. Ken said that somebody'd be certain to kill him sooner or later."

"To kill—Chet?"

"Yes."

Marge had removed the ruby and was rubbing the gum off the
side of her nose with the tip of a middle finger, like a professor pondering a point at a blackboard. "Have the police talked to Kenny yet
about that?"

"I'm not sure."

"When was Chet killed?" Mr. Crouch asked.

"He died at twelve-thirty—"

"Yesterday afternoon—in San Urbano—"

"Yes. The coroner thinks that he could have lived for as long as an
hour and a half or as little as less than an hour with that much
poison in him."

"Then he took the poison," said Mr. Crouch, "sometime between
eleven o'clock and eleven-thirty—"

"Or a little later. Although probably no later than twelve."

"Between eleven and twelve then."

"Yes."

Close above LoSordo's, a police helicopter flapped through the
poisoned sky, eastward toward the clogged freeway, to goggle down
at a fresh traffic death, today's decapitation. When the din had
diminished, Mr. Crouch patted his bare scalp softly and brought his
hand over the short gray hairs at the back of his head. "The boy," he
said, "was with me from nine o'clock until ten minutes past two on
Saturday."

"Nobody's accused him of anything," Marge said.

"No? All right, I'm just telling you where he was." The bruised
eyes moved to Blixen. "He got out of the truck twice, once at a Tex-
aco station, to go to the men's room—and once to make a phone call
from a public booth on Edgemont."

"To Jennifer Muir?"

"I don't know."

Presently Blixen said: "I'd like to meet the boy, Bert."

"I think you ought to."

"Today?"

"He's at Santa Anita today."

"When's his next day off?"

"Wednesday."

"Do you think he'd like to see a studio?"

"I think he probably would."

"My office, then. Two o'clock Wednesday. Okay?"

"All right."

"What's the boy's name?"

"Kuszleika," Marge said.

Blixen glanced around.

"K-U-S-Z," Marge said, "L-E-I-K-A. Ken Kuszleika."

Blixen wrote it down. "Thank you."

"And don't forget to give us your home phone number."

"Oh. Right. It's six-four-four three-one-three-one."

"Any more R.A.'s?" Mr. Crouch asked.

Blixen deliberated. "Were you ever carried off by a dead man?"

"*Gevalt*," Marge said.

"Dead man," Mr. Crouch muttered, "dead man . . ."

"I'll see you Wednesday."

"Yes. Wednesday. Dead man?"

"True initials C.C.," Blixen said, and waved and left with the gray suit over his arm.

Outside, the morning sun already had begun to wilt the dichondra along Fountain. Less than a mile away the police helicopter continued to swirl and squat over the blood-soaked freeway. But Blixen, climbing into his Colt, paid it little attention. He was wondering, instead, how a girl so opposed to a boy could recall so difficult a name as Kuszleika so effortlessly . . .

XIII

The attendant at Klein Brothers, a pre-med student who said he was moonlighting, gave Blixen a receipt for the gray twill suit and added that they expected to have the body in their possession by noon. The coroner had released it, he said; it was simply a matter now of springing the hearse. He showed Blixen the modest gray coffin Mrs. Muir had selected, and notified him that the services were scheduled to be held at eleven in the morning on Tuesday.

Bypassing the freeways, Blixen spent a contented hour driving along the shaded surface streets of Pasadena and through the sun-struck old villages napping against the flank of the San Gabriel range. It was nearly noon by the time he came poking into San Urbano, and it took him another fifteen minutes to locate Children's Hospital, but there was still no sign of Schreiber's Lincoln in the tiny parking lot so he left the Colt conspicuously by the entrance and strolled up a ramp bordered by marigolds into the hospital foyer.

Inside, color assaulted him like a happy shriek. Sunshine-yellow runners sprayed across the tile floor; the admitting desk was a bright blue; finger-painted oils covered the walls. A rosy-faced Caucasian woman in a tumultuous Afro hairdo sat at the desk behind a stuffed giraffe.

"Hello," Blixen said. "Mr. Surmelian, please?"

The woman continued to write distractedly in a ledger. "Who?"

"The administrator."

"Mr. Surmelian's out."

"We had an appointment."

The busy pen halted.

"Blixen?" Blixen said helpfully. "I called earlier this—"

"Yes, I remember . . ." The fingers, like fingers in a science-fiction story, detached, living a life of their own, resumed pushing the pen along.

"Maybe," Blixen said, "you ought to give him a buzz—"

"No use. He's gone. I saw him leave." The high, rather pretty voice coarsened a little and the woman coughed to clear it. "He must have forgotten."

"He must have. Or else he's exceptionally rude."

"He's not rude."

"Frightened?"

"I'm sorry. I don't know what you mean."

"I told him I wanted to ask him some questions about a man who died here yesterday. The name was Muir."

The woman shifted her ample haunches; the wicker chair creaked.

"I'm a friend of the family," Blixen continued. "Muir worked for me."

"Blixen!" the woman said sharply and suddenly.

"Yes—"

Grunting, the woman dropped her pen, retrieved it. The flush in her face had grown darker. "Yes. Well. It was a dreadful thing. We've already commiserated with the widow. The *hospital* has com—"

"Excuse me," Blixen said, "have you heard my name before?"

"What?"

"From Muir?"

"You see—"

"Were you the nurse on duty?"

"I'm not a nurse."

"The clerk, then."

Demoralized, the woman closed her mouth.

"May I have your name?" Blixen asked.

"You see, I've been advised that I'm not obliged to answer questions from anyone except the police."

"Advised by whom?"

"By the hospital authorities."

"And the hospital's insurance carrier?"

The woman pushed her chair back. "Pardon me, please."

"Let me put it this way," Blixen said. "Either someone can answer a few simple questions now, or you and Mr. Surmelian can answer a great many far more complex ones in court." He beamed at her. "With that understood, you're pardoned."

The woman walked to the edge of the yellow runner, hesitated, and returned.

"Do sit down," Blixen said.

"I'd rather not."

"Now may I have your name?"

"It's Geraldine Styne."

"How did my name come up, Geraldine?"

"He told me he worked for you. You were a reference. He—wanted to be admitted. And obviously I couldn't do that." Her hands, pressed tight against her tweedy hips, moved in rigid small circles.

"It's not obvious to me."

"Well—we don't have the facilities for—for—"

"Don't you have emergency service?"

"We—there's an emergency hospital on Oak—"

"And suppose someone is knocked down in the street outside by a car. Would you send him to the hospital on Oak, or would—"

"Oh, don't be silly."

"You'd care for him here?"

"Well, of course!"

"Then why—"

"It was a matter of personal judgment!" Tears shook in the angry eyes; blunted fingernails jabbed at the tweed. "At first I thought he was drunk. I *never* thought he was as sick as he said. He looked—do you know what he looked like to me? A junkie. They come in all the time. Although they're usually kids. He even asked me for some morphine—"

"To ease the pain—"

"Oh, I guess so." She took a deep breath and arched her head back, eyes closed, neck muscles prominent.

"Do you know what it was that killed him?"

"Doctor said he was poisoned. I don't know with what."

"Oxalic acid."

"Oh."

"Aren't you trained to recognize poisoning symptoms?"

"I told you I'm not a nurse!"

"Still, children must be brought in occasionally who—"

"All *right!*" Geraldine Styne exclaimed. "I should have recognized it! I don't know why I didn't. But *he* didn't say anything. Except that he had an ulcer—"

"In other words, he had no idea himself that he'd been poisoned?"

"He didn't say anything about it. At least—"

Blixen waited. "At least what?"

Her eyes were puzzled. "Well—just before he lost consciousness, I—" She hesitated. "It was just an impression—"

"Right," Blixen said. "What happened?"

Her arm described an arc. "Well, he fell on his face, but I thought he said something just before he fell—or while he was falling, 'My leg aches,' or something like that. And then he got the oddest expression on his face—"

"Yes . . ."

"As though he'd figured something out—or—come to a conclusion or something. I don't know . . ."

Blixen studied her for a second or two. "Did he mention any names?"

"Then? No."

"Was that the first time he'd spoken about the leg?"

"Not the first time. He was talking about it when he came in. But he wasn't limping or anything. He seemed angry. He was mad at one of his brothers—"

"Which brother?"

"Does he have a brother named Emmett?"

"Yes."

"Emmett. He was going to get even with Emmett. Or I *think* that's what he said. He was almost impossible to understand."

"What else did he say about Emmett?"

"That's all. I asked him what he was talking about, and he said,

Emmett, my brother Emmett, the *musician*—like that, very contemptuously."

"Contemptuously . . ."

"Very contemptuously."

"Then what?"

Miss Styne closed her ledger and arranged the pen and a number
of pencils squarely across its top. "Well—then he began to lie and
carry on . . . He said he had a reservation. He wanted to give me a
deposit—"

"A check?"

"No, cash."

Blixen found himself leaning forward slightly. "How much?"

"Oh, I can't remember." Impatiently Miss Styne pushed at her
dandelion-shaped hairdo. "Fifty dollars, something like that. But it
was all talk. He didn't have the money."

"None?"

"None in his wallet. No bills. We found some loose change in his
pocket later."

Blixen stared at her.

Miss Styne's fingers went to the top button on her jacket, found it
closed, dropped again. "What's the matter?"

"In other words," Blixen said, "he brought the wallet out—and
opened it—and saw there was no money—"

"Yes . . ."

"What was his reaction to that? Was he surprised? Was he—"

"*Well*, I can't—"

Intently Blixen said: "Of course you can. Think about it."

Round-eyed, Miss Styne said: "Reaction." She looked at her silent
telephone for support, touched the heels of her hands to the desk
edge. "I don't remember any reaction at all. He wasn't *surprised*."

"Angry? Mad?"

"No . . ."

"No? You're sure?"

"He was a little irritated. As though he'd forgotten for a minute
what he'd done with it—and then remembered—and it exasperated
him. It was quite a performance. It was exactly the way a junkie
would have acted. He looked like a junkie, he smelled like a junkie,
he was simply a mess. He'd vomited all over everything and there
was blood on his sweat shirt—"

Blixen roused himself. "Blood? From what? The vomiting?"

"No, I wouldn't think it had come from that—"

"He had an ulcer—"

"This blood was on his right shoulder. Right sleeve. Separate from
the—the vomit."

"Separate . . ."

"As though he'd fallen down and cut his hand or something, and then tried to wipe it off."

"Did you notice any cuts like that?"

"Well, there were a number of scratches—" Miss Styne was focusing on something beyond his shoulder. "Is that man waving at one of us?"

Turning, Blixen saw Wade Schreiber at the door, slanted inward a little at the waist, hand to his eyes, like Bligh on a poop deck in a high wind, contemplating mutiny. He was jacketless, dapper in flared trousers and a fitted checked shirt. A walrus mustache, designed to add years to his young face, floated in the soft breeze. He gave a further tentative wave with his raised hand.

"At me," Blixen said. He waved back, rubbed a finger meditatively across his temple. "Where's the sweat shirt now, Geraldine?"

"The police took all his clothes."

Blixen sighed. "All right. Thank you very much."

"Is that all?"

"That's all."

"You know—"

Blixen stopped.

"Really," Miss Styne continued miserably, "I can't tell you how sorry I am that all this happened. I'd give anything to be able to turn the clock back . . ."

"I doubt that you could have helped him."

"Stomach pump—antidotes—"

"No, I think he would have had to live a different life," Blixen paused. "That seems to be the only antidote to karma."

"To what?" Miss Styne asked.

"Talking to myself," Blixen said, and went to join Schreiber.

XIV

Schreiber, who feared and mistrusted hospitals, had retreated to the bottom of the ramp, where he could smoke and lean against the handrail and watch the young pant-suited nurses come and go. At the sound of Blixen's footsteps, he tossed his cigarette into a nearby urn and held his hand out. "Nils, good morning," he said. "I didn't mean to break up your meeting—"

"No problem," Blixen assured him. "We were through."

"I'm sorry I'm late. What time is it?"

"Half-past twelve."

"I was almost out the office door when Pep called."

Alerted, Blixen said: "You engaged Cisneros?"

"Yeah, well, I'll tell you," Schreiber said, "Peppy's expensive, but after talking to Robert last night I figured this was no time to start counting pennies."

"No, of course not."

"I told Pep the first thing we had to do was check up on Robert's alibi. So he contacted an investigator he knows in Tijuana."

"Come up with anything?"

"Enough. He called at eleven-thirty and I didn't get away from Hollywood until after noon. Do you want the complete version or the meat of the thing?"

"Short as possible."

"Robert Muir hasn't been at Rosarita Beach since the summer of 1970."

"God *damn* it! How sure are they?"

"They're sure. The desk clerk knows him. On top of that, Robert called late last night and asked the clerk to alibi him. The clerk promised he would."

"What changed his mind?"

"An even fifty," Schreiber said.

"Christ."

"There's more."

"Naturally there's more. There's always more."

A brace of nurses, black and white, passed them curiously, and Schreiber said: "You want to go back to the car now?"

"What's the matter," Blixen asked, "don't you think I can take it standing up?"

Schreiber laughed and said: "Come on," so Blixen trailed him across the warm, scented grass to the parking lot. He waited while Schreiber unlocked the Lincoln and then got in. Schreiber trotted in a thoughtful way around the Lincoln's blunt snout to the driver's side. "Too hot for you in here?" he asked.

"No, it's fine."

"Let me turn the air conditioning on." He started the engine and raised the windows and adjusted everything there was to adjust while Blixen regarded him out of moody half-closed eyes. "If you get too—"

"Wade," Blixen said.

"Yes—"

"It's not going to go away no matter how you fuss. Is it."

Schreiber opened his mouth, shut it, and hooked his hands over the top of the steering wheel. "No, it isn't," he said.

"I'm a television producer, I can take anything," Blixen said. "Let the other shoe drop, for God's sake."

"Pep's also extremely thorough," Schreiber said. "For a private eye."

"I'm aware of that."

Inhaling deeply, Schreiber said: "So he drove by McKinley Drive in the early hours of the morning and went through Robert's car. He thought he might pick up a clue as to where the car had been."

"Well?"

"Well," Schreiber said, "he picked up a beaut." He glanced at Blixen and then returned to an examination of his hands on the wheel. "He found a Shell credit card receipt on the floor. Dated Saturday. Signed by Robert. From a station in Pasadena." He waited for a tense moment, shifted his eyes to Blixen. "Why are you so quiet?" he asked.

"I'm very noisy inside," Blixen said. "I'm screaming inside."

"Of course it isn't the end of the world or anything, even if it does place him within ten miles of the scene of the murder," Schreiber resumed. "I mean Pep and I between us were able to account for that receipt in half a dozen innocent ways."

"Jury proof?"

"That was the problem. No."

Chin on his chest, Blixen said: "All right. Robert was lying or he was set up. Let's assume he was set up. The first thing we'd better do is talk to the Shell attendant."

"Pep's already done that," Schreiber said. "Let's assume Robert was lying."

"Hell. Definite identification?"

"From the newspaper photo. Absolutely."

"When did Robert buy the gas?"

"Half an hour after Chet died. Around one o'clock Saturday afternoon."

Blixen shook his head in despair.

"Now it's not going to take the police long to catch up with Pep," Schreiber continued. "So I'd suggest we have a heart to heart talk with Robert while he's still loose. Like this afternoon."

"They're all going to the hospital this afternoon," Blixen said. "The old man's worse. It'll have to wait."

"We can't let it wait too long, Nils."

"I'll get to him tomorrow morning."

"You're meeting with Irene Nicholas tomorrow at eleven."

Blixen considered. "Well. Do you know the abandoned railroad spur in Simi? The trestle?"

"I think so . . ."

"Meet me there at eight. That'll give us an hour or so with him. Meanwhile—what's Pep doing?"

"Trying to trace Robert's movements. He apparently stayed away from the College Inn. Chet had made a reservation, but none of the clerks recognized Robert's picture."

Blixen nodded, musing.

"I still think there's an explanation," Schreiber said. "Probably a very simple one. That man's not a murderer. Nothing murderous in his background—"

"Pep been over that, too?"

"He checked out the whole family. . . . Did you know that Emmett tried to kill Chet when they were kids?"

"Um."

"*That's* murderous. There's a story, too, that he used to be in love with Chet's wife. And that's motive."

"Is Emmett your choice, Wade?"

"I wouldn't mind knowing where Emmett was from eleven to twelve on Saturday."

Moodily Blixen said: "I wouldn't mind knowing, for a fact, where any of them were." He watched a wasted Chinese child in leg braces hitch a walker up the ramp. "Why don't you put Peppy on that, too."

"Alibis? Okay. Who in particular?"

"Brother Spencer's supposed to have been in Vegas. Let's make sure of it."

"Right—"

"Wanda was teaching a quilting class—"

Surprised, Schreiber said: "Do you doubt it?"

"The daughter," Blixen went on, "claims she was at the public library."

Presently Schreiber resumed writing his notes. "Anything else?"

Blixen hesitated. "Not at the moment." He pushed himself upright. "I passed the bus office when I drove in. Let's see if anybody there recognized Robert Saturday."

"And suppose they did. Suppose he was hanging around with a glass of oxalic acid in his hand."

"Then," Blixen said, "we're in trouble."

XV

The Valley Transit terminal, crushed between the Golden Years Hotel and a pornographic motion picture theater, was a pungent, narrow, concrete cavern, twice as long as it was wide, a former shooting gallery. Empty gum-studded benches lined the western wall; opposite them, three Mexican children raced boisterously up and down past a magazine rack, a broken water fountain, the ticket counter, a hot-dog stand, and two rest rooms. In an alley beyond the rest rooms, an orange and silver bus stood poised to leave. Half a dozen white-haired passengers sat in scattered window seats, stunned with waiting.

While Schreiber tarried by the magazine rack, Blixen stooped to peer through the ticket grill. The booth was empty, although its small side door stood open.

"Hello?" Blixen began.

"Yeah, hello, hello, just a minute, okay?" a woman called.

Leaning back, Blixen saw that she was hunkered down behind the hot-dog stand, breaking out a crate of buns. She was hawk-eyed and heavy, dressed in white overalls and a short stiff chef's cap.

"She'll be with you in a second," the man on the other side of the stand said. He sipped at his coffee. "Where do you want to go, Hollywood?"

"Well," Blixen said, "actually—no—I—"

"Upland bus has already left," the woman said. She bobbed up, rested her bosom on the counter, panting. "Next one's at one twenty-three."

"Well, to tell you the truth," Blixen said, "I'm not waiting for a bus." He pulled one of the stools out. "As a matter of fact, I wanted to ask you a couple of questions."

"Oh, shit," the man beside Blixen muttered.

The woman had stiffened. "Questions about what?" Her eyes blazed. "Listen, to begin with, I haven't laid eyes on that son of a bitch since August, and if he thinks he's going to screw one more dime out of me, he's looney. How did he find out I was working?"

"Cora and him haven't been married for ten years anyway," the man snapped. "Tell him to go drink himself to death and leave decent people alone."

"Oh, save your breath, Floyd," Cora said. She pushed tight gray curls back under the chef's cap. Her heavy face was white as dough, empty and longing. "Oh, hell," she said. "All right, what gutter is he in now and how much does he need?"

"Cora, Jesus Christ," Floyd began.

"Shut up, just shut up," Cora said. And to Blixen: "Well?"

Blixen lifted his hands a little from the counter, let them fall. "Wrong problem," he said. "Sorry."

Floyd frowned. "What do you mean, wrong—"

"Wait a minute," Cora interrupted. She examined Blixen's face intently. "Didn't Ed send you here?"

"No."

"Well, for Christ's sake," Floyd said, "why didn't—"

"Floyd, will you please just close your mouth!" Wiping her upper lip, Cora stared at the counter.

Floyd watched her for a moment from under lowered, baffled brows, and then chuckled and struck her plump shoulder. "Bastard's probably dead by now anyway, Cor."

Pain flashed like sunshine off a knife blade through the woman's wet dark eyes. "Yep," she said, and lumbered off to fiddle with the Silex behind her. "Okay, who wants coffee?"

"I'm good," Floyd said.

"Please," said Blixen.

"Cream? Sugar?"

"Black."

The eyes were controlled and irascible when Cora swung back. She slapped the coffee down in front of Blixen and spread her soft large hands on the counter before her. "So," she said, "who are you? Police?"

"So they've been around," Blixen said.

"Who?" Floyd asked. "Oh, about the poisoning?"

"Yep, they were around," Cora said to Blixen. "I know because I always make it a point to check everybody's ID."

Nodding, Blixen said: "My name's Blixen. The man who was poisoned worked for me. I'm carrying out a private inquiry of my own."

"Uh huh." Cora tilted her chin toward Schreiber at the magazine rack. "Is he with you?"

"He's my lawyer," Blixen said.

"Uh huh."

"Tell me," Blixen said, "what in particular did the police want to know?"

"You're newspaper, right?" Cora said.

Blinking, Blixen said: "What? No."

The rounded chin picked out Schreiber again. "He your photographer?"

"No, no. Really—"

"Listen, I don't give a hoot," Cora said. "I just like to set all the square pegs in all the square holes. My name's Mrs. Cora Foss. F-O-S-S."

Blixen looked at Floyd, who was grinning slyly, and then back at Cora. Then he got out his ball point and a scrap of paper. "F—" he said.

"O-S-S," said Cora. "Double S."

"S-S . . ."

"Seven eighty-two West Foothill, Apartment B." She wet her lips and glittered at Schreiber when he strolled up.

"Good," Blixen said. "Now—"

"Okay—first they wanted to know exactly what time the noon bus from Hollywood got in Saturday, and whether I noticed this Muir." Cora pulled a folded newspaper from under the counter. "This man." She tapped at a studio portrait of Chettie next to the headline story.

"Yes," Blixen said, "and had you?"

"I was out on the platform when they unloaded. Muir got off and asked me where the men's room was and I told him."

"And what was his attitude then?"

"I don't know what you mean by attitude."

"Well—was he—how were his spirits?"

Cora shrugged. "He was all right. I wouldn't have noticed him except for the sweat shirt."

"Why? What was wrong with the sweat shirt?"

"He'd bled on it, on the arm. It said 'Stolen from Something Productions.'"

"Was there anything else on the sweat shirt?"

"Just 'Stolen from—'"

"No, I mean—he hadn't gotten sick? Or—"

"Sick? No."

Blixen said: "Mrs. Foss, this is vitally important. Are you positive about that?"

"He wasn't sick *then*," Cora said, "no."

"Then," Blixen repeated.

"Can I tell this in my own way?" Cora asked. "Without you hopping in every—"

"Sure. Please. I'm sorry."

"Okay," Cora said. She glittered again at Schreiber to show that she wasn't too aggravated to have her picture taken if that's what Schreiber wanted. "The bus was a little late. She's due in at eleven-fifty, but it was—oh—a couple of minutes after twelve before she turned up."

"You're buckin' that Saturday noon traffic," Floyd said, "is what you're doin'."

"Anyway, me and the driver gabbed a while and then I come back to the stand here, and pretty soon along comes Muir again."

"Yes—"

"White as a sheet. And he says he wants an Alka-Seltzer. Well, I said we didn't have any Alka-Seltzer out at the stand. I told him there was an Alka-Seltzer dispenser in the men's room, but he said he'd already took the last one, and I says, well, I'm sorry then, but that's it."

"And this," Blixen said, "was around noon . . ."

"Right about noon—little later."

"Okay, what happened next?"

"That's it. Then he left."

"Didn't get sick? Physically?"

"Not in here," Cora said. "He'd already gotten sick in the men's room, because the janitor told me this morning he'd had to clean up this mess."

"Right," Blixen said. "Now—here comes the tricky part . . . Was he alone all this time?"

"That's the first thing the cops wanted to know, too," Cora answered. "Yep, he was all alone."

"You're sure about that?"

"Well, I didn't see him talk to nobody. Of course, I wasn't watching him every minute."

"Didn't see him meet anyone outside?"

"Nope."

"Didn't see—" Blixen folded the newspaper to show only Robert's face. "—*this* man hanging around anywhere?"

"Listen, I wish I could help you people but I can't," Cora said. "If the cops ast me about that fella once, they ast me a thousand times. All I can tell you is what I told them. I personally did not see that man in this terminal."

"Absolutely certain?"

Laughing in annoyance, Cora said: "Hey, what do you want from me, an affidavit?"

"We might."

"All right, I'll give you an affidavit."

"How about a man with a beard?" Schreiber asked. "Notice any beards around here yesterday noon?"

"Beards, beards," Cora said. "No . . ."

"Any kids?" Blixen asked.

"Little kids?"

"Teen-agers."

"Oh, sure. Half a dozen. You know, from the colleges."

"Boys? Girls?"

"Mixed . . ."

"Any as young as—oh, say, fourteen?"

"Listen, they all look fourteen to me," Cora said.

Blixen tapped the ball point against his knuckles. "Is this bus run a limited from Hollywood?"

"It's limited past Santa Monica and Western, where he gets on the freeway there."

"But he'll pick up passengers between Vine and the freeway?"

"Right, yeah."

"Who had the noon run yesterday?"

"That was Charlie Washoe."

"And where could I get in touch with Charlie Washoe?"

"Well, Big Bear, if Charlie don't change his mind and go on up to Sun Valley or Timberline or someplace. Charlie's a skier."

"She-er," Floyd said, and laughed.

Smiling, Cora said: "He's on vacation. Left last night."

After a beat, Blixen said: "And when will he be back?"

"Two weeks from Monday . . ." Cora put her head on one side. "Why? What do you want to see Charlie about?"

"I wanted to know who got on where."

"Well, Charlie's never going to remember a thing like that after two weeks," Cora said.

"No," Floyd said, "but Stell would."

Cora pushed her lips out speculatively. "By God, I believe she would," she said.

Schreiber glanced from one to the other. "Who's Stell?"

"Old Stell Burns," Cora replied. "Stell was on the noon bus Saturday. She's eighty-two but she's got a mind like a steel trap."

"Eighty-three," Floyd said.

"Eighty-two. Interested in everything. She lives right next door if you want to talk to her."

"Bright as a penny," Floyd said. "For eighty-three."

"I wonder," Blixen mused, "if she happened to notice Mr. Muir—"

"Oh, she must have," Cora said. "I seen the two of 'em when the bus pulled in. They were right up front." Cora grinned. "Sittin' in the same seat . . ."

XVI

The Golden Years Hotel smelled of mice and urine and very old powdered ladies. There was no one at the dusty reception desk. But a toothless man clutching a cat in a rocker under a rubber plant said that Mrs. Burns was in because he'd seen her go up and nobody'd fell out past the front window yet. He laughed to show he was kidding and added that Mrs. Burns would be in three-oh-eight.

Someone was frying fish on the third floor. A baby carriage stood in an alcove opposite the elevator under a sign that said No COOKING IN ROOMS.

"Baby carriage?" Schreiber muttered.

"For groceries," Blixen explained.

"Can't they steal carts like everybody else?" Schreiber grumbled. "Here. Three-oh-eight."

He knocked.

"Can you hear anything?"

"Just the TV."

"Try it again."

But before Schreiber could raise his hand, the door cracked open. Knobby fingers gripped the jamb below the restraining chain.

"Hello?" Blixen said.

"You've got the wrong place," a lipsticked mouth below a red-tipped nose said. "Now split before I sic my two Dobermans on you."

"Mrs. Burns?"

"Back Kirk! Back Heidi!" Mrs. Burns shouted.

"Very silent types, for Dobermans," Schreiber said.

"Maybe they're well trained, smart-ass, did you ever think of that?"

Blixen put a hand on Schreiber's arm and said: "Mrs. Burns, my name's Blixen—this is Mr. Schreiber. . . . We're here in connection with the Muir poisoning?"

"All I know about that is what I read in the papers."

"We understood you were on the bus with Mr. Muir yesterday."

A gleaming eye swept them both. "Police?"

"No, no."

"If we were police," Schreiber said, "we would have beaten your door down by now and bullied you into submission. Don't you ever watch S.W.A.T.?"

The mouth grinned. "You're FBI, right?"

"Wrong."

"Why do you think we're FBI?" Blixen asked.

"I can tell. You look it. You've got the look. Like Zimmie."

"Like—"

"Efrem Zimbalist, Jr."

"Oh, you're an FBI fan, is that it?" Blixen grinned.

"I'm an Efrem Zimbalist fan."

"What do you think of Murphy Smith?" Schreiber asked.

"Stagg?"

"Yeah."

"Why?"

"This man produces *Stagg at Bay*," Schreiber said.

The gleaming eye narrowed in on Blixen. "You don't mean it."

"He means it," Blixen said uncomfortably.

"Well, for pity sakes," said Mrs. Burns. "What is it you do again?"

"He produces it," Schreiber said.

"Uh huh," said Mrs. Burns. "Now just exactly what is it a producer does?"

"That's a very good question," Schreiber said.

"A producer," Blixen said, "spends every day trying to keep order from deteriorating into chaos, and he always loses."

"Uh huh," said Mrs. Burns. "Say, tell me, what's Efrem really like?"

"He's a warm and charming gentleman. Very good golfer—tennis player—"

"How about Robert Redford?"

"I don't know Mr. Redford."

"Aren't you interested in Murphy Smith?" Schreiber asked. "How would you like an autographed picture of Stagg and all the regulars?"

The eyes calculated.

"We just want to ask you a couple of questions, Mrs. Burns," Blixen said. "We'll be out of your way in ten minutes."

"Ah, what the heck," said Mrs. Burns. "If you're rapists, you're rapists." The door closed; the chain rattled; the door creaked open again. Mrs. Burns stood behind it, apprehensive and winded. "Well, come on in."

The room was thinly furnished, small and light, dominated by a massive Spanish TV set placed opposite a rump-sprung easy chair. A robust red azalea on the one window sill nearly blocked the alley view. They were playing basketball on TV. Five elongated men waved frantic hands at five leaping men until Mrs. Burns snapped them all off. "Local," she explained. "Bunch of klutzes. If they'd have been the Lakers I wouldn't even have answered the door."

She was a short woman, fat and vulgar, painted like a soubrette. She was still a little leery of them; she left the door ostentatiously open. "Okay," she said to Blixen. "Shoot."

"Okay," Blixen said. "Well—you know Mrs. Foss, of course—"

"Who? Oh, Cora? Yeah . . ."

"Mrs. Foss thought you might be able to help us. We're trying to trace Chet Muir's movements from—"

"Wait a minute, wait a minute. Help you do what?"

"Catch Chet Muir's murderer," Schreiber put in.

The old eyes brooded at him out of their green shadows. "Why? Who are you two anyway, the Lone Ranger and his Faithful Indian Companion? What do you care about anybody's murderer for?"

"Ah," Schreiber said. "Well. Mr. Blixen's a friend of Chet's and I'm a lawyer."

"Uh huh," said Mrs. Burns. "Lawyer for the boy they arrested?"

"Well," Schreiber said. "Yes."

"Uh huh," said Mrs. Burns. "Okay, now we know where we're at. Disinterested people scare the bejeesus out of me. Go ahead."

"Okay, we're after three things," Blixen said. "First—did Muir speak to anyone on the bus besides you and the driver? Did he seem to know anyone? Recognize anyone? Second—"

"Let me work on number one for a minute," Mrs. Burns said. She waddled pensively to the easy chair, picked up a half-filled water glass, sipped. "Who wants some gin?"

"I think I'd better pass," Blixen said.

"If he won't," Schreiber said, "I won't."

Mrs. Burns shrugged and clicked her teeth against the tumbler. "Did he speak to anybody . . ." She munched meditatively on a piece of ice. "He asked to borrow this one person's paper. Or do you count that?"

"Did you notice the person?"

"Yeah—"

"Man with a beard?"

"No, this was a girl."

"How old?"

"Oh—thirty?"

"All right—what happened?"

"Well," Mrs. Burns reflected, "let's see . . . The bus was pretty well filled up when I got there, so I took the first seat I seen, which was this one right behind the driver."

"Yes," Blixen said, "and Mr. Muir was already *in* the seat?"

"He was in the seat," Mrs. Burns said, "looking out the window. And he turned and he kind of smiled, and I smiled, and just then this girl across from us folded her paper and started to stick it down next to the wall and Mr. Muir he leaned out and he says 'Oh, pardon me, miss, but could I borrow your paper?' Like that."

"Yes . . ."

"And she smiles and says 'Why, certainly,' and hands it to me and I handed it to him."

"No sign of recognition between them? No—"

"I wouldn't think they ever laid eyes on each other before."

"And of course *you'd* never seen her before either?"

"Nope."

"How often do you take the bus into Hollywood and back, Mrs. Burns?"

"Oh, lord—two or three times a week—"

"So you must know quite a few of the regulars . . ."

"I guess so."

"Were there many regulars on the Saturday run?"

"I couldn't tell you," Mrs. Burns said.

Schreiber leaned forward, intrigued. "Why not, ma'am?"

Cocking an eyebrow at him, Mrs. Burns said: "I was in the front."

"Yes . . . ?"

"Well, you don't look behind you much in a bus. *I* don't. There could have been a two-headed zebra back there and I wouldn't have seen it."

Schreiber leaned back again. "Of course," he said thoughtfully. "A two-headed zebra, or a man with a beard, or a fourteen-year-old girl—"

Mrs. Burns gave an unexpected smirk. "That's the second time somebody's mentioned a man with a beard."

Blixen frowned. "Why—is that funny?"

"It is if you live near a pornographic movie theater," Mrs. Burns said.

Blixen looked blankly at Schreiber and Schreiber said: "Beaver," and Mrs. Burns started whooping and sneezing and sipping her gin, red-faced and delighted. If she'd had an apron, she would have thrown it over her face.

"A beaver—" Schreiber began.

"I know, I know," Blixen said.

"I think of that now every time I see a beard on a man," Mrs. Burns gasped. "Talk about generation gap." She wiped her streaming eyes. "Poor Muir kept asking me what was wrong Saturday and I couldn't tell him—"

Blixen stiffened. "Saturday? You saw a bearded man Saturday?"

But she was off again, hooting and breathless. "Oh, a pip," she said.

"I thought you told me there were no beards on the bus—"

"Not *on* the bus. Not that I saw anyway. This was a man waiting on the corner. Bearded man. The bus stopped to pick him up, but he stepped in and then seemed to change his mind. He turned right around and got off."

"Did Muir see him?"

"No! That's what made it so funny—"

"How old was he?"

"Young man. Forty—fifty—"

"Do you think you'd recognize him if you saw him again?"

"Not him. Just the beaver." Whooping, Mrs. Burns choked over her gin.

"Maybe you'd better go on to question number two," Schreiber suggested.

"My lord, yes," Mrs. Burns wheezed.

"In a minute . . . Did the bus stop for anyone else?"

"No . . ."

"Nobody else got on in Hollywood after you left the terminal?"

"Nobody."

"Except the bearded man."

"No. Well—he was just inside the door for a second or two—"

"What do you think he did, Nils," Schreiber asked, "throw the poison at Chettie?"

Blixen rubbed a finger across his closed lips. "Okay, question number two," he said. "Did Mr. Muir show any signs of nausea while he was sitting next to you, Mrs. Burns?"

"Now there's a pretty compliment," said Mrs. Burns.

"Ah, they don't call him old Honey-tongue for nothing," Schreiber said.

Laughing, Mrs. Burns tipped her empty glass coquettishly at Schreiber. "Sure I can't buy anybody a little snort? No obligation."

"Well, maybe I will," Schreiber said.

"Mr. Producer? No?" She splashed gin into a tumbler for Schreiber, filled her own glass. "The answer to your question is that I did not nauseate the man. I don't *think*."

"When did you get on the bus, Mrs. Burns?"

"Quarter to eleven. Thereabouts."

"And you sat with Muir until twelve, when the bus pulled into San Urbano."

"True."

"Was he in pretty good spirits all that time?"

"Oh, I think so."

"What did you talk about? Or did you talk?"

"You bet we talked. I always talk on the bus." She swirled the gin in her glass and narrowed her eyes. "Well, let's see. We talked about Nixon. We talked about TV. He told me he was a film editor, and what an editor did, and how he used to go to college at Southern San Gabriel. He said he was married. He said he was going to spend the weekend at the College Inn—"

"Alone?"

"Now that he didn't say."

Blixen walked back and forth in front of the window, rubbing his forehead.

"Although I did get the feeling," Mrs. Burns continued, "that he just might have had a little slap-and-tickle on his mind."

"Slap-and-tickle?" Schreiber asked.

"The old slap-and-tickle," said Mrs. Burns.

"Why?" Blixen inquired. "I mean—what gave you that impression? Did he mention another woman? Or—"

Hesitantly Mrs. Burns said: "No . . ."

"Then—"

"Well," Mrs. Burns said, "it was more in his attitude, don't you see. He was all bright-eyed and bushy-tailed. He was putting something over on somebody, but he wasn't 100-per-cent sure of himself yet. He was like the little kids who walk past the porno box office down there. They want to go in—they might get stopped—but they're bound to try it."

"The game," Schreiber said, "is worth the candle."

"The game is worth the candle," Mrs. Burns agreed.

Bleakly Blixen picked a dead leaf off the azalea plant.

"What's question number three?" Mrs. Burns asked.

Blixen dropped the twig into a heavy glass ashtray. "Question number three," he repeated. "How did Chettie get all that blood on his sweat shirt?"

"Yeah, I was wondering when we'd come to that," Mrs. Burns said.

"Were you?"

"Listen, that was the craziest thing that happened all day. That was when I whacked him on the nose."

She had a strong sense of the dramatic; she reveled in the looks they flung at her, beaming at them over the lip of her gin glass. "I was trying to kill the wasp," she said. "Don't you see."

Desperately Schreiber said: "*What* wa—!" but Blixen held up his right hand, palm outward, and Schreiber bit his words off and contented himself with puffing.

"Mrs. Burns?" Blixen said in his gentlest tone. "What wasp?"

"Maybe," said Mrs. Burns, "I had better begin at the beginning."

"Maybe you had," Blixen said.

Mrs. Burns made a dainty dab at her ginny lips with the cuff of her polka-dotted blue dress. "Well. The minute I heard this sound—this hum—I told Mr. Muir, I says, I know what that is, that's a wasp, stop the bus. I says the only thing I'm more scared of than a wasp is a snake and I won't stay here. I says—"

"Now when was all this?" Blixen asked.

"This was just when we turned onto the freeway."

"Santa Monica and Western—"

"Yes. So I says—"

"Where did the bearded man try to get on?"

Irritated, Mrs. Burns said, "Oh, somewhere in there. Western and Sunset or someplace."

"Nils—" Schreiber began, but Blixen held his palm up again and Schreiber went on puffing.

"Go ahead, Mrs. Burns," Blixen said.

"Now you've thrown me all off," Mrs. Burns said crossly.

"I'm sorry . . ."

Mrs. Burns stared out the alley window for a moment and then coughed and settled her dress around her hips. "So I says to the driver, I says there's a wasp in here, Charlie. I says if you don't stop this bus I'm going to jump out the window. So Charlie says, why, we're on the freeway, Stell, we can't stop, you know that. I says all right then, kill it, kill it. I says, Mr. Muir, you kill it. And he grabs his folded up newspaper and he says okay, where the hell is it, and I says, oh, my God, it's *there*, it's on you, on your shoulder—so I grabbed the paper myself and just then he turned his head—"

"And you hit him in the nose," Blixen finished.

"And I hit him in the nose," Mrs. Burns echoed. "Whammo. Thank heavens I didn't break it. But what did he turn his head like that for?"

"It bled, though—"

"It bled and it bled. He wiped it off on his sleeve, and finally he held his finger over his lower lip and it stopped. I really felt terrible, but he laughed and he said there was no problem, and I guess there wasn't because the nose didn't swell or anything. But if there was ever a time I wanted to crawl in a hole, that was it."

Schreiber was still watching Blixen. "When are you going to let me say something?" he asked.

"In the car," Blixen said. "Mrs. Burns? What happened to the wasp?"

"Mr. Muir pushed it out the window with his newspaper."

"Did it sting anybody?"

"Nobody said anything."

"Didn't sting Mr. Muir?"

"No, I think we scared it away first."

Blixen caressed the azalea plant contemplatively and then nodded. "Okay, Mrs. Burns. Thank you very much."

"*Now* are you ready for that gin?"

"Next time—"

"Thanks, Mrs. Burns," Schreiber said.

"I wish you didn't have to go . . ."

"So do we—"

She accompanied them to the elevator. "Don't forget my autographed picture!"

"You'll get it—"

"Have him sign it, to my good pal, Stell, with love and kisses!"

Blixen waved and nodded while the elevator door closed.

The last they saw of her was the smile on the lipsticked mouth, and the gin glass in the jaunty hand, and the terrible, terrible loneliness in the Golden Years eyes . . .

XVII

"All right," Schreiber said, "let's recapitulate."

They hesitated for a moment outside the hotel lobby, squinting against the unexpected glare of the high afternoon sun, and then automatically, without discussing it, they turned their backs on the Lincoln and headed obliquely across the street toward the cool edge of the campus. They proceeded, hands in their pockets, through a laurel hedge and down a shaded gravel path. Students lay under the trees on either side of them, sleeping or studying or making lazy discreet love.

"Who wants to go first?" Schreiber asked.

Blixen paused beside a water fountain to wash his dark glasses. "Strange word, 'recapitulate,'" he said. He used his handkerchief to dry his lenses before dropping them back into his shirt pocket. "Capitulate. To give up. Then why doesn't 'recapitulate' mean to give up again?"

"I suppose it does. Or could." Schreiber bent over for a drink and rose dripping. "The one that always got me was 'sanguine.' I knew it came from 'sanguinary'—'bloody.' So I always imagined that anyone who was sanguine about his prospects had beaten his head bloody and was ready to fold."

"How does anyone ever learn this lunatic language?" Blixen asked.

"Now there you've got me," Schreiber said. "Anyway, how do you feel about giving up again on Robert's problem?"

"Oh, I couldn't be bloodier," Blixen said.

Laughing, Schreiber said: "Well, at least we're easily amused." He pointed to a metal bench under an oak tree and Blixen nodded and followed him across the bumpy lawn. But the bench turned out to be uncomfortable as well as chilly so Blixen spread his handkerchief on the ground and sat on that while Schreiber reaped a number of long grasses and shuffled back and forth, chewing them. "Okay," he said, "first of all, what do we do about that rutting wasp?"

"We forget about that rutting wasp," Blixen said.

Schreiber swung about, but before he could open his mouth, Blixen continued tiredly: "Wade, we aren't writing a *Stagg* script. We're trying to find out who could have poisoned Chettie Muir."

"I'm aware of that."

"And what possible part could a wasp play in a poisoning?"

"Listen—" Schreiber began hotly and then stopped.

"Go ahead, give your imagination free rein," Blixen said.

"People have died from bee stings—"

"Did Chet?"

"Well," Schreiber said, "no . . ."

"Was he stung at all?"

"What about the man with the beard?" Schreiber countered.

"All right, let's take the man with the beard," Blixen said. "Either the man with the beard was Emmett—or he was not Emmett. If he was not, he's of no more interest to us. If he *was*, then we've practically cleared him—"

"How have we practically cleared him?"

"He didn't get on the bus, did he? He didn't speak to Chettie. He didn't touch him—"

"Why couldn't he have hopped in his car and raced out to the terminal and met Chettie there?"

"He could have," Blixen admitted.

"Okay then," Schreiber snapped, and stomped back and forth, chewing his grass stems. In a growl he added: "I still don't think we've explained the wasp."

"We don't have to explain the wasp," Blixen said. "The wasp explains the blood on Chettie's sweat shirt. That's what's important."

"I remember one story," Schreiber said. "It seems that this fellow had these killer bees. I forget how he got them to attack—rubbed flowers on his victims? No . . ." He sneaked a glance at Blixen, who was listening politely. "It was a hell of a yarn."

"It sounds like it," Blixen said.

Schreiber spat out a grass stem. "All right—forget the wasp. Suppose the poison was on the folded newspaper—and when Mrs. Burns hit him with it—"

"Are you serious?" Blixen asked.

"I'm spitballing," Schreiber replied. "I'm also a little tired." He sat down on the bench with his knees apart and his clasped hands dangling between them. "We're really dead as far as the bus goes, aren't we. . . . He couldn't have gotten the poison on the bus. . . ."

"Not unless he swallowed it just before he got off," Blixen said. "I'm told there's an immediate reaction to oxalic acid. Severe stomach cramps."

"And the first time we hear of him with stomach cramps is when he comes out of the San Urbano men's room . . ."

"After drinking an Alka-Seltzer . . ."

"Right." Frowning, Schreiber stared at his toes. "Question: who was in the men's room with him?" He glanced at Blixen. "Or was he alone? *Was* it suicide?"

"I'd sooner believe in the flower-mad wasp," Blixen said.

"Ah, so would I," groaned Schreiber. He was silent for a time. Then: "Men's room," he grunted. "What we're saying, then, is that he met his murderer in the men's room—"

"Yes—"

"Which would seem, at least, to eliminate the women on our list of suspects. Wouldn't it?"

"Would it . . . ?" Blixen said.

"Don't you *want* to eliminate the females?"

"If anyone can be eliminated, yes, I want to eliminate them."

"Well, surely you don't think that Chet Muir would arrange a rendezvous with some female in a men's lavatory?"

"We live in unattractive times," Blixen said. "I'd never rule something out just because it appalled me."

"You ruled out my flower-mad wasp."

"Not because it appalled me. Because it was comic."

Schreiber sighed. "So you still want Pep to check out everybody's alibi. Male and female."

"Yes."

"Which brings us right back to where we started," Schreiber said. "We haven't learned a thing."

"One thing," Blixen corrected him. "We know that Chettie wasn't robbed."

Schreiber, who was brushing the dust off his shoes, paused to turn his head. "How do we know that?"

"Wait a minute, you weren't there, were you," Blixen said.

"No, I wasn't," Schreiber replied. "Where?"

"With the hospital receptionist."

"No . . ."

"And what does that signify?"

"She told me that Chettie had taken his wallet out to show her that he had enough money for a room. But the wallet was empty. She said he didn't seem surprised."

"And what does that signify?"

"Well, for one thing," Blixen said, "it might mean that he'd given the money away, and had forgotten for a moment."

Schreiber screwed his face into a scowl. "Given it away to who? Whom?"

"I don't know. A gambling brother? A wife? His daughter's boy friend? To send him packing?"

"But, Nils," Schreiber said, "what does it matter? Nobody's going to murder him for money he's already given them, are they?"

Blixen looked at him for a long while and then gripped both hands behind his neck and pressed his forehead against his knees.

"Of course," Schreiber went on, "it's always darkest before the dawn. That's a psychological fact."

"Really."

"And our cloud has a silver lining in any event. Look at all the chaff we've blown away. We've managed in one way or another to eliminate almost everybody who could have killed Chettie. Keep that up and we're bound to get to the true murderer."

"There's one person we haven't eliminated," Blixen said. He stood upright, brushed his pants off, put his handkerchief away.

"There you are," Schreiber said cheerfully. "Who?"

"Robert," Blixen said.

"Let's go home," Schreiber said.

Heads down, lost in thought, they trudged together across the lumpy lawn toward the break in the laurel hedge.

XVIII

"How much farther?" Murphy Smith kept panting. "We should have brought the jeep."

"Hang on, Murf," Blixen said. He blew his breath out through rounded cheeks, wiped his nose and pointed. "There's the trestle. Fifty more little yards."

"Fifty, Jesus," Murf groaned. "I'll never make that."

"Yes, you will. Come on."

"How high are we here?" Murf asked. His face was flushed and wet beneath the Panama hat and the crisp casual curls at the edge of his hair-piece. He turned heavily to gaze back at the Chinese-colored valley, black and bronze in the Monday morning sun. The studio drivers had followed them in as far as they could; Murf's limousine lay across the mouth of the draw like a slaughtered bug. Murf groaned and cranked his head around to squint up at the trestle spanning the windy sky.

"Are you okay?" Blixen asked.

"You mean apart from wondering why the bloody hell we're shooting up here instead of against a blue backdrop in a civilized studio?"

"Apart from that, right," Blixen said.

"No, I'm not," Murf said. "My back aches and I'm nauseous and I don't understand the bloody scene anyway."

"You're saving the girl. What do you have to understand about that?"

"I have to understand my *motivation!* *Why* am I saving her?"

"Love," Blixen said.

"You know what I have to say to that, Mr. Executive Producer? Balls!"

"And very prettily put, too," Blixen said.

"I also want to talk to you sometime about the quality of writing I get on this series."

"Go ahead and talk."

"It's crap, it's all CRAP! Doesn't anybody ever read this junk before it's mimeographed? Do you realize I have to rewrite 99 per cent of every script I get? Take this script—"

"Yes—"

"Who wrote this shit?"

"I did," Blixen said.

"You did," Murf repeated.

Blixen nodded and smiled, waiting politely.

"Uh *huh*," Murf said. The mountainside had grown brighter, warmer. A dog barked, miles away. On the trestle above them, wind sang through the old spans, and the grips horsed around while the cameraman checked his exposure meter and argued with the art director. "Oh, there's Fitz," Murf cried, and waved at a wiry yawning man who was slumped in a canvas director's chair under an umbrella at the base of the trestle, talking to Robert Muir. Fitzwilliam waved back, shouting something thinly at Murf, and Murf laughed and grimaced and clasped his hands over his head and muttered: "What'd he say, what'd he say" out of the corner of his mouth.

"Couldn't make it out," Blixen answered.

"Well, it couldn't have been important," Murf growled. "The man's too bloody dumb to ever say anything important. That's the real bottleneck on this series. Directors."

"Rather," Blixen said, "than scripts."

"Oh, come on, boss, for Christ's sake," Murf said, and struck Blixen playfully on the back, "can't you tell when you're being put on? I was putting you *on*, man."

"Ah."

"But you don't believe that."

"No."

"I blotted my copybook?"

"Yes you did, Murf."

Murf shrugged and jammed his hands in his pockets and plodded on up the slope for a little way and then stopped. "Listen, you understand that there's nothing personal when I have to change a line or two on the set, Nils, eh?" He smiled boyishly.

"Absolutely," Blixen said. "And I know you feel the same when I have to chop out your changes in the cutting room, right?"

"Right," Murf said, and started jauntily up the hill again and then slowed.

"Oh, by the way," Blixen called, "would you send Robert down when you get up there?"

Murf thought about that and a number of other things, waved once more without turning, and continued on.

"What did you do to him?" someone muttered glumly in Blixen's ear. "You've crushed the man."

Kapralos, corpselike in decent black, had materialized out of a stand of straggly pines at the edge of the path.

"Well, good morning," Blixen said.

"I know. You told him we were going to pay actors according to their talent from now on."

Still watching the ugly dogged figure in the Panama hat toiling up the hillside, Blixen said quietly: "No, Socrates, I'd never dare do that. He'd break us. That's the man's strong suit—talent."

"His strong suit is sleep," Kapralos said. "He bellyached and bellyached to have a limousine pick him up in the mornings, so we gave him a limousine and a seven o'clock make-up call, and he got here at a quarter after nine. We won't get our first setup before noon."

"We'll make it," Blixen said.

"Well, it's not my problem," Kapralos said. "You're the one who has to sign the budget overages. You're going to be eighty thousand over on this picture if you're a penny. I'm just warning you."

"Fine, you've warned me."

"And now music's sent me an authorization I'm going to have to rescind."

"What authorization?"

"They've hired a composer."

"For this picture? Who?"

"George Ireland," Kapralos said.

"Excellent man."

"I've put a call in to his agent. I can hold the commitment off until next season."

"You can cancel the call," Blixen said. "I want the episode scored."

Horrified, Kapralos said: "With the music library we've piled up? *Why?* We must have five thousand cues—"

"We don't have the cues I want for this story," Blixen said.

"But, Nils—"

"Socrates," Blixen said gently, "do it."

Kapralos raised his thin hands, let them fall against his black pants, and turned to go back down the hill.

"Oh, just a minute," Blixen said. He gazed for a time at the trestle.

Kapralos waited, drained and beaten, haunted by the specter of economic ruin.

"Yes," Blixen said. He snapped his fingers. "Let me have your script."

Kapralos handed it over and Blixen drew two music staffs rapidly on the back cover. Kapralos watched him fill in the notes he'd found at the laundry. "What's this? Kapralos asked gloomily. " 'Blixen's Theme'?"

"You're going back to the studio now?"

"Yes . . ."

"Give this to somebody in Music. Tell them I want to know what it's from."

"What it's *from?*"

"I want the name of the piece—the words that go with the notes, if there are any—name of the composer—everything—"

Kapralos was holding the script at arm's length, eying the music doubtfully. "And you don't know who wrote it?"

"No."

"I don't think you've given them enough."

"Tell them to do the best they can."

Kapralos shrugged, rolled the script into a cylinder, started off,

stopped abruptly. "Oh!" he said. "I knew there was something else
. . . You got a phone call. Wade Schreiber."

"Now what? Is he lost?"

"He told me to tell you he wouldn't be able to make it," Kapralos
replied. "I think he said he was waiting to hear from somebody
named Cisneros?"

"Yes—"

"He said in the meantime to tell you that everybody's alibi does
check out, except the bearded man's, and they can't confirm that because he was alone. He said you'd know what he meant."

"Did he say anything about Spencer?"

"He said that's who he was waiting to hear from Cisneros about.
He said he'd fill you in when he saw you at eleven."

Blixen pondered silently.

"Okay?" Kapralos inquired.

"Okay," Blixen said.

Wrapped in despair, Kapralos wended his melancholy way
through the thorns and around the rocks down the mountainside
while Blixen struggled on up the path to meet Robert, who had re-
ceived Murf's message and was sliding toward him down the trail.

Always slender, Robert—Blixen thought—looked now as if every
excess ounce of flesh had been whittled off his frame. His bony
calves seemed suddenly incapable of holding up his loose socks; the
points of his shoulders could be seen through his thin shirt; the skin
over his nose was tight and paperish. He caught himself against a
gnarled tree. "Yes, Nils—"

"Everything under control?"

"Well, Fitz is a little behind, but he thinks he can be through by
three-thirty—"

"I didn't mean that."

Robert kept his eyes on the ground. "Well—'control'—I guess
so. . . . Wanda finally collapsed."

"About time."

"Yes. The doctor gave her a shot and put her to bed. Lupe's with
her."

"Who's Lupe?"

"Lupe's kind of our community maid. She kept house for Pop
when he was home, and she cleans for all of us. Good girl."

"Have you heard from Spencer?"

"Spencer called," Robert said. "He saw the story on TV."

"How'd he take it?"

"Rocked him."

"How'd he react to the idea of you being arrested?"

"He didn't like it much," Robert said. He stretched his tense back muscles and stared up at the top of the wind-swept trestle. "He wanted to scrub his assignment right then and there and come on home, but I said, 'Spence, it was a tempest in a teapot, they just asked me a couple of questions and let me go, it's over with.' He finally calmed down."

Presently Blixen said: "Will he be able to make it back for the funeral?"

Robert shook his head. "He can't. They're way off schedule. They had a power outage Saturday. The whole city was blacked out from about eleven in the morning until three. So they won't get to the main stunt before Tuesday. Chettie would have understood." Flushing, Robert added in a low tone: "Incidentally, Nils, I want to thank you on behalf of the whole family for closing the company down tomorrow. I hope you know how much we all appreciate it. Pop's the one who would have really been proud."

"Have you told him yet, by the way?" Blixen asked. "About Chettie?"

"We're not going to bother him with it. We'll just let him die."

"I think that's the best."

"That's the best," Robert agreed. "We're bringing him home tonight."

"Good."

"He's always wanted to die in his own bed. The doctor said it wouldn't be long. Maybe a week."

"It's been a rough year, hasn't it."

"Terrible year. Grisly year."

"Robert," Blixen said reflectively, "what were you doing in Pasadena last Saturday?"

All his life, Robert's blood had betrayed him at crucial points, flooding into his ears when he was pleased or scared or undone, tinting his cheeks like make-up, lying in dull patches around his poker-cool eyes. He arched a casual brow now; his mouth was amused and perplexed; his face flamed. "Pasadena," he said. "Who told you I was in Pasadena?"

"Weren't you?"

"No, I wasn't."

"Didn't stop for gas around one in the afternoon?"

"No."

"At a Shell station?"

"No."

"Robert," Blixen said, "I must also tell you there's a record. You signed the credit voucher. The attendant identified your photograph." He paused. "Now—"

A Cessna bumbled across the mountains. A smell of disturbed

earth and bruised grass rose from the path. The blood gave a copperish Indian look to Robert's high forehead.

"Robert?" Blixen murmured.

"When I was ten," Robert said, "I was sent to a new school. And one day—the second or third day I was there—I wet my pants in class. No one knew it at the time, but the teacher must have found the pool under my seat when we left. Because she asked me the next day—very gently and in private—if I had had an accident. And I said no." He brushed something away from the brown of his hot balding head and scanned the sky for the Cessna. "I seem to have this infinite capacity for running down blind alleys. I don't suppose you know what I mean."

"How did your teacher react?"

"She pretended to believe me. She dropped the subject. She was a very considerate person."

"But a very poor teacher."

Robert shrugged. "What should she have done? Ridiculed me? Reported me? Punished me?"

"I think she should have helped you find out why you were too frightened to raise your hand when you wanted to leave the room."

The clown's smile widened, joyless and white-edged. "But aren't there some things one just doesn't talk about? Even to one's teacher? Especially to one's teacher." His gaze held Blixen's for a moment more, and then he tucked his chin against his chest and said: "Well," and started past Blixen down the trail.

"Robert," Blixen said.

Robert stopped.

"What were you doing in Pasadena, Robert?" Blixen asked.

But Robert shook his head mutely.

"Were you alone?"

"I won't tell you, Nils."

"Then you were *not* alone."

"I won't tell you."

"Do you have an alibi for the hour between eleven o'clock and noon on Saturday?"

"Apparently I haven't."

"You'll be rearrested as soon as the police find out you were less than ten miles away from Chet when he died."

"I can't help that. They'll be wrong. I didn't kill Chettie."

"Can you prove it?"

"I guess not."

"Robert, I don't understand," Blixen said. "Forget about your own neck. Why are you doing this to your family? To Gail?"

Above them, the Cessna was back, as excited as a moth by the reflectors on the ground and the studio equipment trucks. Shading his eyes, following the Cessna, Robert said: "To Gail? Oh, I don't know, maybe it's a matter of love."

"Were you with another woman?"

"I won't tell you."

"Why do you think Gail wouldn't understand that? Gail's not a child."

"Gail's more of a child than you realize. In many ways."

"You know, it's academic in any case," Blixen said. "I've got a firm of private detectives on the thing and they'll retrace your steps if it takes forever."

Robert's ears had grown scarlet. "Please let it alone, Nils."

"You're too valuable to me. Who were you with in Pasadena?"

"Nils—"

"Ah, man, man!" Murphy Smith cried behind Blixen. "Quit ragging the boy!" He pointed a finger at Robert. "Fitzwilliam's screaming for you," he said. "Hop it."

Robert stared up at the trestle and then set out at a run.

"Nice chap," Murf said fondly. "I liked the way he stood up to you."

"He's a fool," Blixen said.

"Oh, maybe not," Murf replied. "You were talking about Pasadena? Friday and Saturday? I heard him ask you to let it alone. Suppose I asked you, too. For the sake of the show, boss?"

Blixen had turned his head. Now: "Why? What do you know about all this?"

"Oh, a lot," Murf said. His eyes grinned mischievously at Blixen.

"See, I was the one he was with," he said.

XIX

Above them, on the trestle, the stand-ins strolled back over the snaggle-toothed ties to the bank and Fitzwilliam called something to Robert Muir, who shouted: "First team!" through the clear morning air.

"Ah," Murf said, "the voice of the massa. Lif' dat barge, tote dat bale. Another day, another two thousand dollars. Well, what the hell, it's a living." He patted Blixen on the arm and headed again up the overgrown trail.

"Murf," Blixen said quietly, "freeze."

"Freeze?" Murf said. *"Freeze?* Good grief, man, that's an ad lib even I wouldn't use. What are you going to do, shoot me?"

"It's a thought," Blixen said.

The grin widened, but the intelligent ape's-eyes grew speculative and watery. And the ugly figure remained still.

"Murphy," Blixen said, "what did you mean, you were the one he was with?"

"Mr. Smith!" Robert bawled.

"Excuse me," Murf said, "I'd better—"

"I told you to hold it."

"They're waiting—"

"Let them wait."

Murf pushed his lips out, folded his arms, and leaned against the gnarled tree. He pointed an elbow up at Fitzwilliam, who had come to the edge of the trestle and was gawking down in disbelief, his hands on his hips. "Look at that," Murf said. "I always maintained that that man should have been an actor. Look at those vivid emotions chase each other across that mobile face. 'God damn all rotten lazy actors, god damn all dumb rotten producers who come on sets and delay everything.' "

"He'll be with you in ten minutes!" Blixen shouted through his cupped palms. He smiled broadly and nodded. "Ten minutes, Fitz, okay?"

Fitzwilliam—the director, the set's dictator—numbed by outrage, the bereft spoiled man who had heard everything now, threw himself into his canvas chair.

"Wonderful," Murf murmured.

In the meantime Robert, alone in the middle of the span, had turned his back on the valley and was gripping the rail, staring up at the mountains.

"There's the man you're really giving fits to, by the way," Murf continued. "We agreed we wouldn't say anything about Pasadena."

"It's true, then."

"Oh yes."

"How long have you known Robert?"

"Do you mean in a biblical sense?" Murf squinted up at the figure on the trestle. "Oh—about a month." He glanced back at Blixen. "I think you're shocked, boss."

"Surprised."

"Why? Because he doesn't lisp? Because he's married?"

Blixen buttoned his jacket and clasped his hands behind his back. "All right," he said. "The point is that he has an alibi—"

"Well," Murf said, "that's not *quite* the point, is it." His mouth

crinkled in his special *Stagg* smile. "The point is that you and
Robert and *I* know he has an alibi."

"And so will the police in a day or two—"

"Maybe, but not *this* alibi."

Blixen turned to examine the other. "You know, Murf," he said,
"sometimes you can be a little difficult to understand without a
script."

"Ah, damn it, it's these new caps," Murf said, and gave his wolfish
front teeth a regretful flick.

"Not *this* alibi? What does that mean?"

"Okay," Murf said briskly. "You traced Robert as far as Pasadena,
didn't you?"

"Yes."

"And you're afraid the police may do the same—"

"Sooner or later."

"And that they may even find the motel he registered at."

"Yes."

"Okay, but they won't find me," Murf said. "So in a way, it's no
alibi at all."

Presently Blixen said: "Why won't they find you, Mr. Bones?"

"Because no one saw me go in. No one saw me leave—"

"Cleaning woman? Manager?"

"Nobody."

"You can't possibly be sure of that."

"Oh yes," Murf said, and winked. "I can. I made sure of it. I was
very careful. I've been careful all my life. I've got a reputation to
keep up, bubby. I know the routine."

"Nobody gives a damn about your private life in this town, Murf."

"Nobody?" Murf said, and gave an Italian hoist of the shoulder.
"Almost nobody. You don't. My friends don't. The studio doesn't."
He sniffed softly. "But the network? Pablo?"

"Pablo's odd," Blixen said, "but he's not psychotic."

"Pablo," Murf said, "is an Iowa boy who parlayed a small-town
TV station into the presidency of the network. The things that
shocked Pablo in Adel still shock him. He likes me because I call
him 'sir.' He told Art Todd that he hoped I'd fall in love with his
daughter because he'd be proud to have me for a son-in-law. Did you
know that?"

Blixen shook his head silently.

"Now what do you suppose would happen," Murf went on, "if
Robert was to be quoted in the national press as saying that he
couldn't have killed his brother because he was rolling in the hay
with Murphy Smith at the time?"

"Murf—"

"How long do you think it would take Pablo to buy out of his commitment?"

"Stars have been known to survive scandals before this."

"I'm not concerned with them. I'm concerned with me. Could *Stagg* survive?"

"I don't know," Blixen said.

"Did you expect a pickup this season?" Murf continued. "Normally?"

"We figured we'd have to work for it."

"Then you've got to know a scandal would kill you."

"It might," Blixen said.

Murf lifted his hands a little, let them drop to his sides. "So good luck, bubby," he said, and started away.

"Just a minute, Murf."

Warily the smaller man stopped.

Blixen ungripped his hands, pushed them into his hip pockets. "One question. Where does all of this leave Robert?"

"Where he's always been," Murf replied. "Innocent."

"That might be hard to prove without an alibi."

"Yes, that's true," Murf agreed. "Why don't you buy him one?"

"Buy—?"

"Here's a thought if you're really worried. Why don't you hire some nice girl to swear she was with Robert Friday and Saturday?"

"Are you serious?"

Murf held up his palm. "Bubby. Suit yourself. It was just a suggestion. I don't care what you do. So long as you leave me out of it."

"I can't leave you out of it. You're in it up to your ears."

"All right," Murf said patiently, "I'll explain it to you again. Nobody's ever going to find out about me and Robert, so—"

"I found out. What did you tell me for if—"

"I told you," Murf interrupted, "so you'd call off your dogs. I wanted you in the picture. I knew you'd see the economics of it—"

"Economics!"

"Ah, come on, Nils, get off the pot! Robert doesn't want this story out any more than I do! What do you think it would do to his wife? His family? Either you keep your mouth shut and let those Keystone Kops flail around until they all get tired and go home, or you make an accusation I'll sure as hell deny, and you'll run the risk of ruining everything—me, Robert, the series, the studio, yourself—the whole goddamn shebang!"

From the trestle, Fitzwilliam shouted, "Gentlemen, are we going to rehearse this sequence or are we going to spend all day picking our noses!"

"Ten minutes," Blixen whispered. "Get to work."

Murf's smile was humorless. Straightening, he whipped up a salute
and dug his toe into the dirt to execute an elaborate about-face.
"Yassuh, general," he said, "right away, general, can't delay the war,
general," and marched up the hill like a lame soldier, to the sound of
his own whistled fife.

XX

It was twenty minutes to eleven when Blixen pulled into his studio
parking stall—too late for dailies, too early for his meeting—so he
unclipped his safety belt and rested his forearms on the steering
wheel and let his thoughts nose like lost mice through the maze of
unacceptable options he'd been given.

It was a drowsy bright blue forenoon, full of the natter of low-
geared trucks, and sprinklers ticking. In front of the Administration
Building, a flag snapped and buckled in the breeze. Directly ahead, a
red warning light at the corner of a a vaultlike stage door hummed
and blinked, hummed and blinked . . .

Someone was staring into his ear.

With a grunt, Blixen jerked his head to the right and around,
shying away from the unexpected face in his left-hand window.
"What—!"

"What! What?" the old man shouted. He was husky and white-
haired—white-faced as well, now—wrapped in sweaters. Walter Tibbet. As leathery as the books he reigned over. Head of Research. He
gripped his chest, breathing hard.

"My God, Walter," Blixen said, "what were you trying to *do*,
scare me to death?"

"Scare *you* to death!" Tibbet howled. "Screaming at me like
some—"

"Well, you come creeping up—"

"I didn't *creep!* I saw you and I said, 'Nils?', I said, 'Nils?' and you
just sat there—I thought you were dead—"

"Bolt upright—eyes wide open—"

"The only place on earth where people die with their eyes closed is
TV!" Tibbet roared. "You're a producer. I thought you'd had a
heart attack."

"I'm not sure I like the way you've got those two thoughts
linked," Blixen said.

"Then get out of this asinine trade while there's time," Tibbet snapped. He pulled a tablecloth-size handkerchief from his hip pocket and blew his nose vigorously into it. "Who needs all this grief?" He glared at the handkerchief. "How are all the Muirs, incidentally? Speaking of grief."

"They're bearing up."

"Uh huh," Tibbet said. "I understand the police busted Robert."

"He's out. They didn't even book him."

"I wonder if he could have had anything to do with that murder—"

"Don't wonder. He didn't."

"I think you're right. But a lot of people remember how him and Chettie were always scrapping—"

Blixen looked over. "Have the police been through here, Walter?"

"Like a dose of salts," Tibbet said. He folded the handkerchief and tucked it into his pocket. "I kind of got the feeling that they'd already made their minds up. About Robert. I told 'em to *cherchez la femme* and they looked at me like I was crazy."

"*Cherchez la femme*," Blixen repeated.

"Detective rule number one," Tibbet explained. "I'll bet you a hundred dollars—when this is all over—you'll find a woman at the bottom of it."

After a thoughtful moment Blixen said: "Walter—you've been out here since the year one . . . Have you ever heard any rumors about Chettie playing around?"

"Never. Why?"

"I keep wondering why he went to San Urbano Saturday."

"Yes—that's where they found him, wasn't it . . . Well—to meet somebody?"

"Possible."

"Well," Tibbet speculated, "if Chettie Muir ever made a date with a woman in a strange motel, it'd be his wife. I can tell you that much."

"Wife . . ."

"People do a lot of crazy things these days. On water beds."

"Yes . . ."

"And Chettie was always crazy about that woman, you know."

"How did Wanda feel about him, Walter?"

"There's always one who loves and one who lets himself be loved," Tibbet said. "Another old French phrase. I read a lot."

"How about movies," Blixen asked. "Do you see a lot of movies?"

Puzzled, Tibbet said: "I guess I see my share . . ."

"Somebody told me once," Blixen said, "that you knew more about old movies than anybody else in this town."

Tibbet simpered modestly. "Oh—well—"

"I'm trying to run a certain plot down . . . I have the title."

"Yes—"

"*Daughter of the Red Death.*"

"Serial?"

"No, I wouldn't think so. . . . Wanda Mills starred in it."

"Oh—for Universal . . ."

"Probably. Although it might have been independent—"

"Wanda Mills, Wanda Mills," Tibbet said. "Are you sure you've got the right title?"

"Fairly sure."

"Any co-stars?"

"No. I'm sorry."

"Wanda did a picture in '58 or '59," Tibbet said, "called *Red Plague* . . ."

"Science fiction?" Blixen asked. "Monster from outer space?"

"No, this was an anti-commie thing," Tibbet said.

"That's not it."

"*Daughter of the Red Death,*" Tibbet muttered. "*Red Death.*" He combed his spindly fingers through his soft white hair. "My goodness, I've never been so embarrassed in my life."

"Well, listen, Walter, never mind, I just—"

"Well, wait a minute," Tibbet said. "I'll tell you what I'll do. Are you in a hurry?"

"No, no," Blixen replied. "So long as I can have it by noon."

"Seriously—"

"Seriously," Blixen said, "I wish you'd forget it. It was just—"

"Listen, let me call a couple of guys I know, all right?" Tibbet suggested. "I'll get back to you by the end of the day, all right?"

"All right," Blixen said, "but it really isn't necessary—"

"Not to you," Tibbet said. "To *me.*" He pushed himself away from the car and headed brittley down the studio street, mumbling "*Red Death, Red Death,*" in a querulous voice and striking his forehead with the end of his clenched fist.

Blixen sighed, saw that it was eleven by the clock on his dashboard, and nearly opened his door into the fender of a stubby black Toyota that was sliding into the space beside him. The Toyota gave him a surly raspberry of a honk, but before Blixen could bend down for a little outraged eye-to-eye contact, Irene Nicholas waved her hand at him over the roof and got out, slim and smiling.

"Oh," Blixen said. "Well—hi."

"Hi," Irene said. "Can I park here?"

"Suppose I said no?"

"I'd ignore you." She held her tanned wrist out to him. "Eleven o'clock on the nose. How about that for timing?"

"How about that for a pretty dress?" Blixen said.

"Do you like yellow?"

"I like yellow, I like pleats, I like high, rounded collars—"

"How does it happen," Irene asked, "that single men usually notice what a woman's wearing, but married men never do"

"Don't they?"

"Never. Did you, when you were married?"

"Never."

Blixen was still holding her gloved hands. "I don't suppose," Irene speculated, "that it would do at all for two business persons to kiss each other directly before they went into a cut-throat conference."

"Why don't we risk it?"

Softly she bent to him, brushed his lips with her own, rested her cheek against his. "Oh, what a lovely day," she whispered, "for a knock-down-drag-out contract fight . . ."

"Lovely."

But there was a hesitation in the word—a faint distance between them—and she sensed it. She drew her face away.

"So," Blixen smiled, and took a deep breath. "How was Disneyland?"

After a meditative moment, she returned the smile. "Well, it was delightful. Charming."

"And did Curtis behave himself?"

"Curtis was a perfect gentleman. Except for one little lapse on Mr. Toad's Wild Ride. . . . He was terribly interested in you, by the way."

"In *me*?"

"Well—in the man who called. He wanted to know what your intentions were."

"And what did you tell him?"

"Of course that it was none of his business. Sometimes I think Curtis forgets that we're separated."

"I still can't understand why he took you out. Or is that none of *my* business?"

Irene smoothed the fingers on one glove. "I—think he's growing a little tired of his fat friend."

"Ah-*hah*."

"Yes." She met his gaze head on. "He spoke in a roundabout way of coming back home.

"Well, well, well."

"He's worried about me. He's afraid I have no business sense."

"Really? Why?"

"He thinks I've put all my eggs in one basket."

Frowning, Blixen said: "I don't believe I understand—"

"Yes—well—I'm really not sure I ought to clarify it for you."

"Why not?"

"Well—think of the unfair business advantage you could take—if
—I should tell you that Murphy was my only major client."

The words at first were quite meaningless. Blixen continued to
wait.

"Did you hear me?" Irene asked.

Slowly Blixen straightened. "Your *only* major client," he said.

"I couldn't seem to explain to Curtis that no agency starts out
fully grown—that one client attracts another. Obviously Murphy's
waiting to see what I can do for him before he recommends me."

"And suppose you can't do anything—"

"Darling," Irene said, "this studio has got to have *Stagg* to survive.
And there's no *Stagg* without Murphy Smith. Those are the condi-
tions that prevail." She hooked her arm through Blixen's. "So why
don't we go in and talk facts now."

"I think it's time," Blixen said.

"And anyway," Irene laughed, "even if you toss us both out on our
ears, I'll still have Curtis to go back to." She smiled brilliantly.
"Won't I—"

XXI

Miss Firebush, Blixen's remarkable gray-haired secretary, was draped
over the radiator like a pile of clothes tossed down in a school cloak-
room. A surprised nose poked out of a nest of tweed when Blixen
opened his outer office door. "Oh! It's you! Good morning!"

"Good morning—"

"We'd begun to wonder if you'd deserted us—"

"Soon," Blixen said. "Not yet, but soon."

Miss Firebush laughed uproariously and hurried, shivering, back to
her desk. "You've had some calls—"

"I'll get to them later," Blixen said. "You know Murf's agent,
don't you, Muriel? Miss Firebush—Mrs. Nicholas—"

"I know her on the phone," Miss Firebush said. "Hi."

"Hi, Muriel."

"Can I fix you a nice cup of hot coffee?"

"To help keep you warm in this steam bath," Blixen explained.

"He always thinks it's too hot in here," Miss Firebush confided.
"All the girls call this the Refrigerator. I don't understand men."

"Nobody understands men," Irene said.

"I don't suppose *you* want any coffee," Miss Firebush said to Blixen on her way to the hot plate.

"Not unless it's iced," Blixen said. "Incidentally, would you try Mr. Todd for me? I'll—"

"Oh!" Miss Firebush exclaimed and stopped dead, fingers to her brow. "He's here," she whispered.

"Who's here? Authur?"

Mortified, Miss Firebush nodded. "He came down about fifteen minutes ago—never said a word—just sailed right on into your office and slammed the door. I couldn't stop him—"

Blixen ran his hand gently over the back of his head.

"I'm sorry, Mr. Blixen—"

"It's all right, Muriel," Blixen said. "Never mind. It doesn't matter."

"Yes, but I don't like that—"

"No problem at all . . ." Blixen dropped his hand finally and glanced at Irene. "I know what he wants. This shouldn't take long. Can you give us five minutes?"

"Absolutely not," Irene replied. "Throw the s.o.b. out on his ear."

"Don't think I won't tell him what you said," Blixen warned her and murmured to Muriel when he passed: "I want to be notified as soon as Wade Schreiber turns up."

"Sheiva, yes, sir," Miss Firebush said. . . .

Arthur Todd, spiffy in a blue blazer and ice-cream colored yachting pants, was standing by the courtyard window, near Blixen's seven-foot philodendron, thumbing through a sheaf of papers. The shadows cast by the thin slats of the window blind fell like branding bars across his face; he'd never looked older. "Don't you ever knock?" he asked.

"Rarely," Blixen said, "on my own office door. Good morning."

"Is it? Check again."

Musingly Blixen closed the door, snapped on the overhead light, and walked to the hissing steam radiator.

"Now where are you going?"

"To turn the heat down. Isn't it a little warm in here?"

"Intolerable."

"Then why didn't you do something about it?"

"It's not my office."

"Are those your papers?"

"They concern me." Todd threw the papers heavily against the herd of ceramic hippos foraging across the green blotter on Blixen's desk. The calves seemed to scatter; the largest bull pitched onto his broad face, his outraged rear flung high into the jungle-wet air.

In the silence that followed, Blixen righted his hippo, picked up the stapled papers. The thick pages, he saw now, were the complex and fanciful proposals that made up *Stagg*'s third-year pattern budget, starry-eyed suggestions out of Leo Newmarket's office for holding the production line, as pretty and as impractical as Levis spun from glass. Blixen placed them on the coffee table beside him and regarded Todd patiently.

"Well?" Todd said.

"Well, what?"

"You usually have something cutting to say to me after I've made a dramatic gesture."

"Is that what that was?"

"Don't bug me, Nils. It's the wrong time for it. I'm feeling my age today."

"Let me see if I can guess why," Blixen said. "You've just come from an emergency conference with Leo, and Leo has warned you to crack down now or to risk losing control of the situation."

Intently Todd said: "Do you deny that those crazies of yours out at Simi were still rehearsing their first sequence at ten minutes past ten?"

"Can't deny that, Arthur."

"Or that they'll probably have to go back tomorrow for pickups?"

"Wednesday," Blixen said. "We're shutting down tomorrow."

"Wednesday, Wednesday, that's worse, Wednesday!" Todd shouted. He tramped around the desk, waving his arms over his head. "Nils, don't you understand what that means? *Another* thirty-five thousand! What the hell is Fitz doing?"

"Beats me," Blixen said. "Let's fire him."

"Oh, don't be a fool!"

"All right, let's end the picture here and now."

"Without a climax?"

"Right."

"Are you out of your mind?"

"Can't do that?"

"You know goddamn well we can't do that! We can't do anything!"

"Then, Arthur," Blixen said softly, "what are you screaming about?"

Todd, still stumping back and forth, red-faced, waving his hands, paused by the philodendron.

"Sit down, Arthur," Blixen said.

"No, I'm too jumpy," Todd replied. "I can't."

"You really shouldn't let Leo get to you that way."

Todd measured him for a moment and then turned again to the

window, to the courtyard. "It isn't Leo," he said. "Do you know what it really is? It's the years."

"The years?"

"I've been at this studio forty-two years," Todd said. "I came here in the middle of the depression and I never left."

"Long time," Blixen said.

"Long, long time," Todd said. "And now I'm scared to death it's over. And all I can do about that is scream."

"Budget overages won't end your tenure here, Arthur."

"I know. I even know you spend the money so the pictures will benefit and Pablo will pick the series up. But I have to scream at something." Todd put his hands to his waist and bent backward, testing his sacroiliac. "I suppose my nightmare is that nothing will work—not money—not ratings—nothing. And the series will be dropped, and I'll have to retire and go to Hollywood parties and be sympathized with."

Thoughtfully Blixen drew his black swivel chair out, sat down, and arranged his hippos into a pugnacious British square, bull to the front, cows and calves in the center. "Arthur," he said slowly, "how important do you think Murf is to the series?"

Todd was bent forward now like a fat, white-haired old football player, trying to touch his toes, which was absurd. "I don't think I know what you're driving at."

"Well—what's your personal opinion of Murf?"

"As a man? Or a star?"

"Either."

"Spoiled, ignorant, dangerous fag. Splendid actor." He squinted suddenly at Blixen and then pulled a straight-back chair over and collapsed onto it, puffing. "Oh-ho," he said. "You're talking about the rumors."

"What rumors?"

"Money rumors. Aren't you?"

"What did you hear?"

"That he'd changed agents. That he wants half the studio."

"And what was your gut reaction to that?"

Todd sat for a second or two mopping his face with a Kleenex tissue he'd yanked from a box on Blixen's desk. "This is going to surprise you," he said.

"Arthur," Blixen said, "after today, nothing advocated by man born of woman could surprise me."

"Well," Todd said, "be that as it may, you know how I feel about indulging actors. I don't believe in it. I never have. I think this business of tearing up contracts every two years is pure piracy." He sat staring at the wadded tissue in his hand.

"But what?" Blixen murmured.

Todd flipped the tissue into the wastebasket. "Well, we need him, don't we."

"That was going to be my next question. Do we?"

Surprised, Todd looked up. "Replace *Stagg*?"

"Could the show survive?"

"The show couldn't be given away. You know that. You know how Pablo feels about that man."

Blixen folded his hands on the blotter. The bull hippos roared silent defiance at his knuckles.

Tilting forward in his chair, Todd said: "What the devil are you talking about anyway? I don't understand."

"Talking about survival, Art," Blixen said. "And alternatives. I wanted to make sure of my alternatives."

"Alt—"

The intercom buzzer throbbed delicately and Todd popped out of his chair as if he'd been prodded. "If that's Leo," he muttered, "I'm not here."

"Yes," Blixen said into the phone.

"Mr. Sheiva, Mr. Blixen," Miss Firebush said.

"Oh. Good." His eyes rested momentarily on Todd. Then: "Tell him I'll be out in a minute . . ."

"Is it Leo?" Todd asked.

Blixen shook his head and replaced the phone. "Wade Schreiber. And Murf's new agent."

"To talk about money?"

"Yes."

"So the rumors were true," Todd said.

"Yes."

"All right," Todd said briskly, "what's Murf get?"

"Ten thousand."

"You're authorized to go to fifteen and whatever crap he wants within reason—mobile dressing room, doctor's shots, chauffeur—"

"Art," Blixen said.

"It's cleared, don't worry about it. I've already spoken to Pablo. If the network up the show, they'll pick up the extra tab on Murf, too —up to the limit I've—"

"Arthur, sit down. Please."

"Why? I don't want to be in on this thing—"

"Please."

Todd stopped openmouthed, watching Blixen cross to the door. Blixen waited, hand on the knob. "What are you so serious about?" Todd asked.

"I don't want to go over it again and again," Blixen said. "I'll tell all three of you at once. Will you please sit down?"

"Don't play games with me, Nils."

"No games."

"I've got to have this series," Todd said. But he sat—more or less —against the edge of the desk, his old man's hands on his thighs.

Blixen opened the door and smiled at Schreiber and Irene, who were chattering and laughing on the leather sofa. Twisting around, Schreiber said: "Ah! Finally. Are we ready? I'm sorry I was late—"

"Come in, come in," Blixen said.

"Don't look so grim, Nils. It's only business."

"True."

"Well," Irene laughed, passing him lightly at the door, "here goes nothing."

Schreiber laughed and Blixen smiled and gazed for a moment at the tips of his shoes and then closed the door on them all very quietly.

XXII

Arthur Todd, it turned out, was a yellow-dress man, too.

Dazzled by the swinging pleats, he introduced himself even before Schreiber could do the honors, and went on to declare that he was putty in the hands of any woman who had the sense to wear short white gloves nowadays. Irene told him that she was delighted to hear it and confessed that she was herself a pushover for gallantry and blue blazers and that she had already decided to soften her most rigid demands. Gravely Todd replied that he couldn't let her do that, that he would protect her in spite of herself. He coaxed her into Blixen's best chair and then went to stand by the philodendron with his stomach sucked in. "So," he said. "We're all here, I think. Are we ready?"

Blixen, who had reseated himself behind the desk, put aside the largest of his bull hippos and rested his chin on his steepled forefingers. "I suppose we must be . . ." he said.

"Oh," Schreiber began, and then sank back, shaking his head. "Never mind, Nils. I can get to you later."

"About what?"

"Nothing important. Cisneros."

"Who's Cisneros?" Todd asked.

"You know Peppy," Blixen said. "Private investigator."

"We're using him on the Muir case," Schreiber explained. He glanced at Irene. "You must have been reading about that—"

"Yes. Frightful."

"Well, the police are bound and determined that Robert Muir had something to do with his brother's death, and we're bound and determined he didn't. So we've had Peppy checking around a little."

Todd let his stomach out surreptitiously. "And what's he uncovered?"

"Not very much, I'm afraid."

Blixen stirred. "Has he talked to Spencer?"

Nodding, Schreiber said: "Talked to Spencer this morning." He hesitated. "Apparently Spencer's clear—"

Blixen lifted his eyes. "Apparently?"

"Well," Schreiber said, "he's got an alibi. Of sorts. He says he's been in Vegas for the last two weeks. He claims he spent Saturday and Sunday holed up with a girl named Verna in Verna's home. Verna confirms it."

"Then what's the problem?"

"Verna," Schreiber said. "Peppy doesn't trust her."

"Why not?"

Schreiber shrugged. "He can't put his finger on it. I think it's because Verna's for hire."

"A lady of the night?" Irene asked.

Schreiber looked at her blankly and then said: "Oh. Check. Lady of the night."

Broodingly Blixen said: "Maybe I'd better go up there and talk to her myself. I'll need her address."

"I'll have Pep call you."

"You know," Irene said, "I think this is really extraordinary."

Todd turned to her. "What is?"

"All of this. The fact that they care. Don't you? Robert Muir must be a very special person."

"Oh, I wouldn't say that—"

"I would," Blixen said. He put his hands flat on his blotter. "Very special. Because he's innocent."

"According to who?" Todd asked belligerently. "Even the police—"

"The police don't know what I know," Blixen said.

Schreiber sat up, interested. "Why, what's happened?"

Blixen swung his chair to the window. The sun gleamed through a sprinkler's mist; a gardener raked the stones on the courtyard path.

"Nils?" Schreiber persisted.

"Robert has an alibi," Blixen said.

"You're kidding!"

Blixen shook his head mutely.

"Well—does it hold up?"

"Yes."

"Oh, what a relief for his wife!" Irene cried.

"Well, I'll be damned!" Schreiber said. "Who confirms his story?"

"Murf."

"*Smith?* Wonderful! Where are they?"

"Something's wrong, wait a minute," Todd said. He was staring at Blixen, who shifted his own eyes to Todd's.

"Wrong—how can anything be wrong?" Schreiber exclaimed. "He's out of it! It's over! Where were they?"

"In a motel in Pasadena," Blixen said. "In each other's arms."

An air-horn blared raucously for silence somewhere on the back lot; the cooling radiator clicked to itself in the corner. Blixen pulled his bottom right-hand desk drawer out and rested his foot on it. "Don't everybody talk at once," he said.

"You know what I think I'd like?" Irene asked. "A cigarette."

"I didn't realize you smoked," Blixen said.

"I haven't for years," Irene answered.

Schreiber offered her a crumpled package and Todd struck a kitchen match on his thumbnail and rolled the flame under the end of the cigarette as though it were a Havana cigar.

"Thank you," Irene murmured. "Ashtray?"

Schreiber found her an ashtray.

"Thank you," Irene said, and pressed the cigarette out in it and crossed her knees. "Of course you're certain of your facts," she said.

"Of course."

"Who told you?"

"Murf."

"Damn sap," Todd said almost to himself.

"It's strange that he never mentioned Robert," Irene went on. "I thought I knew most of his boy friends—"

"Apparently this hasn't been going on for very long," Blixen said.

"Now let me see if I've got this nightmare straight," Todd said. "Robert is definitely off the hook because the star of *Stagg at Bay* is willing to confess to Middle America that he's a practicing Sodomite. Is that it roughly?"

"Oh, just a second, Arthur," Schreiber protested. "Middle America's changed a lot since they busted Wallace Reid. Scandal didn't end Bergman's career."

"It isn't the same—"

"But, Arthur, half the male stars in town are light-heeled. You know that."

"I know it, and you know it, but does Kansas City know it?"

"Does Kansas City care?" Irene inquired.

All three men looked at her and Irene sighed and let her chin drop.

"Yes, I guess it does," she said.

"Is the press in on this yet, Nils?" Todd asked.

"Not yet."

"Obviously not," Todd muttered. "Pablo'd be on the phone if they were." He rubbed his hands over his face. "I can hear him now."

Schreiber had begun to pace stolidly back and forth, fists in his pockets, eyes on the carpet. "Who else does know, then?"

"Nobody," Blixen said.

"I don't mean around the studio. Around the motel."

"Nobody."

"No, I'm not making myself clear," Schreiber said impatiently. "Who—"

"Nobody," Blixen said.

Schreiber came to a halt.

Baffled, Irene bent forward a little. "Well—but—"

"Murf told me," Blixen said, "in order to stop my investigations. He doesn't intend to tell anyone else."

"You mean," said Todd, "except the police . . ."

"Including the police. Nobody."

Schreiber sat down.

"Well," Irene said hesitantly, "what about Robert? There's Robert. Robert knows—"

"Robert's not going to say anything about it either."

"Because Robert," Todd guessed softly, "doesn't want his *wife* to hear. Correct?"

"Correct."

Presently Schreiber said in a small awed voice: "Does anybody know where there's a church? I think I'd like to go burn a candle or talk in tongues or something. God exists."

"And He's kind," Irene whispered.

Todd had begun to chuckle. He clapped his hands briskly before him, once, like a man destroying a mosquito, and then hopped backward a step in a ridiculous jig. "Well," he said. "By all that's holy. We're out of the woods then."

Blixen looked up from his hippos.

"Why didn't you *tell* us, Nils—"

"How are we out of the woods exactly, Arthur?"

"*Well*—if nobody knows, nobody has to know—"

"Provided Robert isn't accused of the murder, you mean."

"Why should he be accused of it? We're sure he didn't do it—"

"We aren't the ones with the warrants."

"Yes, I understand that—"

"I don't believe you do. And that's the heart of the matter. Because the police are bound to arrest him again."

"*Why?*" Irene asked earnestly. "I mean, Nils, why should they? They haven't a thing in the world to go on. They arrested him once and they had to release him—" She swung to Schreiber. "Didn't they?"

But something had happened to Schreiber. In front of their eyes, he had grown wizened. He picked at his trouser-legs with arthritic-looking fingers.

"Wade?" Irene said.

From the depths of his chest, Schreiber said: "Didn't they what?"

"Have to release him—"

Schreiber shut his eyes and rested his head against the doily on the back of his chair. "Do you know what I believe I'll do instead of burning a candle?" he asked. "Join the Foreign Legion. I suppose there still is a Foreign Legion."

"Fine," Blixen said, "but before you go marching off, why don't you answer the lady's question."

"I forget what it was."

"All right," Todd cut in, "I've had about all the fancy footwork around here that I'm capable of taking. Irene's right. They haven't got a thing in the world on Robert—"

"Let me tell you," Schreiber said in his elderly voice, "just exactly what they've got on Robert. They've got motive and they've got the poison. Those they've had all along. The only thing they lacked was opportunity."

"But—"

"Hush," Schreiber said. "You wanted an end to footwork. All right, you've got it. Now lie in it."

"Go ahead."

"It took my investigator about an hour and a half," Schreiber resumed, "to place Robert in Pasadena on the morning of the murder. How long do you expect it'll take the police to learn as much? A day? A week? They'll find the motel—and they'll find, to all intents and purposes, that he was alone at the time, unaccounted for. And they'll have him. Unless he explains himself."

Something—a child or an animal—ran wildly across the office overhead. Phones rang and rang down the corridor.

"Anyone else for the Legion?" Blixen asked.

"Boy," Irene murmured, and got up and went to stand in abstract absorption before a picture of two English soccer players on the wall.

Musingly, Todd said: "Okay, let's assume the worst. Let's assume he's arrested—and tried—and keeps his mouth shut—and loses. What's the worst punishment he could get?"

"Right now, life," Schreiber said.

"Which means what? How many years before parole?"

"Seven."

"Seven years," Todd repeated.

"Arthur—" Blixen began.

"Now hear me out," Todd said. He clasped his hands behind his back and went walking along the edge of the carpet, following the design. "Suppose," he said, "that someone were to invest a fairly substantial piece of change for Robert in a reliable Savings and Loan organization. . . . How old is Robert, by the way?"

"Robert's thirty-one," Schreiber said.

"Uh huh," Todd said. "Say someone were to invest a hundred thousand dollars today for Robert . . ." He pretended to calculate. "How much would Robert be worth by the age of thirty-eight?"

"Somewhere around a quarter of a million," Irene said softly.

Schreiber, still with his head against the doily, was watching Blixen.

"Fairly sweet little nest egg for a man not yet forty," Todd pointed out.

"It isn't illegal, is it?" Irene inquired. "I mean, it isn't like blackmail or anything. I understand Robert would *rather* go to jail than hurt his wife and his family. Correct me if I'm wrong."

"You're not wrong," Todd replied. "You're absolutely right." He scuffed his foot over a flaw in the rug's design. "And the money would be his to do with as he pleased no matter what happened in court. Even if he were let off scot free." He squatted down to smooth the flawed design with a concerned finger. "Naturally."

Irene stood back a little to gain a better perspective on the two English soccer players.

Presently Schreiber folded his hands over his stomach. "You're not saying much, Nils."

"I'm thinking a lot, though," Blixen said.

"Come on, boy," Todd chuckled. "Let it all hang up, as the kids say. *What* were you thinking?"

"Well," Blixen said, "I was thinking, 'Sam Ervin, where are you now that we need you?'"

Todd peered up at him and then returned to his work on the design. "Uh huh," he said. "You're—comparing this to Watergate, then, are you?"

"That would seem to be what I'm doing, Arthur, yes."

"Haven't you got your facts a little mixed? The Nixon Mafia ordered a crime committed and then tried to rescue the criminals. All I want to do is help an innocent man."

"By turning him into a wealthy jailbird."

"Nils, it's by his own choice!" Irene protested.

"Have you heard him choose?"

Striding to the desk, Irene said: "Nils, I won't stand for this! I'm not a criminal, and I won't be treated like one." She leaned forward. "I'm trying to protect my client. Is that so terrible?"

"It's worse than terrible," Blixen answered. "It's pointless. You can't protect him."

"What are you *talking* about?" Irene whirled to face Todd. "Is he *crazy*? Throw Murphy away and you lose *everything!* Don't you?"

"Yes."

"*Tell* him!"

"He knows."

"I don't think he *does!*"

But Todd seemed to be puzzling over something else now. Wiping his dry palms together, he said: "Excuse me, but have I missed a point here, or are we all just playing with ourselves? I beg your pardon, madam."

"Playing with ourselves how?" Irene asked.

Todd focused again on Blixen. "Well—*why* can't we protect our clients? I mean—even if Robert cops out, who's going to confirm his story? *Murf* certainly isn't. No one else saw them. Right?"

"So far," Blixen agreed.

"Then who's going to upset the applecart?"

"I am."

"How? You didn't—"

"I can testify about my conversation with Murf."

Appalled, Irene said: "Nils—!"

"Wait, wait, wait," Todd said, and hunched a little further forward. "Wade? Isn't that hearsay?"

Slowly Schreiber said: "It can be gotten to the jurors—"

"Why should they believe Nils and Robert over Murphy?"

"No reason. Except for the men involved. Who would you believe?"

"Well, we're dead," Todd grunted.

"No, we're *not* dead!" Irene cried. "Damn it, this is just ridiculous! Nils, what's the matter with you? Why are you doing this?"

"You're kidding," Blixen said.

"No!"

"Then I can't explain it."

"All right, Samson," Todd said heavily, "pull the whole temple down, it'll be on your head, too." He turned toward the door. "When are you going to tell the police?"

"The minute they arrest Robert."

"Every reporter in town'll have the story," Schreiber warned.

"Yes."

"Oh, God," Irene groaned.

Todd had halted with the knob in his hand. Blixen met his eyes steadily. Todd nodded without speaking and turned and left.

"Oh, God," Irene said again and fled.

In the stillness, Schreiber let his hands fall on his knees—finally rose. "Well—"

"How long have we got until they arrest Robert?" Blixen murmured.

"Oh—a week at the outside. A day or two probably."

Blixen swiveled to the window. "Doesn't give us much time . . ."

"To do what?"

Blixen continued to gaze into the cool wet courtyard. "Find the real murderer and save the temple," he said.

XXIII

By ten-thirty Tuesday morning, the McKinley Drive cul-de-sac was still crawling with cars although the final services for Chester Kenneth Muir, aged forty-two years, three months, sixteen days, would begin in Klein Brothers' Chapel of Memories on Santa Monica Boulevard in little more than half an hour.

It was almost a Mexican day, dominated by sword-bright sunshine and black shadows, busy grief, unfamiliar blue suits. A lizard drowsed on top of a hot white wall. The moonlighting pre-med student to whom Blixen had spoken on Saturday loitered beside the open door of the limousine sent to carry the family through the respectful streets. The two recognized each other simultaneously, smiling like the saddest of old friends while Blixen locked the Colt and ambled up the sidewalk. "Well, hello," said the attendant.

"Good morning. Little crowded down here."

"I think it must be curiosity seekers."

"I expect you're right."

"Although a number of people have called at the big house in the middle," the attendant said. He indicated the shaded colonial at the very end of the street.

"That's the father's house," Blixen said. "He's very ill. He's just home from the hospital."

"Is that so. He probably won't be attending the services then."

"I'm positive he won't."

"Well, good, that'll help," said the attendant. "I don't like to take more than four in the limousine. I don't think it looks right."

Blixen calculated. "Won't you be taking five?"

"Four, they told me," the attendant said. He drew a piece of note-paper from his breast pocket. "Mrs. Chester Muir, Miss Jennifer Muir, Mr. Emmett Muir, Mr. Robert Muir . . ."

"What about *Mrs.* Robert Muir?" Blixen asked. "Gail Muir?"

"Well, she's not down here," the attendant said doubtfully. He refolded the paper and then said: "Oh! By the way, there was a note attached to that gray suit you brought me, did you realize that?"

"A note?" Blixen said.

"Little note in a cellophane package. I gave it to the widow."

"Well," Blixen said. "And—what was her reaction?"

"She just read it and tore it up," said the attendant. "It couldn't have been important."

"No," Blixen said slowly. "Couldn't have been . . ." Beyond the limousine he could see someone emerge from the colonial house and pause on the front step. Walter Tibbet. "Would you excuse me? I see someone I know . . ."

"Surely," the attendant said, and folded his arms and leaned against the limousine's fender while Blixen moved off.

Tibbet had wandered halfway down the flagstone walk toward the street, but then had paused and was gazing back numbly at the house when Blixen reached him.

"Hi, Walter," Blixen said.

Tibbet turned. His eyes were red and rheumy; tears gleamed on his loose chaps. "Oh, Nils, boy," he said, and started to weep again. "Oh, hell," he said, and covered his face in his hands.

"Let it go, Walter. You're among friends."

"It's dumb, it's so dumb," Tibbet said. "Never get old, boy. You can't hold a thing back."

"Maybe that's good."

"Terribly dumb." Still keeping one hand over his mouth, Tibbet pulled the huge handkerchief out of his hip pocket and covered the rest of his face with that. "It's just that me and Bruce Muir go back so far—"

"I know . . ."

"We were kids together. We used to shoot jack rabbits where Western and Sunset is now."

"Unbelievable."

"Western and Sunset," Tibbet insisted. "We were a lot kinder to them jack rabbits than God is to Bruce, too."

"Is he conscious?"

"Off and on."

"I thought I'd go up and say hello."

"He'd appreciate that," Tibbet said. "But don't expect anything."

"No, I won't."

"And don't say anything about Chettie. He don't know Chettie's gone."

"Incidentally," Blixen said, "Walter—"

"Yes—"

"Did you get a chance to check out that picture I mentioned?"

"The—?"

"Wanda's picture. *Daughter of the Red Death.*"

Startled, Tibbet said: "Didn't I get back to you about that last night? No, of course I didn't. . . . I was *going* to and then my prostate started acting up and I went home instead. . . . I warned you never to get old."

"I'll watch it like a hawk," Blixen promised. "What about the picture?"

"You really picked a dilly, I suppose you know that," Tibbet said. "I finally contacted an archivist I know and he looked it up for me. Do you want the credits?"

"Just the story. The end of the story, really."

"Well. The heroine, of course, is married to this thing from outer space, this beast in human form—"

"That part I know."

"All right, so after a series of adventures, she decides to kill him. But nothing works. Well, to make a long story short, he's gloating about this terrible power over her one day and he asks for a glass of water. So she gets him the glass of water and he drinks it and he dies."

"Of what?"

"Poison. The normal microbes in the water were poison to him, you know, because his system had never met them before."

"Ah," Blixen said. "And—what happened to the heroine?"

"What always happens to heroines?" Tibbet countered. "She married the man who'd loved her all along."

"Of course, why ask," Blixen said. He rubbed his finger gently along his lips. "Okay, Walter, thanks . . ."

"What did you do, have a bet with somebody?"

Blixen glanced up. "In a way," he said.

Sighing, Tibbet folded his handkerchief and stuffed it back into his pocket. "Well, I suppose I'd better shove off. Sometimes I think I'd rather have a tooth pulled than go to a funeral. Wouldn't you?"

"Almost."

"Well—I'll see you there . . ."

Tibbet shambled reluctantly on down the flagstone path while Blixen made his thoughtful way across the shaded lawn to Bruce Muir's front door.

A gong—baritone and Chinese—reverberated in the hallway when he pushed the bell. Footsteps approached from the back. The door was opened by a sallow young woman in a white smock and heavy flat shoes. She regarded Blixen disinterestedly.

"Yes," Blixen said. "Uh—are you Lupe?"

A nod.

"My name's Blixen, Lupe. I'm a friend of Mr. Muir's. I know how sick he is, but if he's awake I'd like very much to see him."

"Sure," Lupe said. "Come on in."

Blixen waited until she'd shut the solid door behind them, and then followed her down a narrow hall that smelled sweetly of corruption and wax. "How's he feeling?"

"Dopey. Nobody's supposed to stay very long."

"I'll be out in two minutes."

"Okay."

She had rounded a dark corner ahead of him, disappeared for a second. When he reached her, she was holding open the door to a dim overheated bedroom.

"Thank you . . ."

Muir was on his back in bed, drowning in covers. He had reached behind him to grip the top of the bedstead in porcelain-white hands. His arms were fleshless, sticklike in lavender-and-white-striped pajama sleeves. It was the size of the man that clutched at Blixen's heart, the dwarfishness. The barrel-chested giant was gone, and all that was left was pain.

Evidently he hadn't heard Blixen enter. The sunken eyes remained closed; the fingers pulled and pulled on the bedstead. All the curtains in the room had been drawn. There was one chair, next to the bed. No plants, although someone had placed a tall vase of five colorful wire and paper Mexican flowers on the dresser. A beaded pitcher of water sat on a silver tray by a bedside radio.

Quietly Blixen drew out the chair, sat down.

It was the creak of the chair's cane bottom that disturbed Muir. The swollen neck tendons hauled the old death's-head around.

"Bruce—good morning . . ."

The eyes were buzzard's eyes, fierce and puzzled, lost in blue film.

"Nils Blixen," Blixen said.

The eyes cleared. The white lips barely moved. "*Stagg . . .*"

"That's right."

"Where's Chet?"

Unsure of the words, Blixen bent forward.

"My son Chettie works for you—"

"Oh, *Chettie.* Yes."

"He won't come by . . ."

"Chettie? Yes, Chettie's been here."

"No . . ."

"I think you've forgotten."

It wasn't beyond reason. The gray face reflected the possibility. The perplexed eyes remembered the needles, the little white pain pills as shiny as agate chips. The mental distortions that followed.

"Chettie's been very concerned about you," Blixen said.

Cautious satisfaction gleamed between the crusted eyelids. "Well, well . . . Chettie's a good boy."

"He is."

"I think I raised four good boys."

"So do I."

"Although I wonder how sometimes."

"Was it hard?"

"Oh, baby," Muir said. The clenched fists tugged at the bedstead. "You do the best you can, but you always wonder. At least they never took drugs, never got a girl into trouble. I had to whip 'em all half to death, but I kept 'em in line." The fists worked on the bedstead railings like a milker's hands, stretching and tugging. "Lion tamer," Muir said.

Again Blixen bent forward.

"You crack the whip," Muir said, "and you shoot the gun and you hope they don't tear each other to pieces. Set each other on fire."

"Well—brothers—"

"No, that was a terrible thing. None of us ever got over that." The old head probed restlessly for a drier place on the wadded-up pillow. "I was too easy on Chet from then on. Maybe too hard on Em."

After a moment, Blixen said: "You were? Why Em?"

The fists stopped. "Don't you know that story?"

"Well—"

"Emmett lit him."

Presently Blixen nodded.

Muir said: "I see you did know."

"I did. Em told some of us. But—he seems to be under the impression that he and Chet had kept it a secret . . ."

"From me?" Muir gave a short choked yap of a laugh. "How?

With the two of them skulking around, whispering and arranging pay-offs. Oh, I knew. I just never said anything. . . . Lion tamer. Keep 'em apart. Watch out for fires. What else could you do?"

"Not much . . ."

"They still showed their teeth. Both always had to have the same piece of meat." The bed quivered; the old man was laughing again. "I suppose Em thought he had me fooled there, too."

"About—?"

"The meat. The woman. I'd see him waltz into their house the minute Chettie'd leave." The fists had resumed their pulling. "Maybe I shouldn't have told Chettie that."

"You *told* Chettie that Em was—"

Querulously the old man complained: "Why does she keep it so effing dark in here? Open the blinds."

After a moment, Blixen rose, walked to the window. The huge fulgent paper flowers on the dresser brushed his arm, rustled dryly in their vase, smelling of dust. He held the black-out curtain back— stopped short. Directly across the way, Wanda was testing her locked front door while Jennifer and Emmett waited part way down the walk. Gail, in a quilted housecoat, was brushing dandruff specks off Robert's blue suit collar near the limousine. The attendant stood respectfully by the rear door.

"Open it. What's the matter?"

Blixen let the draper fall. "It's stuck, Bruce."

"Call the girl."

"Listen—what did you mean when you said you told Chettie about Em and Wanda?"

"I didn't *tell* him." Muir groaned and cleared his throat piously. "It was none of my business. Well. I may have hinted. I asked him if he knew they were passing notes like school children. . . . What time is it?"

"Almost eleven."

"That damn girl's late with my pill again. Call her. *Call* her."

"I'll see you later, Bruce."

The great cords in the wasted neck stood out like cables under the sting and goad of the pain. "Chettie said he'd look into it. The note. But I can't believe that. Chettie's never been one to face a problem head on. That's his trouble."

"He may have faced this one head on all right," Blixen said.

But Muir, involved with the multiplying cells in his tormented body, apparently hadn't heard. The head rolled back and forth on the wet pillow. The arms pulled and pulled. "Lion tamer," he said . . .

XXIV

Klein Brothers, alerted by the publicity surrounding Chet's murder, not only had opened their largest chapel for the services but had prudently crowded more than fifty folding chairs into the back of the hall. When it became evident that even these would not be nearly enough, electricians were sent to install speakers in a second chapel, Lilyland, and seats were found for an additional two hundred guests there.

Blixen, who was late, was standing at the edge of Lilyland, reading his program, when the pre-med attendant touched his elbow. "They want you in the Family Room," whispered the attendant.

Blixen folded his program. "The—? Where is that?"

Beckoning, the attendant led him through an antechamber into the sunshine, down a rosebush-bordered path by the side of the building. At the end of the path, a man leaned dully against a gray door. Robert.

The attendant pointed.

"Thank you, I know this gentleman," Blixen said. "Thank you very much . . ."

Robert had heard the steps on the gravel, and was watching him through obsidian-black glasses.

Blixen waited for the attendant's retreat and then nodded silently.

"Nils," Robert said.

"Where are the others?"

"They're inside. I couldn't stand the smell of the flowers."

"Gail?"

"Gail's home. Gail wasn't feeling too well. She may be getting a cold."

"I'm sorry to hear that."

"She's sensible. She takes care of herself." Robert seemed to be following a flight of sparrows past the top of the mortuary; sunlight glistened off the impenetrable glasses. "I rode back to town with Murphy yesterday."

"Did you?"

"He told me about your conversation."

"Robert—" Blixen began.

"We'd made a deal. He broke his word. I said I never wanted to see him again."

"That may be a little difficult—working on the same series—"

"I quit last night."

"What did you tell Gail?"

"About quitting?"

"About Murf."

Robert took off his glasses to examine Blixen's face. "You know, Nils," he said, "for a sensitive man, you can say some of the dumbest things I've ever heard."

"Meaning you don't intend to tell her?"

Presently Robert reset the glasses on his nose and studied the sky.

After a moment Blixen said: "Robert—has this sort of thing ever happened before?"

"It's none of your business. Once or twice."

"It is going to happen again?"

Robert lifted his hand to his glasses, but the hand had begun to tremble, so he lowered it and thrust it into his pocket. "It's my life," he said. "It's the only life I've got. I'll live it any goddamn way I choose."

"Fine—but if you live it with guilt, you'll kill yourself."

"I know what I'm doing."

"What about Gail?"

"What about her?"

"Are you being fair to her?"

"Marriages have survived worse problems."

"I didn't say they couldn't survive. I asked if it was fair."

"She'd never—she couldn't understand! I *love* her! Can *you* understand?"

"But you can't trust her. Is that it?"

"I can't trust her to—!" Robert broke off. "It doesn't matter. It's not going to come up."

"Suppose you're arrested."

"I won't be." The high forehead wrinkled pugnaciously. "Arrested for what?"

"What do you mean, for what? For murder."

Plainly baffled, Robert said: "But they've already arrested me. And let me go. They can't arrest me again."

"Well, of course they can. What's going to stop them? You've—"

"Double jeopardy," Robert said.

Astonished, Blixen said: "Robert—that refers to trial—not arrest. It means you can't be retried after acquittal. You can certainly be rearrested on the same charge whenever further evidence warrants it. Didn't you understand that?"

Blood washed into Robert's neck, flamed like sunburn in his

cheeks and ears. "Oh, certainly I *understood* it. I'm not a lunatic, Nils." He rattled the change in his pocket. "I simply meant that there *wasn't* any further evidence. There couldn't be—"

"There's proof that you and Chettie were in the same area when he was killed—"

"Well—but—"

"But what, for the love of God!" Blixen snapped, infuriated. "Can't you see that that's the knot in the noose! What's the matter with you? They already had method, motive . . . By the way—was Murf the cause of the fight at Chasen's?"

Robert wouldn't look around, but he managed a nod. "Chettie'd found a note Murf had written to me. I don't know how, unless he'd sifted through our trash. But that was typical of Chettie. He threatened to tell Pop."

"Why?"

"Why, why, how do I know why? Because it was his nature. Why do dogs bark?"

"Anyway," Blixen said, "all the police need now is opportunity and Schreiber expects them to uncover that before the end of the week. So don't give me any of that 'well—but,' business. You're in trouble."

Robert released the change in his pocket and gripped both hands behind his back. "All right, I'm in trouble."

"And if you *are* indicted, Robert, I can tell you right here and now that the only chance on earth you'll have is to tell the truth."

"And wreck Murf's career."

Blixen hesitated. "Probably," he said.

Robert hunched his shoulders. "That's what he was thinking about then . . ."

"When?"

"Oh—when we were driving back to town yesterday. He—said he knew I'd keep my mouth shut—but he told me he wanted to take care of me in case something screwy happened and I had to go to jail for a while."

"Take care of you how?"

"I gathered he was talking about an income."

Blixen shook his head tiredly. "How much did he offer?"

"We didn't get down to specifics."

"Were you tempted?"

Robert considered. "I think I was. For a minute. And then he said there was no way they could give me more than ten years, and I began to think about that in terms of days—hours . . ."

"You'll use your alibi, then, if you're arrested . . ."

"Damned if I do and damned if I don't," Robert said.

Judiciously Blixen said: "There is one way you could draw the sting of it a little. . . . Tell Gail first."

"Jesus," Robert said. And then: "That still wouldn't save Murf. Or the series."

"No. It wouldn't."

"And who's to say a jury'd believe me anyway?"

"Or me, when I back you up. But it's worth a try, isn't it?"

Robert stared at him. "*You'd* back me up?"

"Certainly."

"Why?"

"Did you kill your brother?"

"No."

"That's why."

Again the tip of Robert's tongue explored his lips, testing, moistening them. "Maybe we'll never have to face the problem. Maybe they'll find the real murderer first."

"Maybe," Blixen said.

Behind them, the gray door cracked open. The organist was playing "In the Garden." Emmett's bearded face was thin and strained. "Well?" he said. "Are you going to stay out here all morning? Come on in. They're ready to start."

XXV

But it was not quite true.

The mourners were ready to listen; the minister stood behind his lectern, ready to speak. But no one had told the organist, who *segued* resonantly from "In the Garden" to "Rock of Ages," and flatted on "Cleft," to make it worse.

The Family Room, dim as a crypt, looked through gauzy curtains toward the lectern and the open, flower-banked casket. Klein Brothers had provided two rows of chairs for those closest to the Loved One, but apart from Wanda in the center of the first row and Jennifer at the end of the second, the seats were empty. Robert preferred to stand by the door, breathing through his mouth. Emmett, his face set and bellicose, dropped heavily into the chair on Wanda's right and put an arm at once about her shoulders. Blixen sidled pensively down the second row toward Jennifer.

As he passed, his hand brushed a black feather on Wanda's small black hat and she turned wet eyes toward him. "Oh, Nils," she said. "Darling. Hello."

Blixen leaned down to kiss the cool cheek she raised.

"I'm so glad they found you," Wanda continued. "I thought you ought to be here with us. You're part of the family . . ."

Blixen squeezed what he presumed was her shoulder but which turned out to be one of Emmett's wrists. Emmett scowled at him. Blixen murmured, "Sorry," a word that covered everything, and moved on to Jennifer's side.

"Just *listen* to that," Jennifer said miserably, looking up. "He did it *again*."

"Did what?"

"*Cleft* for me," Jennifer sang, and flatted *cleft*.

"Poor ear," Blixen said.

"It's all such a barbaric *farce*," Jennifer groaned. "I can't believe adults. What are all these idiot people doing here?"

"Showing respect, perhaps?"

"Oh, nertz. To *Chet*?"

"Where's Kenneth?"

"Working."

"Wouldn't they let him off to come to a funeral?"

"I suppose they would have. He didn't ask. The one thing he is not is a hypocrite. Unlike every other living soul at this circus. Including me." Her face grew despairing. "I'll never understand myself. I always know what I ought to do, but I never *do* it. I *wanted* to stay home. Even *Gail* stayed home."

"Gail's getting a cold."

"Sure, right." She smoothed her dark blue skirt. "Incidentally, I've got a message for you."

"Oh?"

"From Ken. He says thanks, but he's just as soon pass on the studio tour. I guess he was supposed to come out and see you tomorrow?"

"Yes, he was."

"He says he just doesn't have any feeling for the boob tube. He says he'd rather drive me to the track on his day off. He says no offense meant."

After a moment, Blixen nodded. "Tell him none taken."

She was regarding him curiously. "What did you want to talk to him about?"

"Nothing important. One thing and another."

Jennifer shrugged and stretched her neck. "Did you notice a water fountain around here anyplace?"

"In the back . . ."

"Excuse me—"

She brushed by him. Blixen hooked his hands over his knee, thinking. When the organist abandoned *"Rock of Ages"* for *"The Lord's Prayer"* Wanda whispered something to Emmett, who rose and left the room. Blixen studied the black feathers on the small black hat until Wanda, as though feeling his eyes, turned her head to him. She managed a dismayed smile. "Isn't this getting a little tedious?" she asked.

"Guests may still be coming in."

"It's a tremendous tribute to Chettie, don't you think?"

"Very moving."

She began to turn away, but stopped when Blixen leaned forward and rested his crossed arms on the back of the seat ahead of him. "Wanda—" he said.

"Yes, darling—"

"Some time ago—before Christmas—you were robbed, I believe . . ."

Arching her thin eyebrows, Wanda said: "I was *what?*"

"Weren't you robbed last December? Gail said—"

"Oh, at the *house.*" Her expressive actress's face registered the barest flinch of distaste, the wryest stumble of astonishment over the number of irrelevant topics that could be introduced at a funeral. "Well, I suppose technically we were robbed, yes. Although it was such an insignificant business—"

"Still, it must have frightened you—"

"Not much."

"Wasn't that when you had all the locks put on?"

"Oh, Chettie insisted on that. The Manson syndrome."

"What was taken?"

"Oh, darling, I don't ever remember—"

"Money?"

"A few dollars. Luckily they missed some diamonds I had in a bedroom drawer. It was a very amateurish effort. Just kids, according to the police."

"Kids," Blixen repeated.

"It's strange how much times have changed," Wanda said. "When I was young, a robber was someone in a black mask, with a gat. Now he's a rich kid who hates his mother."

"You say a few dollars—"

"Two or three. They were in an imitation leather bag of mine, in a secret little mad-money compartment. The police told me that he'd probably throw the bag away as soon as he emptied it, but it's never turned up."

"And what else was in the bag?"

"Little wispy handkerchief. Gum. Lipstick, I think. Odds and ends."

"Wallet?"

"No, no. Nothing valuable."

A door slammed and presently Emmett came tramping down the aisle. "Dumbbells," he muttered.

Swinging around, Wanda said: "Who?"

"Everybody," Emmett growled. "The crowd threw 'em into a panic, so they told the organist to vamp till ready and then they left him alone back there. I've straightened it out."

"Are the doors closed?"

"They can't *get* 'em closed." Emmett dropped into his seat again and struck Blixen's hand when he looped his arm around Wanda's shoulder. "Excuse me, Nils," he grunted.

"My fault," Blixen said, and sat back in his chair.

The organ dwindled flatly away.

"I am the Resurrection and the Life, saith the Lord," said the minister.

"*Farce*," Jennifer groaned . . .

XXVI

Blixen opted against joining the auto procession to the cemetery, got a sandwich and a beer at Musso's, and was back in his studio office before three. Miss Firebush, chilled to the bone, insisted on bringing him a steaming cup of coffee along with his list of messages, and then sat down to hear all about the funeral. Blixen assured her that it had been a beautiful ceremony from start to conclusion, and Miss Firebush declared mistily that she wasn't surprised. "Look at the weather," she said. "'Happy is the corpse that the sun shines on today.' My mother always said that."

Blixen removed his burned lips from the coffee cup. "Isn't that 'bride'?"

"Same thing," Miss Firebush said obscurely. "Oh. I've ordered flowers, of course, for Mr. Moore, but I didn't know where to send them. I said I'd call the florist back. I suppose it'll be Climb Brothers?"

Blixen continued to peer at her until Miss Firebush looked up from her note pad. "You suppose what'll be Klein Brothers?" Blixen asked.

"The funeral."

"The funeral has already been held," Blixen said. "The funeral was today."

"No, no," said Miss Firebush. "Well, *yes, that* one was held. I'm talking about the next one. The father's."

Blixen put his coffee cup down.

"Weren't you informed?" Miss Firebush asked.

"You're telling me, I take it," Blixen said, "that Bruce Muir died this afternoon—"

"If that's the father, yes."

"When?"

"Well, let's see—I'd just gotten back from lunch when they called. That was about one-thirty—"

"Who is 'they'?"

"This person said she was Mr. Moore's daughter-in-law."

"Gail."

"I don't know."

Blixen swung about to face the courtyard. "Try her for me, would you, please? She's Robert's wife. We have the number."

"Yes," Miss Firebush said, and scurried out.

Blixen was still gazing blankly into the courtyard when Miss Firebush's two buzzes indicated that Blixen's party was on the wire. He lifted his receiver. "Gail?"

"Hi, Nils." Her voice was harsh and exhausted. "Listen, I told her you didn't have to call back—"

Exhaling, Blixen said: "Well. It's true, then."

"About the old man? Oh yes, it's true. We can't even have a funeral around here for all the deaths—"

"I don't know why I should be so shocked, but I am," Blixen said.

"Isn't it weird? We really ought to be *grateful*," Gail said. "I don't think any man ever tried harder to die."

"Never."

"I hated him and at the same time I was so sorry for him—"

"What happened exactly, Gail?"

"I don't think anybody knows for sure. I went over there around noon for something, and when I peeked into his bedroom, I could see he was dead. Boy, this has been the craziest day—"

"Wasn't Lupe there?"

"Lupe was in the kitchen. Fixing lunch. She didn't hear a thing. He didn't call out or anything—"

"You must be numb. All of you."

"Comatose."

"Everybody get back from the cemetery?"

"Yeah, about ten minutes ago."

"How did Wanda take it?"

"I think she's in a state of shock. She sat down and she started to laugh. Em's the one who really went to pieces."

Surprised, Blixen said: "Em did?"

"Oh, he's *still* crying. And after the fights those two used to have."

"Maybe that's the trouble . . ."

"What is?"

"Well," Blixen said, "maybe Em wanted to settle accounts—have one last talk with the old man."

"Maybe. Although he was the last one to see him as it was."

"Except for me," Blixen said. "I looked in just before eleven. Em and the rest had already left for the mortuary."

"Uh-huh, but they came back," Gail said. "Wanda wanted some extra Kleenexes, so Em ran into Bruce's place and got a box from Lupe."

"And the old man was all right then?"

"Well, he was in pain, but he was always in pain. He was alive."

"What was Robert's reaction to all this?"

"Scary. Indifference. You know, I'm really worried about Robert. Robert and I used to be able to talk to each other, Nils, but something's happened. He just walks around here like a stranger now. Of course, all those meat-headed cops out in the street don't help either."

"What do they do?"

"Oh, they don't *hurt* anything, they just watch, but—"

"All the time?"

"*All* the time, every minute. It's as if they're just waiting for him to make one false step, and then wham, they've got him. Is this what we're paying taxes for?"

"Apparently it is."

"Well, I just wish they'd all go back to arresting kids at rock concerts and leave us alone. I don't know how much more of this Robert can take."

Pensively Blixen arranged his hippos into a trekking formation, two abreast, headed for the water hole. "It'll probably get worse before it gets better. He'll need a lot of extra patience for a while, Gail."

"Tender loving care. Tea and sympathy."

"That's it."

"Well, that I can always give. I always have. This is one boy who's always had a bed to come home to."

Blixen closed the hoppo ranks. "Good . . ."

"A cook in the kitchen—a whore in the bedroom. What more can a tired man want?"

"I can't imagine," Blixen said. "Unless it might be an understanding friend in the long watches of the night."

"Fine. He's got that, too."

"So have you," Blixen said, "in case you ever need a producer-type party to talk to."

"Even in the long watches of the night?"

"Especially then."

Her voice was pleased and puzzled. "Well—thank you, Nils. I'll remember."

"Now—where's the funeral going to be?"

"Oh, Klein Brothers. But private this time."

"I don't blame you."

"If this keeps up, we might as well open a charge account . . . Listen—did you want to talk to anybody else? Wanda? Em? Robert They're all here."

"I don't think so. Just give them my condolences."

"I will."

"Good-by, Gail."

"By-by . . ."

The phone clicked, but Blixen continued to hold the receiver to his ear, gazing down at his list of messages and remembering the sticklike arms tugging at life in the florid pajamas, the waxen face . . . He depressed the intercom buzzer.

"Yes," said Miss Firebush.

"It will be Klein Brothers again. You were right."

"And will you be going?"

"No, it's private . . ." He rubbed two fingers against the ache in his neck. "Let's clear away some of these calls—"

"Mr. Crotch was the first—"

"Mr—?"

"'Crotch.' C-R-O-U-C-H. Shall I get him?"

Pondering, Blixen said: "No—I know what he wants . . . Try Derek for me . . ."

Derek Kirk, lean and English, head of the Music Department, said: "Kirk here," in his best public school accent when the secretaries finally had completed their complex protocol dance and had buzzed their bosses simultaneously.

"Derek," Blixen said. "Nils. Did you call me earlier?"

"Oh! Yes, I did, Nils. I have your music—"

"Now, which—"

"Didn't you want us to trace a musical phrase for you? Socrates brought it in—"

Astonished, Blixen said: "You don't mean you've got that already!"

"Oh, we don't mess around, boy," Kirk said.

"You certainly don't."

"Eckshually," Kirk said, "it wasn't nearly as difficult as I wish I could pretend. The fact is we'd already traced it once. For poor Chettie Muir. Chettie'd brought the same thing to us."

Blixen leaned forward. "Really," he said.

"He told us he thought it was probably from an opera. He said his brother Emmett—you know Emmett—"

"Yes—"

"Well, he said that Emmett had taken Wanda to several operas at the Music Center last fall and that they'd both come home whistling Verdi's Greatest Hits and so forth. You see?"

"This is from Verdi then?"

"Debussy," Kirk said. "*Pelléas.*"

"Ah."

"Fourth act, when Pelléas and Mélisande first declare their love for one another. In the note you had, Pelléas says the first phrase— '*Je t'aime . . .*' and then Mélisande answers, '*Je t'aime aussi . . .*' Do you understand my miserable French?"

" 'I love you—I love you, too . . .' "

"*Précisément . . .*"

"Derek," Blixen inquired reflectively, "do you have any more of the scene there?"

"Oh, I have the whole thing . . ."

"Read me a little more of it, will you?"

"All right. . . . Well, then Pelléas says: '*Oh, qu'as-tu dit, Mélisande! Je ne l'ai presque pas entendu!*' And so forth and so on. '*Tu m'aimes? Tu m'aimes aussi? Depuis quand m'aimes-tu?*' How long have you loved me? And Mélisande answers: '*Depuis toujours . . . Depuis que je t'ai vu . . .*' Forever. Ever since I first saw you. . . . And they go on like that, and Pelléas says: '*Tu ne mens un peu, pour me faire sourire?*' "

"What's '*mens*'?" Blixen asked. "Lie?"

"Lie, right. You aren't lying just a little bit, to make me feel better? And Mélisande says: '*Non, je ne mens jamais, je ne mens qu'à ton frère . . .*' No, I never lie to you—I only lie to your brother . . .'"

"Brother . . ." Blixen said. "And that's—"

"That's her husband, Golaud. The eternal old triangle . . ."

"How does it end Derek?"

"Well, Golaud's overheard all this lovemaking and he rushes in and kills Pelléas."

"Kills Pelléas," Blixen mused.

"And then he runs after Mélisande and wounds her and *she* eventually dies. Very bloody business all around."

"They'd have done better to kill the husband first, wouldn't they . . ." Blixen said.

"Oh, much better. But opera heroes and heroines never do the intelligent thing."

"I suppose not . . ." Blixen roused himself. "All right, Derek, thank you very much."

"Any time, luv."

After he'd hung up, Blixen paced for a minute or two behind his desk, thinking about the note in the two separate hands—of Emmett scrawling Pelléas' anguished cry, *'Je t'aime . . .'* and then passing the note to Wanda, and Wanda writing, *'Je t'aime aussi . . .'* and of the old man seeing the exchange, and telling Chet, and of Chet learning the truth . . . And confronting them?

Blixen picked up the telephone.

"Yes," said Miss Firebush.

"I want to speak to a Sergeant Fries, in the sheriff's office downtown. I don't know the number."

"Fleas, yes, sir," Miss Firebush said. "And while you were on the phone, a Mr. Peep called—"

Blixen, adrift, cast about for a straw. "Peep . . ."

"When I asked him his name, he said to just tell you Peep."

Groping, Blixen said: "Could it have been 'Pep'?"

"No," said Miss Firebush.

"What did he want?"

"He said the address you were after was one forty-seven Del Rio Street, Las Vegas. The girl's name, he said, was Vera."

"Verna," Blixen said.

"Verna, Vera," Miss Firebush said. "It makes sense to you then?"

"Oh yes."

"I'll get Sergeant Fleas now . . ."

But the sergeant, according to the voice that answered, was away from his desk and wasn't expected back before five-thirty or six. Could Deputy Bacon help?

Blixen was tempted and considered it, but then abandoned the idea as complicated and impractical, thanked Deputy Bacon, and said he would try Sergeant Fries later.

"Okay, that clears everybody up except Mr. Smith and Mr. Crotch," Miss Firebush reported.

"Did Murf say what he wanted?" Blixen asked.

"Yes, a Church Youth Group has voted him the hero they'd most like to emulate, and he wondered if he could go pick up the award on Sunday."

"So long as he's ready to work on Monday."

"I'll tell him."

"Incidentally, I want him to autograph a cast picture—"

"All right—"

"It's to 'My good pal, Stell, with love and kisses—'"

"Yes—"

"And when he sends it over, mail it to Mrs. Stell Burns, Golden Years Hotel, San Urbano, California."

"Okay. . . . Shall I get Mr. Crotch now?"

"Get Mr. Crotch."

"Lord, if I had a name like that, I'd sure change it quick," said Miss Firebush.

"I don't blame you," Blixen said.

"Whew-ee," said Miss Firebush, and cut herself off.

Blixen waited with one hand on the receiver, his thoughts a million miles away, until the two buzzes summoned him, and then he pressed the lighted button. "Hi Bert . . ."

"You're back," Mr. Crouch said.

"Finally back."

"I forgot that you'd probably be going to that funeral. . . . How was it?"

"Gigantic."

"Uh—" Mr. Crouch cleared his throat. "Mr. Blixen, let me tell you why I called—"

"I think I know why," Blixen said. "Is this about Ken?"

"Oh ho," said Mr. Crouch, "so the little girl told you."

"I saw her at the funeral parlor."

"He's a fine boy, Mr. Blixen, but he's as independent as a hog on a hot tin roof."

"Well, there are worse sins."

"Yes, but a lot of people can't stand that attitude. Marge can't."

"Maybe Marge is more attracted to it than she wants to admit."

"Oh ho again," said Mr. Crouch. "So you see that, too."

"How does he feel about Marge?"

"He likes Marge, I think, but she confuses him."

"And Jennifer doesn't?"

"Well, Jennifer's younger," said Mr. Crouch. "Safer?"

Blixen's eyebrows rose. "That's very perceptive."

"Don't you remember how Andy Hardy always ran from the complex older women back to Ann Rutherford?"

"Of course."

"By the way, I give up on your last R.A."

"Ramsay Ames," Blixen said.

"Ramsay *Ames!*" shouted Mr. Crouch. "Of course. Who was the dead man who carried her off?"

"Lon Chaney, Jr. *The Mummy's Ghost*, 1944."

"You're right. C.C. Creighton Chaney. No, I'm not Ramsay Ames. Okay. Ask me a question."

"Are you male?"

"Yes, I am."

"Do you stutter?"

"No, I'm not Roscoe Ates."

"Were you one of Paramount's great stars?"

"These all have to be men from now on," warned Mr. Crouch.

"This was a man."

"Paramount, Paramount . . . Just give me a minute . . . Incidentally, I still wish you could talk to Kenneth. Maybe he could come out some Wednesday in between racing meets . . ."

"He likes the horses, does he . . ."

"He likes the betting."

"How did he do Sunday, by the way?"

"He won."

"Big?"

There was a moment's silence before Mr. Crouch said: "Pretty big."

"Several hundred dollars?"

"You just don't trust him, do you?" asked Mr. Crouch. "I can hear it in your voice."

"I don't have any reason not to trust him," Blixen said. "Chettie himself knew the money was missing. Which means that he must have given it away. Or at least that he knew where it had gone." He paused. "As for the murder—well, there's no way Kenneth could have done that—"

"Not unless he's learned how to be in two places at once," Mr. Crouch said.

Blixen tapped his fingers on the desk. "Bert—you're dead sure, are you, that the boy was out of your sight only on those two short occasions?"

"Absolutely. Ask anyone on the route. We talked to a dozen people . . . What was the critical time again?"

"Noon."

"All right," said Mr. Crouch triumphantly, "ask Emmett Muir!"

It was a shockingly long while before the full implication of the statement began to sink in—far longer, probably, than it would have been if Blixen had not come to his prior, obstinate, subconscious belief in Emmett's guilt. And even then all Blixen could do was stare at the truth round-eyed, like a child at an ostrich, still only half-convinced of so ill shaped a fact.

"Hello?" said Mr. Crouch.

"You saw *Emmett* Saturday?"

"Emmett—yes—"

Blixen hunched forward. "Where?" he demanded, and then tried to neutralize the rage in his voice by saying: "I'm not angry, Bert, I'm just surprised," which only seemed to unman Mr. Crouch the more. "Talk into the mouthpiece," Blixen said. "I can't understand you—"

"Uh—I said out back—in the—by the—"

"At his house?"

"At his house—on the back porch—"

"What was he doing?"

"Well—he was feeding his cat—"

"And what time was this? Exactly?"

"I don't know *exactly*—about two minutes to twelve?"

"It *couldn't* have been!"

Suddenly stubborn, Mr. Crouch said: "Two or three minutes, yes, it was. I know because the pasta factory on Edgemont always blows a whistle at noon, and Saturday they blew just when Ken and I were walking back to the truck, and we checked our watches—"

"*Ken* was with you?"

"Sure—"

"And you both saw Emmett?"

"Saw him and talked to him."

"What did you say?"

"Well—I don't know—good morning—got anything for us—and he said no, and that was it . . ."

"I really can't believe this."

"Oh, there are a lot of times when Emmett doesn't have anything—"

"No, I mean—" Blixen groaned. "Why the hell would he lie? I don't understand! Why would he maintain to the police that no one could corroborate his alibi?"

"That I wouldn't know."

"Bert—are you *positive* it was Emmett you spoke to?"

"Certainly I'm positive. . . . I don't know what you mean—"

Sighing, Blixen rested his cheek on his fist. "I don't know what I mean either," he said. "Well. Okay, thanks very much."

"You sound the way those World War One aviators used to look when the Germans shot them down in *Wings*."

"That's just about how I feel."

"*Wings!*" Mr. Crouch exclaimed. "Paramount! No, I'm not Richard Arlen!"

"You're too good for me," Blixen said. "Good-by, Bert."

"Good-by, Mr. Blixen."

After he'd hung up, Blixen sat for a moment with his head in his hands, looking at the closed door to his private bathroom, and then he buzzed Miss Firebush.

"Yes," Miss Firebush said.

"What was the address again that Mr. Peep gave you?"

"Uh—one forty-seven Del Rio Street."

"See if you can get me on the six o'clock flight to Vegas."

"What about return?"

"I'll arrange that myself. I'll be back in the office tomorrow."

"My goodness," Miss Firebush said, "that won't be much of a vacation, will it."

"No, it won't," Blixen said. "Not much."

XXVII

By seven, Blixen had landed at McCarran Field, lost a dollar and a half in the airport slot machines, and acquired a car and a map of Las Vegas from a winsome rental agent who resembled a stewardess.

It was a plum-colored evening, reddish and warm. In his shirt sleeves, feeling like a self-conscious Lew Archer, Blixen drove east and north, across the gaudy, exhausted Strip into a development dominated by churches and neat homes behind sand lawns and cactus gardens. One forty-seven Del Rio bordered on a crisp new grammar school; a battered tricycle lay on its side in the driveway.

Spencer Muir, long-nosed and balding, answered the doorbell, looking more like Chettie than Emmett, smaller than Robert. He carried a wadded-up paper napkin in one hand and his tone was quarrelsome. "You're early," he said.

"Spencer?" Blixen said.

Suspicious, Spencer said: "Who's this?" and then, "Well, for—"

"Hey, man, how've you been?" Blixen said.

"Well, by God, not bad," Spencer said.

Behind him, a brown-haired young girl in a green and gold muumuu came curiously to a dining room arch, wiping a dish.

"Listen, what did I do, get you at dinner?" Blixen asked.

"No, no, we just finished," Spencer said, and laughed. "Do you know who I thought you were? The studio car. I'm doing a bike spill up at Mead." He beamed fondly and wiped his mouth with the napkin. "Well. What are you doing in Vegas, Nils?"

"Oh, I came over to see the show at the Grand—"

"Yeah . . ."

"And I ran into a friend of yours and he told me where you were staying—"

"What friend?" Spencer asked.

"Gaffer—heavy-set fellow—"

"I wish you'd called first," Spencer said. "We could have saved you some dessert."

"Not with the weight I've been putting on."

"How about some Sanka and Sweeta then?" the young woman in the muumuu asked. Her voice was wispy and distant, as innocent as a daisy.

"Oh," Blixen said. "Well—all right. Thank you."

Spencer's hesitation was barely perceptible. "Good," he said, and unhooked the screen door and pushed it open. "Come on in . . ."

The woman had vanished. The room was cluttered with racing forms and plastic toys. Spencer dug an earless hippo out of a worn overstuffed chair. "She has a three-year-old kid," he explained. "Sit down, Nils."

"This is obviously one child I'd get along with," Blixen said, and added, when Spencer looked blank: "The hippo."

"Oh! Right. You're the hippo freak."

"Now there's a splendid reputation to carry to the grave."

"Well, what the heck, how are you going to fight love?" Spencer asked, and flopped down on the sofa opposite Blixen, where he could watch the door. His right hand kneaded the napkin ceaselessly. He leaned back, clearly forcing himself to relax. "By the way," he said, "I've been in touch with the family, and—I want you to know how much—how—important your support—"

"Oh, please," Blixen said.

"No, I mean it," Spencer insisted. "They appreciate it, and I appreciate it. . . . I just wish I could have been at the funeral myself, but—" He spread out the tattered napkin, crumpled it again, and tossed it into an ashtray. "Well, I'll be back for Pop's. We ought to wind this thing up tonight."

"It's been a long location," Blixen said.

"Been endless," Spencer replied. "Especially with all those crap tables around."

"You've been up here—what?—two weeks now?"

"Fifteen days."

"What's been the main problem?"

"Oh, this terrible weather," Spencer said.

"They give you Saturday calls?"

"They tried. But they had to cancel both of 'em."

"So what did you do with your spare time?"

"Well—Verna and me, we'd fool around—go downtown some-times . . ." He hesitated, fidgeting. "Except for last Saturday. We stayed home last Saturday. That was when Chettie was—" Again he broke off. "We just lazed around," he said. "The two of us. Reading —listening to the opera broadcast. . . . She feels the same way about opera as you do about hippos. Just a lot of yelling to me."

"What did you hear?"

"Huh?" Spencer said.

"I said, what did you hear? I'm quite a fan myself."

Spencer poked at the napkin, flicked it with his thumb. "I think it was *Aïda*," he said.

"It was *Così fan tutte*," Verna said. The muumuu rustled as she put Blixen's cup down on an end table beside him. "Cream?" she murmured.

"Black."

"I thought it was *Aïda*," Spencer said.

"No, you didn't, they aren't anything alike," Verna said, and ar-ranged herself on the floor between them, slim and sober, make-up free, her baby-fine hair held in an old-fashioned pony-tail. Her cool gray eyes sought Blixen's. "Roberta Peters sang Despina," she said. "I'm really just crazy about Roberta Peters."

"So am I," Blixen said.

"Your voice is as good as Roberta Peters', honey," Spencer said.

"Oh, Spencer, stop it," Verna said.

"She's shy," Spencer said to Blixen. "What's that pretty song you sing to me, Vern?"

"'*O, mio babbino caro*,'" Verna muttered.

"You always want to make it in Hollywood. Well, here's a big Hollywood producer. Sing '*Bambino Cairo*' for Nils."

"Oh, Christ," Verna groaned.

"Go ahead."

"No!"

"Go on, he'll—"

A mellow toot from outside stopped him. A car had turned into the drive; headlights shone through the bulging screen door.

"Whoops, saved by the horn," Spencer said, and clambered to his feet, laughing. "All right. Well, I'll bring her to the studio some-day and she can give an audition, Nils. You like '*Bambino Cairo*'?"

"Love 'Bambino Cairo,'" Blixen said.

Spencer laughed again and shifted from one foot to the other, waiting. "Well—" he said.

"Right," Blixen said reluctantly, "I'd better go, too. It's—"

"Hey, you're not going without finishing your Sanka, are you?" Verna asked. "Sit down."

"Well—I—"

"Sit, sit, sit—"

Spencer was gazing meditatively at the back of Verna's head, but Verna wouldn't look around, and finally, when the inquisitive toot sounded for the second time, Spencer shrugged and turned. "Okay," he said. "See you, Nils."

"Good luck, Spencer."

Verna continued to stare at the floor until the car door outside had slammed and the headlights had disappeared and then she raised her fists like a child and whacked them down on her crossed knees. "*Jesus*, that man makes me mad sometimes," she said.

"Great tease," Blixen said.

"Great pain in the behind," Verna said. "He just loves to bug me about my singing. I've just about had it."

"Maybe he's proud of you—"

"Proud of *what?* He doesn't have any judgment. I've got a sweet little voice. I'm like the woman in *Citizen Kane*. Little tiny voice, big fantasies."

"What do you fantasize?"

She threw him a mercurial, mischievous glance. "About what you'd expect. I do Mimi at the Met. Gilda." She gave a choked chuckle. "Once I was even Turandot."

"Brünnhilde next," Blixen said.

"Never. Even fantasy has its limits."

"Have you sung professionally?"

"Not sung. Acted."

"Where?"

"New York porn," Verna said.

"Oh," Blixen said.

"I'm twenty-five," Verna said, "but I've got this dumb teen-age face and they like that. And I like New York. When I'm not working, there I am at Lincoln Center, fantasizing."

"Is that what you were doing Saturday?"

"When?" Verna asked.

"Saturday."

After a moment Verna said: "I don't follow you."

"Well, it's simple enough," Blixen said. "I'm suggesting that you fantasized hearing Roberta Peters in *Così* Saturday and that you forgot to tell Spencer that the opera wasn't broadcast."

"But it *was* broadcast—"

"It was in the rest of the country, yes. But I understand there was a power outrage in Vegas last Saturday between eleven and three. Broadcast time. Wasn't that true?"

Verna watched him steadily.

"Then how," Blixen inquired, "could you hear *Così?*"

"Battery radio," Verna said. "We got Salt Lake or someplace . . ."

"Can I see it?" Blixen asked politely. "The radio?"

"We gave it away," Verna said.

"He wasn't here on Saturday, was he, Verna?"

Verna tapped her fists mildly on her knees for a moment and then got to her feet. "More coffee?" she asked.

"Verna?"

"No," Verna said. "He wasn't here."

"Where was he?"

"That hostile son of a bitch really hurts me when he makes fun of my voice," Verna said.

"Verna? Where was he?"

"Why, he was in Los Angeles," Verna said. "Where else?"

XXVIII

Tuesday night was plum-colored in Vegas and black as outer space in L.A. Thunder clouds from the west hid the moon and threatened rain. On Temple Street, the young whores scared each other with dreadful ghost stories and clung, for the most part, to the Cuban ballrooms. Everyone smelled murder in the air.

"Well," Lupe said in Spanish from the bathroom, "I guess I'm ready. I don't know when I'll be back. Don't wait up."

"What?" Guzman asked. He was her paternal uncle, an enormous brute who existed, apparently, on Coors beer and beans. At least she'd never seen him take anything else. He was stretched out on the couch in front of the TV set, scratching his bedbug bites and watching a Mexican soap opera.

"I said—" But it was like talking to the wind, to a beer belch. "Nothing." She pressed her lipsticked lips over a tissue, tossed it away, tugged her jacket down. "Tell Mama not to lock the door, okay?"

Guzman pulled his eyes away from the set to frown at her while she walked in front of him. "You're all dressed up," he said.

"Yeah."

"Why?"

"I told you why."

"Me? You didn't."

Sighing, she said: "Oh, Uncle—"

"It's funny out. It's going to rain. I want you to stay home."

She shook her stubborn Indian head. "I'll be perfectly all right. I'm just going over to the police station."

The alarm on his face was so ludicrous, his consternation so great, that she nearly laughed aloud. "No, no, no," she said, "nothing to do with you . . ." He peddled a little heroin on the side. She knew it, everyone knew it.

"But then—"

"I just want to talk to them about Mr. Muir," Lupe said. "I told you that."

"You keep away from those people," Guzman warned her. "What about Mr. Muir?"

"I told you that, too. I think I finally figured out how they killed him."

"How?"

Wearily she said: "Uncle, I've been over the whole thing with you half a dozen times—"

"All right, all right, forget it," Guzman said. His lower lip hung pendulously.

Curious but wounded, Lupe said to herself. *He'll pout for two days now.* She considered explaining her theory again to him, and then decided against it when his paw went for the Coors can and his eyes strayed back to the TV set. He'd never in the world hear her. "Well, good night, Uncle," she said.

He didn't even hear that. He didn't even wave.

Outside, Temple Street was misty and abandoned. The local gang had splashed a new threat in spray paint on the alley wall beside the house to re-establish territorial dominion. SHIT ON THE TIGRES, the paint read. Bemused, Lupe opened her automobile door and sat heavily behind the wheel. She was settled, really, before she saw the figure on the passenger side. And then there was no way to get out.

The odd thing was that she wasn't surprised. There was hardly time to be frightened. "So it's you—" she said—and the knife fell like ice across the side of her neck, across the jugular, slicing toward her murderer, beneath the jaw, through the windpipe . . .

She couldn't have screamed. She hadn't the time or the breath.

And yet in two separate ballrooms, whores said: "What was that? Did you hear that?" to their friends. But in each case they were chided and mocked a little because they'd been imagining screams all night long . . .

XXIX

The phone rang at nine o'clock Wednesday morning, while Blixen was lifting it from his crowded breakfast table to the pass-through bar so that he'd have room for his coffee and eggs. "Hello," he said.

"Hello?" Irene said blankly.

"Oh," Blixen said, and transferred the receiver from his awkward right ear to his more comfortable left. "Hello."

"Boy, for someone who hates telephones," Irene said, "you certainly answer fast. I didn't even have time to sit down. I just finished dialing."

"Well, I was—"

"Do I sound a little off-stride? I feel it."

"I'm sorry. Maybe we both ought to hang up and start over."

"Maybe we should. . . . I tried to call you last night."

"I went to Vegas."

She seemed to draw in her breath and to expel it again harshly. "Oh, this is never going to work," she said. "This is terribly difficult for me."

"Evidently," Blixen said.

"You don't even grasp what I'm trying to do, do you?"

His attitude was cautious. "Well—"

"I'm trying to apologize," Irene said.

"Apologize," Blixen repeated. "For—"

"For Monday. For the scene in your office. No—not exactly for that . . ." There was a crash in his ear.

"What did you do, drop the phone?"

"Dropped the phone," Irene said. "Excuse me. Can you wait a minute? I need a cigarette."

Blixen waited, smiling.

"Hello?" Irene said.

"Hello."

"What I'm apologizing for, really, I *think*, is my own fear."

"Then you're apologizing for being human."

"A person can be human without also being all greed and a yard wide. Now I know what the Victorians must have meant when they'd warn each other that they'd hate themselves in the morning."

"I think they were referring to illicit sexual adventures."

"So am I. I screwed myself. How illicit can you get?"

"Screwed yourself how?"

"With you."

"Never," Blixen said.

"You hate me because of my bourgeois soul," Irene said.

"I think you have a perfectly splendid soul. A very honest soul."

"No, you don't," Irene said. "Do you know what happened? I panicked. All I could think of was the network reaction. I could just see everything going down the drain. The series. Murphy. My agency. . . . I didn't give a hoot about Robert—"

"There's no reason you should have been concerned with Robert—"

"The truth should have concerned me!" She paused; her breathing was ragged and fierce. "Well, it does now," she said.

"What happened?"

"I called my client, among other things."

"Ah."

"And I asked him where he'd been Saturday—whether he'd been with Robert or not—and of course he said he didn't know what I was talking about. He claimed he'd been home with a good book. Well, I knew he was lying. And I thought, dear Jesus, is *this* what I'm trying to protect?" The ragged breathing stopped and was held for a moment and presently released with a whoosh. "Anyway—I told him what I thought of him—and then I thought about what I was turning into—and about you—and—so—I called . . ."

"I'm glad."

"Still plan to pull the temple down if Robert's arrested?"

"Still do, yes."

"Well, for what it's worth, I'll be applauding when it happens."

"It's worth a great deal," Blixen said.

"Good," Irene whispered. "Good."

"Incidentally, what are you doing Saturday?" Blixen asked.

"Nothing. Why don't you come over for a swim? Provided we're not all murdered in our beds."

"It's a date."

"I don't suppose," Irene said, "that this last one makes any difference to the situation. Robert's situation, I mean."

"This last what?" Blixen asked.

"Last murder," Irene said in surprise. "Didn't you read the paper?"

"Not yet—"

"Lupe was killed last night. Their cleaning woman."

"Lupe!"

"Someone cut her throat."

Deeply shocked, Blixen said: "But—my God—*why?*"

"Robbery, according to the man in charge. She lived in a horrible neighborhood—"

"Who's the man in charge?"

"Uh—just a second . . . A lieutenant named Cohen."

"Is the name 'Fries' mentioned? F-R-I-E-S. Sheriff's department—"

"They don't say anything about sheriffs here. Just L.A. police. Do those two groups even talk to each other?"

"They do," Blixen replied, "when their cases overlap. Or they should . . ." He stared at the congealing eggs on his plate, still unable to assimilate the news fully, anxious as a child in the dark over the pointless, unexplained violence. "Irene," he said, "let me call you back. . . . I think I'd better talk to Fries."

"Don't you believe the robbery story?"

"I don't like the odds. I want to know how it happens that a woman so close to that family should end up in this fashion."

"It is grisly, isn't it . . ."

"Anyway—I'll see you Saturday."

"Come for lunch."

"All right."

"By-by, darling."

"Good-by . . ."

He pressed the receiver bar, and then dialed 411 and got the number of the sheriff's office downtown, and called that. He was dabbling in the eggs when the sheriff's switchboard connected him with Fries.

"Sergeant Fries," Fries said.

"Good morning, Sergeant. Nils Blixen."

The voice on the other end seemed to gather itself, like a cat, for jumping. "Oh, hello, Mr. Blixen—"

"Are you busy?"

"Well, now, that might depend on what you've got in mind—"

"I'd like to ask you a couple of questions."

"Not about pre-trial deals, I hope. Those are against my religion."

"Pre—?"

"Mr. Blixen, may I give you a little well-meant advice?"

"Why not?" Blixen said. "Everybody else does."

"You see, we know that you have a considerable influence over this boy—"

"By 'this boy,' I take it you're talking about Robert Muir. . . ."

"Talking about Robert Muir, right."

"Go ahead."

"We also know," Fries continued, "that he severed his connection with your organization last Monday night."

"You know a great deal."

"Yes, sir. . . . Was that on your recommendation?"

"Certainly not."

"He isn't preparing to leave town? On your advice?"

"This is ridiculous," Blixen said. "Why on earth should he want to leave town? He hasn't done anything wrong—"

"I applaud your loyalty," Fries said. "But you're really not helping him."

"He doesn't need help."

"He needs guidance. I wish someone like you could convince him that the longer he runs the harder the law's going to crack down on him."

"Sergeant—"

"We traced him to Pasadena, Mr. Blixen."

Blixen shook his head silently and pushed the plate of eggs away.

"Are you there?" Fries asked.

"Yes."

"We've placed him now within ten minutes of the scene of the crime on the day the murder was committed."

"Have you indeed."

"You don't feel that's significant?"

"Not very."

"The District Attorney does."

"Suppose someone were to tell the District Attorney that Robert Muir had a cast-iron alibi for every single second he was in Pasadena?"

The silence lengthened. Then: "So you knew he was there all along."

"Not 'all along,' no. I learned about it by accident."

"Why didn't you tell us? Why didn't *he* tell us?"

"The alibi's cast-iron, Sergeant—but—he's a little ashamed of it. He hoped he wouldn't have to use it. He still hopes so. Please keep the case open—"

"Why? To give him time to take off?"

"How is he going to take off with half your department watching him?"

Fries's chuckle was smug and indulgent.

"You *are* watching him, I suppose?" Blixen said.

"Twenty-four hours a day, yes, sir."

"Good."

"Why 'good,' Mr. Blixen?"

"Because you're his alibi now."

"Oh? For what?"

"Oh—any other unsolved murders around town—"

"Like—"

"Lupe's."

"Mr. Blixen," Fries said softly, "what makes you think that watching a man gives him a alibi? We don't have a tap on Muir's phone. And I can tell you that the going rate for a murder around here is under five hundred dollars."

"I can't believe this," Blixen said. "Are you suggesting that Robert *hired*—"

"I'm suggesting that it's possible."

"You can't be serious—"

"Semi," Fries said.

"But why in the world—"

"All right," Fries said, "suppose Lupe saw him fiddling with the oxalic acid. She was taking care of the old man that morning. I don't know whether you're aware of it, but his bedroom window looks directly into Robert's garage—"

"I'm aware of it," Blixen said. "Certainly I'm aware of it. But all of this has got to be pure speculation on your—"

"Not altogether," Fries interrupted. "She was on her way to the police station when she was killed."

Presently Blixen said: "How do you know that?"

"She told her uncle."

"Told him—that she had seen Robert take the acid—?"

"No," Fries said. "Well. Hang on. Have you got a minute?"

"Of course."

"Here's his statement." Papers rattled crisply. " 'It must have been about midnight. I didn't want her to go out. But she said she had to. She said, "I finally figured how Mr. Muir was killed." She wanted to tell the police. Question: Didn't you ask her what she'd figured out? Answer: I asked her but she didn't want to tell me. She said she already told me. Question: Told you what? Answer: I just remember it was something about the room. She said something was funny when she looked out the window.' " Fries paused. "End of statement."

"Something was funny when she looked out the window," Blixen repeated.

"Right into Robert's garage," Fries said.

"That window overlooks the entire cul-de-sac."

"Mr. Blixen," Fries said, "your young friend's caught. He's truly through. I won't deny that there are a couple of loose ends. There are always a couple of loose ends. But if you've really got Muir's best interests at heart, you'll convince him to start co-operating with this office. I was kidding about pre-trial deals. They aren't really against my religion. I'm a pragmatic agnostic, actually."

"The man's innocent, Sergeant," Blixen said.

"Uh huh," Fries said. "Is that your last word?"

"That's *his* last word."

"Okay," Fries said. "There's nothing to do except ask for the warrant, then. But I can tell you it's going to be Murder One. I'm sorry."

"Sergeant—!" Blixen began.

But the connection was broken.

XXX

A bony girl in a baseball cap and a long green dress was dribbling a basketball down the middle of the street when Blixen swung into McKinley Drive. He honked and the girl shouted something, dodged, gave him the finger, and missed her easy lay-up shot. Blixen parked in front of Robert's house, his eyes on the closed front draperies and the empty garage.

The girl had spun ferociously, but was standing now with her hands upstretched while the ball bounced unattended into Wanda's azaleas.

Blixen slammed his door. "Jen," he said.

"Oh, it's you," Jennifer said.

"Who were you expecting?"

"I thought you were my date."

"Is that the way young ladies greet their beaux in the drug culture?"

"*Beaux?*" Jennifer snorted, but she was blushing. She retrieved the basketball and went dragging across the lawn, pink and clumsy, to Blixen's side. "What are you doing over here again?"

"I wanted to talk to Robert. I called, but there was no answer."

"They're gone."

"Do you know where?"

"Gail and him go for a lot of rides. I guess they went for a ride."

"How about your mom?" Blixen asked. "Is she home?"

"Huh-uh . . . Did you hear about Lupe?"

"Dreadful—"

"They cut her throat from ear to ear," Jennifer said. She shivered and let her chin rest on the basketball. "I wonder what she thought

—how it felt . . ." She touched the back of her hand to her thin neck. "I can't imagine a thing like that. Can you?"

"No."

"I told her she'd get mugged someday. I used to warn her to shake that crazy neighborhood. Those people would just as soon rip you off as look at you. She could have had a room with one of us. Grampa used to ask her to move in there. Or she could have stayed at our place. Or over at Mr. Robert's. I think she was a little leary of Mr. Emmett and Mr. Spencer—"

"What's all this 'Mr. Robert, Mr. Spencer' business?" Blixen asked.

"That's what she always called them," Jennifer said. "Mr. Chet, Mr. Spencer—"

Slowly Blixen said: "Mr. Bruce?"

"No, Grampa was the boss. He was always Mr. Muir."

Blixen had turned to stare at the shaded colonial house next door.

"Now what's wrong?" Jennifer asked.

"Always?" Blixen inquired. "She wouldn't even have referred to Chet as 'Mr. Muir'?"

"Huh-uh, never," Jennifer said. "Why?"

She said, I finally figured how Mr. Muir was killed. She wanted to tell the police. She said something was funny when she looked out the window . . .

"Hey, man, let's sit down," Jennifer said uneasily. "Okay? You sit on the curb here and I'll get you a nice glass of—"

But Blixen was walking like a robot away from her, up the little bank that separated the two lots. "Hey!" Jennifer called, and trotted after him.

The spongy earth under the old man's front bedroom window had been watered recently; ferns as wide as palmetto leaves drooped and swayed against the pane. On tiptoe, Blixen could see past the greenery into the spartan room. The bed had been stripped; the mattress was sweat-stained. Someone had pushed the single chair against the wall, but nothing else appeared to have been moved. The paper flowers bloomed dustily on the dresser; the water pitcher still sat on its silver tray by the bedside radio . . .

"What's in there?" Jennifer asked. "What are you looking at?"

Twisting his head, Blixen stared back across the lawn to Chet's house and closed garage—and beyond that to Robert's. It wasn't true that one could see the whole of the cul-de-sac from here. Half of Emmett's house was hidden. All of Spencer's . . .

She said something was funny when she looked out the window. She said, I finally figured how Mr. Muir was killed.

"Not *who* killed him," Blixen muttered. "How. How. *How* he was killed."

"What—?"

Twisting back, Blixen said: "Is the house locked?"

He had startled her into hiccups. "Locked," she gasped. "Naturally."

"Have you got a key?"

Hiccuping: "No—"

"Hold your breath and count to ten . . ."

She swept air into her lungs, clamped her mouth shut, eyes bulging.

"Did anyone order an autopsy on the old man?"

The air came roaring out—followed by the hiccups. "I don't think so. *Damn* it!"

"When you got home yesterday, after the funeral, did you see your grandfather's body, or had it been taken away by then?"

"No, I saw it. I wish I hadn't."

"Why?"

"I don't know . . ."

"Was the bed disarranged?"

"No. Well—no. I wouldn't say disarranged."

"Any sign of blood?"

"Was there any blood!" The voice cracked like a slap across her face.

Meekly Jennifer said: "Yes, everywhere—he was always hemmorrhaging—"

Blixen stared back at the window. Jennifer was holding her breath again; her body quivered rhythmically against the hiccups. "All right, turn around," Blixen said.

She was instantly suspicious. "Why?"

So he spun her himself, gripped her waist, hoisted her to his own height. "Is the room any different?"

She put her fingers into his hands, but didn't try to fight him. The soft explosions convulsed her rib cage. "Different how?"

"Is there anything strange around the window?"

"No . . ."

"Tell me exactly what you see."

"Well—the dresser—the four paper flowers—the base—Kenny—"

He nearly dropped her. "*Kenny?*"

She was waving at the reflection in the window. "Hoo-hoo—"

Blixen turned. A long-haired boy in a headache band, a striped tank top, and torn work pants was crawling stiffly out of a '52 Cadillac.

"Put me down, put me down," Jennifer ordered.

Blixen lowered her to the lawn and she went galloping like a colt down the bank to crash exuberantly into the boy, who glowered over her head at Blixen, but allowed himself to be pulled back across the yard toward the colonial house. He was unco-ordinated and parenthesis-shaped, fashionably cadaverous, designed to grate on the Establishment blackboard like a fingernail. Beside him, Jennifer capered and glowed with pride. "This is Ken," she called.

"Hello, Ken . . ."

He mumbled something, perhaps a greeting, and shifted his sullen, shy eyes to the girl for reassurance again.

"We're going out to the track," Jennifer explained to Blixen.

"Right. Good luck."

She hesitated. "Are you okay?"

"Of course."

"What did you want to know about Grampa for?"

"Crazy brainstorm. Don't worry about it."

"Well, yes, but—" She scowled, dissatisfied.

"Put three rocks in your mouth, stand on your head, and say the first ten words of the Yajur-Veda backward," Kenneth growled.

Jennifer peered at him.

"For hiccups."

"God, I'd rather have the hiccups." She tore off, hiccuping, to the house. "I just want to go to the bathroom *once* more, okay! Wait for me!"

The day had grown heavy and smoggish; there would be an alert in the East Valleys before noon. The men stood at right angles to each other, mute as foreigners, looking into the deep distances the generation gap made.

"Well," Blixen said. "Let's see—they're running out at Arcadia these days, aren't they?"

Kenneth looked around cautiously, ready, apparently, to dodge if Blixen should turn dangerous. "Yeah, Santa Anita," he said.

"I understand you had a pretty good day Sunday."

Bubble gum flared on the pale lips, popped.

"Gospel according to Bert Crouch," Blixen said.

"I did all right."

"Several hundred dollars sounds better than all right."

"You win some, you lose some, it all evens out."

"Karma," Blixen said.

A corset-pink bubble grew out of the pursed mouth like an aneurysm.

"Isn't that what karma is?" Blixen asked. "Eventual justice?"

Shrugging, Ken scrubbed at his chin.

"I thought you were an expert on karma."

"Who told you that?"

"Jennifer."

"Why?"

"She said you prophesied her father's death."

"Bull."

"Didn't you?" Blixen asked.

"If you're a cop," Kenneth said, "show me your I.D."

"Didn't she tell you who I was?"

"I didn't catch it."

"I worked with Chet at the studio. My name is Blixen."

"Oh." It might have made a faint difference. The tilt of the hairy head seemed a shade less truculent.

"You know," Blixen said, "nobody gets along with his girl friend's father."

It appeared to amuse him. "Is that a fact."

"Chet may have thought she was too young to chase around. I think he loved her—"

"*Loved* her!" Astonishment and passion took him by surprise, wrecked his cool.

"I think he loved her, yes—"

"That bastard never—do you know who that mother loved? Himself!"

"I know, but—"

"Everything else was property! *His* wife! *His* daughter!" Snorting, Ken spat the red gum into his hand and threw it violently up the street. "Everything was buy and sell to that—"

"Did he try to buy and sell you?" Blixen asked.

For a moment Ken teetered on the balls of his feet, ready to take off, to run up the street after the gum, or over to the house, or back to the car. Then, flushing, he forced his hands into his tight front pockets. "I didn't think that son-of-a-bitch could still make me so mad—"

"What happened?"

"Show and tell time," Kenneth said, and laughed and looked at Blixen. "All right." He worked a new paper-wrapped wad of bubble gum out of his pocket, began to peel it. "Yeah, he tried to buy and sell me both." Musing, he nibbled at the gum. "Got any kids?"

"No."

"If you had a kid," Ken said, "and she was seeing some cat you didn't like, what would you do about it?"

"I think I'd have a little talk with her."

"Guess who that flaked-out hamburger had a talk with?"

"Your employer."

"That's close. He went to see my old lady." Chewing, Ken

squinted at the white ranch house. "Okay, she don't understand much English. He scared the piss out of her. He said I was screwing his little girl and she was under age and he'd tell my parole officer if she didn't get me to stop."

"How'd he find out you had a record?"

"He found out. I don't know." Impatiently Ken blew a bubble, sucked it in. "Anyway, she just stood and hollered Slav at him, so he went to the P.O. anyway. P.O asks him if he's got any proof, is the girl pregnant or anything, and he has to say no, so the P.O. tells him to relax, he'll have a little chat with me. Which is the first time I even knew the goddamn maniac *objected*."

"He'd never talked to you directly about it?"

"Never said a goddamn word." Ken shook his head wearily. "So I went to see *him*. Well, he hemmed and hawed around, he said it wasn't *me* he objected to, it was Jen's age. He said he didn't think I'd like her to hear about all the trouble I'd been in, and I said, are you kidding? That's the first thing we talked about. Then he said he'd have to tell the laundry, and I said, go, man, they could probably fill him in on some crap he hadn't even picked up yet. . . . Well, the poor bastard looked like he was going to cry. . . . So he takes a deep breath and he asks me how I'd like to earn a couple of bucks— a hundred dollars—"

"A—"

"Well, I tell him to lay it on me, so he says, all right, fifty to spy on somebody and fifty after that to leave town."

Blixen paused with his handkerchief halfway to his nose.

"I advised him to shove it up his ass and light it," Ken said.

Slowly Blixen wiped his nose, put the handkerchief away. "Spy on who?" he asked. "Or did he give you a name?"

"He said he wanted me to watch his wife."

"His wife . . ."

"Oh, this was a very sweet character," Ken said. "I guess he thought she was futzing around a little."

"What else did he—"

"That's all he come up with," Ken said, and, brightening, grinned as the girl came tumbling out of the house and across the lawn to them. "We thought you fell in, chickie," he said.

"I had to lock everything up—"

"Now *I* have to go."

"Tough. Pick a bush. Unless you want me to break back in."

"Don't you have a key?"

"They won't *give* me one," Jennifer complained. "Can't you hold it?"

"Some vulgar conversation—"

"Wait a minute," Blixen said, "wait a minute, *wait* a minute—" and then jumped when the girl gave a cry of pain and alarm and tried to pull her forearm out of his grip. He released her. "What did you say?"

"When—?"

"You've *never* had a key?"

"No . . ."

"Jen, where were you when you heard about Chet?"

Scared, she said: "Well—at Gail's. . . . Mom called from San Urbano—"

"You couldn't get in your house—"

"Nobody was home . . ."

"By God," Blixen said, "by God . . ." He spun on his heel and strode back toward the colonial house.

"Jen . . ." Kenneth began uneasily, but Jennifer squeezed past him and scuttled after Blixen.

"What's the matter—?"

Blixen was staring through the ferns into the bedroom. "Your grandfather was killed," he said, "because he saw something he shouldn't have that morning—before they took him to the hospital—"

"Saw *what?*"

"Now what was it that *Lupe* saw?" Blixen cupped his hands around his eyes and pressed his nose to the pane. There was nothing close to the window except the four huge paper flowers, crinkled and dusty—orange, yellow, red, green. Four. "Four?" Blixen said.

"What—?"

"Where's the fifth?"

"Fifth *what?*"

"Flower, flower! There were five flowers in that vase day before yesterday—"

"Well—but—"

"Hey, what's this?" Ken muttered, and Jennifer whirled to stare at the street, and grabbed Blixen's sleeve and said: "Holy moley . . ."

Blixen turned.

Robert's station wagon had rounded the corner and was bumping erratically down the cul-de-sac, on the curb and off, smashing into trash cans, digging up the lawns.

"Is it Aunt Gail?"

"Lady's drunk," Ken said.

"Stay here," Blixen commanded, and ran across the yard to where the car had sideswiped an oak and come to rest.

He hauled open the driver's door. Gail, alone, smelling like a distillery, had collapsed over the steering wheel. Blixen touched her forehead, probed for the pulse in her throat.

"You get your bloody damn hands off me," Gail said.

"Where's Robert?"

The heavy head turned; the bloodshot eyes flicked over his. "You knew all the time. Did you laugh? About the woman in love?"

"Give me your hand . . ."

"Lay one finger on me and I'll tear your bloody balls off and beat you to death with 'em. Get away. Get away."

"Where's Robert, Gail?"

"How the hell would I know? Buggering some pretty boy. My husband, the fag."

"Let's talk about it inside."

"Let's talk about it here. He said you told him to tell me."

"I thought he needed help. I thought you could help him."

"Help." A tear swelled over one eyelid. "I wanted to kill him. Let's have a drink, he said, I've got a secret for you, I'm a fairy. No —homosexual, he said." She stopped, jaw clenched. "Freak . . ."

Despairing, Blixen said: "Is that what you called him?"

"I called him worse than that. I told him he could take his sodomized little body and dump it in the river if he wanted, but he'd better not try to come back to me."

"Where is he?" Blixen shouted. He knew he was shaking her; her head wobbled back and forth, her eyes were shocked. "Where did you leave him!"

"The Strip. St. Ives Hotel—"

He pushed her away, ran toward his own car.

On the bank, Kenneth and Jennifer were watching, wide-eyed.

"Take care of her!" Blixen shouted, and was gone . . .

XXXI

They stood in casual sun-struck groups, like spectators at an air fair, hands to their eyes and necks craned. For the most part they were well behaved and quiet; what bustle there was came from the circling, restless police and the open-shirted firemen trying to haul the net into place. Now and then someone would call for a little action, and laughter would ripple up and down the block, but if the man on the ledge heard the needling, he gave no sign of it.

Sheriff's deputies were diverting cars off Sunset as far east as La

Cienega, so Blixen double-parked in a yellow zone and slipped past the county sawhorses while everyone was attempting to cope with a majestic negro who claimed to be kin to the mayor and said that no one was about to detour him while there was life left in his black body.

Fries had taken up a position on the southern side of the street, in front of a candy store, where he could watch Robert through binoculars, though when Blixen reached him he had dropped the glasses and was rubbing his sore eyes with his knuckles like a sleepy urchin.

"All right, what the hell happened?" Blixen snapped.

"Great," Fries said, "that's all I need, your nagging." He lowered his hand. "How did you get past my line?"

"Bribery," Blixen said. "I asked you a question."

Again Fries raised the binoculars, centered them on the fourth-floor ledge. "I don't know what happened," he said. "My men followed him and his crazy wife here. They went into the bar and had a couple of drinks and started yelling at each other. The wife left and Muir went upstairs to the men's room and crawled out the window."

"With your bloodhounds watching?"

"They didn't go in. There was no other exit. They figured it was a natural enough action on his part—"

"How natural did they figure it was for him to pick a lavatory on the fourth floor?"

"Now that you mention it," Fries said, "it sounds like they didn't think at all."

"Why didn't they arrest him in the bar?"

"They were waiting for the warrant." Fries tapped his breast pocket. "It just got here."

"Then I'd suggest you tear it up."

"I'll do that," Fries said.

"He's innocent," Blixen said.

"Yeah, you told me," Fries said.

"Sergeant, I know now why Lupe was killed—"

"So do I. She was killed because she saw that man"—Fries pointed—"with a bottle of poison—"

"And why should that surprise her?" Blixen demanded. "It was his poison. He's had it around there for months."

"All right, she saw him doing something else equally—"

"She was killed," Blixen said, "because she figured out how the old man had been murdered and because she certainly would have realized who Bruce's murderer was within a matter of days—"

"Bruce Muir died of cancer of the—"

"Wrong. A sharp thin metal rod was pushed into his brain or his spine sometime after eleven o'clock Tuesday morning."

"Oh, for Christ's sake," Fries groaned.

"Was there an autopsy?"

"No! There was no need for—"

"I want one performed now."

"Look," Fries sputtered, "look—*look—*"

"And then tell me this," Blixen said. "If you find he *was* murdered, tell me how Robert Muir could have gotten away from your tail long enough to do the job. Or why he'd want to do the job in the first place. Or why he'd want to *hire* somebody to do the job—"

"This is the goddamndest, most asinine—"

"Are you going to order the autopsy?"

"No!"

"Tell them the murder weapon was the metal stem of a Mexican paper flower. It may have been inserted through the old man's ear—"

"What in the hell makes you think—"

"That's what Lupe saw at the window," Blixen said. "The vase of paper flowers. And she saw that one of them was gone. And she would have remembered sooner or later who the last person in the room had been—"

"And who was that, Sherlock?"

"The murderer."

"And who was the murderer?"

Blixen told him.

Fries stared. "I don't know whether to commit you or laugh—"

"Just order the autopsy."

"But why kill a man with terminal cancer!"

"Because he *had* seen something through the window."

"Seen what!"

"Something that could have wrecked the murderer's alibi, probably."

"Then why didn't the old man tell the police—"

"He didn't know the significance of what he'd seen, Sergeant. Because he didn't know Chettie was dead. But he would have had to be told sooner or later. He might have lived another week—"

A sigh swept through the watching crowd. Fries snapped the binoculars to his eyes again.

Robert had leaned forward.

"Listen—" Blixen said, "will they let me through up there? I've got to talk to him—"

Fries measured him for a moment, then drew a card out of his pocket, scribbled on it. "Show 'em this."

Holding the card, Blixen started backward across the street. "You're looking for a wire about two feet long! The paper on the flower end was pink crepe!"

"Crepe . . ." Fries repeated.

"One other thing," Blixen added. "Ask the lab if they ever classified the blood they found on the sweat shirt—"

"The what on the sweat shirt—?"

"The blood," Blixen called, "the blood! Ask them about Muir's blood—!"

And he vanished into the hotel.

XXXII

Robert had made it clear that he'd kill himself at the first hint of interference, so no effort had been made to reach him through the lavatory since the first shaky attempt.

"He's on a six-inch ledge about a foot and a half to the right of the window," the deputy in charge told Blixen. "What he's hanging onto I can't imagine. I never did notice. I tried to offer him a cigarette, but the minute he seen my hand he said he'd jump if I didn't clear the toilet so I moved everybody back to the hall."

"How long has he been out there?"

"Fifty-two minutes."

"Is this door locked?"

"No, sir, but I strongly advise you not to fool around. I don't think he was kidding."

"Yes, would you give me the cigarettes, please," Blixen said, and took them, and pushed the door open. "Thank you."

The lavatory was large and light. The frosted pane over the neat line of urinals had been shoved up and there were marks of shoe rubber on the cream-colored sill. A pigeon soared past in, looked in, and flapped off. "Robert?" Blixen said. "It's Nils. Can you hear me?"

No answer.

"I'm alone. I'd like to talk to you."

No answer.

"My God, I hope I'm not *that* alone," Blixen said.

There was something—not a laugh, although almost a laugh. A snort.

"I won't try to reach you, Robert," Blixen said, "but I'd rather not shout. I'm coming over the the window, okay?"

No answer.

"Okay," Blixen said. Face turned, listening for the slightest scrape of shoes against the ledge, a sigh from the street, he crossed the dazzling linoleum floor. The urinals were glossy and cool under his palms. Turtle-slow, he pushed his head out the window.

Robert was pressed against the wall, gazing south toward the jumbled Los Angeles skyline. His face was drawn and ashen. The wind plucked at his trouser-knees. Below him, the net looked like a handkerchief in the gutter, absurdly small. He wasn't hanging on to anything; his hands were flat against the yellow brick, reach to push.

"How about that cigarette now," Blixen said.

At first he presumed there would be no answer to that either, but then he saw the faintest nod of Robert's head, and he withdrew into the lavatory, lit a cigarette, leaned out again with it.

Robert held his fingers a little away from the wall and Blixen, straining, passed the cigarette to them. "Thank you," Robert whispered.

"Robert, I'm going to climb into the window where you can see me," Blixen said. "Don't panic."

"Don't *you* panic," Robert said.

Stolidly, never looking down, Blixen hoisted himself onto the sill, rested his back against the sash, facing Robert. Thin cries rose from the street.

"They're yelling, 'Jump! Jump!'" Robert said.

"They're going to be disappointed."

"No, they're not."

It was cooler up here than Blixen had anticipated it would be. A steady light wind blew from the west. Robert smoked silently, coughed once, and began to laugh.

"What?" Blixen said.

Waggling the cigarette, Robert said: "I was just thinking that I'm killing myself with these things."

"It's true. You are."

"You figure they'll get me before I hit the pavement?"

"No question about it," Blixen said. "Because you aren't going to hit the pavement."

Robert drew gently on the cigarette. "That's a terribly foolish dare to make, Nils, to a man in my position."

"I'm not daring you to jump. Or miss the net."

"No?"

"I've got a tougher one than that for you. I want you to re-examine your fight with Gail."

"I don't want to talk about that," Robert said.

"I'll bet you don't."

"You don't know what went on."

"I can imagine."

"No, you can't," Robert said. "She got worse and worse. She started yelling—" He shut his mouth.

"Robert," Blixen said, "your dad was quite a reactionary, wasn't he."

No answer.

"Is your neighborhood integrated?" Blixen waited for a moment and then shrugged. "Well. I know it is. . . . What was your dad's attitude toward the first black family that moved in?"

Robert flipped the cigarette out and away, staring straight ahead.

"Did he accept them?"

"He raised hell," Robert said.

"Kicked and screamed?"

"I don't know what you want me to say."

"I want you to ask yourself why he kicked and screamed."

"I don't know. I'm not a psychologist."

"You don't have to be a psychologist. You've got eyes and ears. You know what pathological disgust tends to cover."

"No—"

"Robert—"

"If you mean attraction—"

"That's what I mean."

"Give me another cigarette."

Blixen lit one, passed it over.

Robert spat a shred of tobacco off the tip of his tongue. "There's no parallel," he said. "Gail wasn't attracted to *anything* I said! She didn't almost vomit because of a hidden lust for gays—"

"Then why did she almost vomit?"

"I can think of a dozen reasons. She was hurt—"

"Do you vomit when you're hurt?"

"She was disgusted! She thought I was lying when I said I loved her all those years—"

"*Were* you lying?"

"No!"

"Then she'd have known that."

"Nils—!" Robert said and stopped. He swayed back and forth, his fingers testing the stone behind him.

Blixen waited.

"You don't *know* she's homosexual herself," Robert said.

"No. I don't. She may not be. She probably isn't."

"Then—"

"It isn't a question of what she is, Robert. It's a question of what she fears she might be."

"What's your point?"

"That human beings are infinitely complex," Blixen said. "Infinitely vulnerable. Infinitely inclined to hide behind masks. You dropped yours. Gail wasn't ready for it."

"She saw a monster."

"Couldn't that enormous reaction of hers indicate that she might have seen Gail?"

Again and again the fingers pressed the stone.

"Robert," Blixen said, "we're not dealing with a fool here, a clod. She was drunk and she was scared. What happens when she sobers up and thinks the thing through and sees what she's done?"

"Listen, I'd be better out of her life," Robert said.

"Maybe you would," Blixen agreed. "But aren't there better ways of leaving it than this?"

"Anyway," Robert said restlessly, "it isn't just that. Just her. It's—"

"What?"

"Everything."

"Are you ashamed of your homosexuality?"

"No!"

Blixen tried to find a more comfortable spot for his back. "It's never easy belonging to an unpopular minority. How would you like to have been an uppity black fifty years ago in Mississippi?"

Robert was still able to muster a partial smile. "I think I'd have worn white-face and stayed in the closet," he said.

"All right, but at least you can join the Gay Liberation Front without expecting to be lynched. Can't you?"

"What can I expect to have happen to a fratricide?"

"Did you kill your brother?"

"No—but that won't stop Fries from arresting me."

"*That* won't," Blixen replied, "although a talk with the real murderer might."

Snapping his head around, Robert said: "*Real* murderer?"

Blixen nodded.

Slowly Robert straightened. "You know who killed Chettie?"

"Chettie," Blixen said, "and Lupe—and your dad—"

"My—!"

"Bruce was stabbed to death because he could have wrecked the murderer's alibi."

"I don't understand—"

"It's a long story—"

"Well—who—"

"Come inside, Robert," Blixen said, "and I'll tell you."

A truck backfired in the street below. The wind had risen. The same pigeon was back, crooked-winged and fishy-eyed, hovering cagily.

"You know what I ought to do," Robert said finally. "I ought to dive off this ledge right now and take you with me."

"Right," Blixen said.

"That's a very cheap shot, Nils."

"Right," Blixen said.

Still studying him, Robert said: "And it's not going to work. Keep your goddamn secrets."

"Okay," Blixen said.

The pigeon circled and disappeared. The sun-warmed bricks were cooling. There was a smell of evening in the air, a taste of fog and salt from Santa Monica.

"I don't believe you know the answer anyway," Robert said.

"Getting chilly up here," Blixen said.

"Give me one clue," Robert said, "if you know so goddamned much."

"Clue," Blixen repeated. "Okay. Not long ago somebody bet me that when all the facts were in, we'd find a woman at the bottom of this business. He was right."

"What woman?"

"Wanda."

Robert continued to regard him unblinkingly.

"More?" Blixen asked.

"Go ahead, Scheherazade."

"If there's a key word to this case," Blixen said, "it's love. It was a very operatic case. The panting lover, the guilty wife, the jealous husband—"

"Em and Wanda," Robert said.

"Yes."

"It didn't shock anybody. We all knew about it."

"It shocked your dad."

"He never said anything—"

"Maybe not to you," Blixen said. "But he saw Em and Wanda exchanging a note—and he told Chettie—"

"Chettie!"

"And the fat was in the fire. Because Chettie couldn't ignore the situation any longer. So he decided to try to catch his wife and his brother *in flagrante delicto*. And it cost him his life."

After a moment Robert said: "You're suggesting that that's why he went to San Urbano? To give them a clear field?"

"To set his trap, yes."

Robert shook his head slowly, stubbornly, but he remained silent.

"He'd already," Blixen continued, "tried to bribe Kenny Kuszleika to spy on them, but Ken had said no. So he turned to his brother—"

"Spencer? Spencer was in Vegas."

"Not on Saturday," Blixen said. "Spencer had flown to L.A. Saturday morning."

"Why?"

"I won't know why. But I can guess. He'd been gambling—and he'd probably been losing. So he decided to ask for a little family help. He called Chettie. And Chettie said, sure, he could let him have three hundred or so—if Spence would help him play a trick on Wanda—"

But again Robert was shaking his head. "Nils, you've got the wrong man," he insisted. "Spencer would never in the world have agreed to spy on someone no matter how much money he needed—"

"He wasn't asked that," Blixen said. "Chettie had thought of a better idea by then. He'd decided to stay home and do the spying himself—"

Bewildered, Robert said: "But Chettie took the bus to San Urbano on Saturday—"

"No," Blixen said. "Spencer took the bus to San Urbano."

The wind sighed down the street. Some teen-agers below, in a picnic mood, had begun a chant: "Jump, coward, jump, coward."

"You see, that's the heart of the matter," Blixen said. "Understand that, and you understand it all."

"I don't understand a bloody thing," Robert said.

"All right, let me try to reconstruct it for you." Blixen rearranged his tormented bones, thinking. "Now—a lot of what I say will have to be speculation until we talk to Spencer. But I believe it all happened more or less like this. . . . Chettie asked Spencer to meet him at the bus station on Vine around half-past ten Saturday morning. He said he had a crazy proposition for his brother. He said he wanted to fool Wanda into thinking he'd gone out to San Urbano. Little domestic joke. But the problem was that Wanda usually called the College Inn to make sure he'd gotten there safely, and if he wasn't there to answer, the whole surprise would be spoiled. However, if *Spence* were there to answer—and so on. Do you follow me?"

Robert nodded.

"Could you tell Spence from Chettie over the telephone?" Blixen asked.

"No . . ."

"All right. Spencer needed the loan. Chettie needed the voice. So the deal was made."

"And you're saying that that's what happened to Chettie's four hundred dollars—"

"That's what happened to most of it."

"But there was no money for the hospital—"

"Let me take this in sequence—"

"Go on."

Blixen pondered. "Anyway, Spencer threw himself into the game like a good stunt man should. He'd doubled half the stars in TV. There was no reason he couldn't double his own brother. They looked alike—you *all* look alike—except for Em, with the beard—and even someone who knew them well couldn't tell their voices apart over the phone. He'd flown in—he didn't have a car—but he could take the bus that was already there waiting. It was probably Spencer, by the way, who insisted on taking the overnight bag and Chettie's sweat shirt, too."

"Why?"

"Verisimilitude. Fun." Blixen shrugged. "He's an actor. . . . I talked to the woman who sat beside him on the ride out. She said that he was having the time of his life, that he was like a little boy trying to get away with something forbidden. . . ."

"Hadn't the police talked to this woman?"

"Probably."

"Wouldn't they show her a picture of Chettie?"

"Of course."

"Then why couldn't she see the difference?"

"She saw a picture that resembled the man who sat beside her. He'd told her his name, his occupation. He was a TV editor named Chet Muir, as far as she was concerned. Do you pay more attention than that?"

"Cigarette," Robert said.

Blixen lit another, passed it along.

"All right," Robert said. "So what was Chettie doing all this time?"

"Waiting," Blixen said. "Drinking an Alka-Seltzer for his tense stomach. Dying."

Slowly Robert looked around.

"It wasn't *just* an Alka-Seltzer," Blixen said. "Someone he knew and trusted had borrowed the oxalic acid from your garage and poured a lethal dose into his drink."

Staring, Robert said: "But Chet must have known—"

"He certainly knew something was wrong," Blixen agreed. "On the other hand, his ulcer had been giving him terrible trouble. It might have been a perforation. I don't think he suspected poison at first—or the poisoner. The one thing he was certain of was that he mustn't be found throwing up all around the house after he'd set off with so much hoopla for San Urbano. So he called a cab—and that, I imagine, took all the money he had left. . . ."

"What time was this?"

"About eleven-thirty. He got to the San Urbano terminal at twelve—"

"Thirty minutes between Hollywood and San Urbano? That's impossible!"

"I thought it was, too—until my lawyer assured me he'd done it in less than that last Sunday."

"Jump, cowards, jump, cowards!" chanted the children.

Robert wiped his mouth on the back of his hand. "All right, go ahead."

"He was waiting when the bus got in. He signaled for his brother to meet him in the men's room. He explained what had happened— that his ulcer was acting up and that he'd have to postpone the surprise—he took back the overnight bag and the sweat shirt—and he sent Spencer on his way."

"But—why didn't Spencer tell us all this—"

"Two reasons, I think," Blixen said. "Originally Spencer hadn't wanted his dad to know that he'd been gambling again or that he'd come to town to borrow more money. After Bruce died, I think Spencer realized that he'd be in an absolutely untenable position with the police if he confessed that he'd been with Chettie in San Urbano half an hour before he died."

"So Spencer left—and Chettie—"

"Chettie probably intended at first to go on to the College Inn. But obviously the pain was too severe. So he decided to look for a hospital. . . ."

"And by then," Robert finished, "it was too late. . . ."

"Yes."

After a moment Robert said: "You tell a hell of a yarn, Scheherazade. You ought to be in TV."

"Don't you believe it?"

"Jump, cowards, jump, cowards!" piped the little voices.

"I don't know," Robert said. "I still can't see a face behind—"

The lavatory door slapped against the wall.

"It's all right!" Blixen snapped. And to Fries: "Stay back, Sergeant!"

In the street, even the chanters fell silent.

The wind swirled and sang against the wall.

Teetering, Robert gazed down at the upturned faces.

"He's stopped in the doorway, Robert," Blixen said.

"Who is it?"

"Fries."

"I'm not going back with him."

"He isn't here to take you back." Blixen turned his head. "Are you?"

"I'm here primarily to apologize, Mr. Muir," Fries said.

"Did you hear that?" Blixen asked.

No answer.

Blixen glanced at Fries. "Where's the suspect?"

"Out in the hall," Fries replied. "My men went by the house. They found the wire probe in the attic. Some of the pink paper. We have a confession. There was no trouble."

"What about the blood on the sweat shirt?"

"AB. Chet Muir's type was O."

"Brother Spencer's?"

"AB," Fries said.

"Did you hear *that?*" Blixen asked.

"Yes," Robert whispered.

Blixen held his hand out. "Then come inside."

Slowly Robert turned his head. Slowly his hand lifted. Blixen gripped it, smiling.

The angry groans from the street outlasted the scattered timid applause.

"Nils . . ."

"Yes."

"Who did it?"

"Haven't you guessed?"

"I'm not sure . . ."

Glancing at Fries, Blixen said: "Will you bring the murderer in, Sergeant? Just the murderer."

Fries nodded, motioned.

A figure hesitated in the doorway.

XXXIII

"Hello, Mr. Blixen," Mr. Crouch said.

"Hello, Bert."

Incredulously, Robert leaned against the window sash. He looked at Blixen, and then back at the doorway.

The Donald Meek face fought against crumbling. "Mr. Muir," he said, "I do want to assure you that your father never felt one second of pain. Nothing. I think I can promise you that."

"Sergeant?" Blixen inquired.

Nodding, Fries said: "The rod was driven into the back of the neck, just below the skull. It would have been very quick."

Robert's face was drained. "And what can you promise us about Lupe?"

"I'll probably go to hell for Lupe," said Mr. Crouch.

"Okay," Fries said. "Mr. Muir, do you want any help getting home? How do you feel? Would you like to see a doctor?"

"No."

"Well—" Fries said, and took Mr. Crouch by the arm.

"Sergeant, just a second," Blixen said. "How illegal would it be to ask your prisoner a couple of final questions?"

"Totally," Fries answered.

"Has he been warned?"

"He told me my rights," said Mr. Crouch. "I've got a lawyer coming over. I'm fine."

"Look behind you," Blixen said.

Mr. Crouch craned his neck. In the open doorway, a uniformed deputy was taking notes. "Oh, I understand all that," Mr. Crouch said impatiently. "How can it matter now? Go ahead."

Blixen glanced at Fries, who shrugged and leaned against the wall. "All right," Blixen said. "First of all—what was it the old man saw, Bert, that made him so dangerous?"

"Me," Mr. Crouch said. "Talking to Chet when I picked up the gray suit Saturday morning."

"When was this?"

"This was about twenty minutes past eleven."

"When Chettie was supposed to be halfway to San Urbano?"

"Yes."

"Which would have cleared Robert," Fries said, "and sent us straight to *your* door."

"Yes."

"Did you know about Spencer's part in the plot?" Blixen asked.

Mr. Crouch peered uncertainly at him. "What part?"

"Spencer took Chet's place on the bus."

After a moment Mr. Crouch said: "No, I never heard that."

"Lucky Spencer," Robert said.

Mr. Crouch glanced at him and then returned his gaze to Blixen. "Why didn't Spencer say something?"

"He didn't want to be implicated."

"All Chester told me," Mr. Crouch said slowly, "was that Wanda thought he was in San Urbano and he was going to sneak in later and catch Emmett and her together. I just figured he rushed over there in a cab after I left and that everybody assumed he'd ridden out on the bus—"

"Wait a minute," Robert said. "Chettie told *you* he was going to sneak in on Emmett and Wanda?"

"Yes, he did."

"When?"

"When I talked to him the Saturday before." Mr. Crouch paused. "That's when I made up my mind once and for all I'd have to kill him."

"But my God," Robert exploded, "why the hell would Chettie take *you* into his confidence!" Appealing to Blixen, he said: "Does that make any sense?"

"Oh, I think it might," Blixen replied. "To a blackmailer."

"How'd you guess that?" Mr. Crouch asked curiously.

"Is it true?"

"Spang in the gold."

"He wanted you to do the spying, then . . ."

"That was the arrangement," Mr. Crouch confirmed, "clear up until Wednesday. Then he called me and said he'd do it himself. So I said fine and I poured myself a vialful of your oxalic acid, Mr. Muir, on my next delivery day."

"Thursday," Robert said.

"Yes, sir."

Fries had unstrapped his own notebook and was writing rapidly. "Now about this blackmail—"

"Yes, sir," Mr. Crouch said and glanced at Blixen. "I'll bet you don't know what it was he had on me. Do you?"

"I'll bet it was robbery," Blixen said.

"Damn, you're good," said Mr. Crouch.

Bewildered, Robert said: "*What* robbery?"

Blixen glanced at him. "Wanda's house was robbed just before Christmas. Don't you remember?"

"Well—they didn't get anything. . . . Couple of dollars—"

"The money wasn't important," Blixen said. "It was the handbag the robber wanted."

"And the handkerchief . . ." Mr. Crouch murmured. "The cough drops. The stub of a pencil she'd used . . ."

Robert's jaw had dropped.

Mr. Crouch smiled tiredly at him. "Didn't you ever collect mementoes?" he asked.

"Maybe he was never star-struck, Bert," Blixen said.

"Then I'm sorry for him. . . ."

"How did Chettie find out you were the robber?"

"He caught me in her room two weeks later. With her gloves in my pocket."

"And he never reported you?" Fries asked.

"No."

"That was Chettie's way," Blixen said. "He'd save up his black-mail items like I.O.U.'s, until he needed them—"

"Vicious man," Mr. Crouch said almost to himself. "Morally vicious. Physically vicious. He beat her, you know. . . ."

"Yes, you told me," Blixen said.

Mr. Crouch looked up. "I told you a lot without knowing it, didn't I. . . ."

"You told me you loved her. That was a lot. It gave me that motive I needed when I finally began to put two and two together."

"I thought I always hid everything pretty well—"

"I wonder how many casual fans would have remembered *Daughter of the Red Death*, Bert? The expert I consulted had to go to an archivist for the plot. You tripped over Ramsay Ames, but you knew everything there was to know about Wanda Mills. Seemed significant to me."

"Where else did I trip?"

"With Wanda?"

"With anything."

Blixen thought. "Well, actually," he said, "Chet tripped you."

Fries frowned. "Chet?"

"I guess I don't understand," Mr. Crouch said. "How?"

"By lowering the garage door that morning after you left."

Mr. Crouch stared at him intently for a moment more, and then, straightening, shook his head.

"It's automatic," Blixen said. "Remote-controlled."

"I know—"

"All right—you told me you'd picked up the gray suit in the garage—"

"That's true. I did."

"But the garage door was down when Wanda and Emmett drove up that rainy night."

"Well?" Mr. Crouch said, and peered at Fries and Robert and then back to Blixen. "What about it?"

"Who lowered it?" Blixen asked.

"Now wait a minute," Fries said gruffly. "*Anybody* could have low—"

But Robert had fixed his eyes on Blixen's. "No," he said softly. And then: "By God, *no!*"

"Well—"

"*Chettie* lowered it!" Robert said. "The car was gone. So it couldn't have been shut from the dashboard. Well, don't you see? The only other button is in the house!"

"Okay," Fries said, "one of the family walked in, pressed the button—"

"The house was locked! Double-locked! And the only ones with keys were Chet and Wanda!"

"And since Wanda," Blixen said, "went directly from her quilting class to San Urbano—"

"Chettie must have been there himself after the laundry was picked up!" Robert finished.

Mr. Crouch took a breath, let it out. "Right," he said. "He was having an Alka-Seltzer when I stopped in. He told me exactly what he was going to do to Wanda when he caught her—so I poured the poison in his glass when he was out of the room—and that was it. . . ." Sighing, Mr. Crouch rubbed his hands over his face. "Of course they'll get it wrong—"

"Who will?" Blixen asked.

"The fan magazines. They'll say it was something sexual. They'll dirty it up. She was like a daughter who never gave me any trouble. She loved Emmett and she was stuck with a man she hated. She needed me like Bette Davis needed George Arliss in *The Man Who Played God*. So I helped her. But they won't understand."

"They might."

"Okay," Mr. Crouch said to Fries. "Oh." He stopped, frowned at Blixen. "You still never got my R.A."

"Um," Blixen said. "Did you ever co-star with a monkey?"

"Hell," said Mr. Crouch. "That's it."

"That's what?" Fries asked.

"Yes, I'm Robert Armstrong," said Mr. Crouch. "*King Kong*. With Fay Wray. There was another of my sweethearts."

"I don't blame you," Blixen said.

"I'll never forget the end of that picture," said Mr. Crouch. "Do you remember it?"

Blixen nodded.

Gently Mr. Crouch said: "They shot Kong down. And Bruce Cabot or somebody says, well, they finally killed him. And Robert Armstrong looks at Fay Wray and he says, oh no, bullets didn't do that . . ." Tears gleamed in the ugly Donald Meek eyes. "No. It was Beauty killed the Beast . . ."

The deputy in the doorway was waiting.

Mr. Crouch smiled once at Blixen and put his arm under Fries's, and walked out and into the hall.

G 4

EPILOGUE

Nothing had altered around the pool on Genesee. The breeze-swept water glittered like coins in the dappled sunlight; a cicada clicked in the pink silk tree.

"More coffee?" Irene asked.

Blixen smiled, shook his head. "Perfectly content. Thank you."

"I'm sorry, I didn't mean to interrupt—" She bent forward on the rustic bench, an elbow on her knee, her chin in her hand.

"Well, that's all, really," Blixen said. "Catalina'll be anticlimactic now that the network's renewed us. Arthur's already a great hero with the Chairman. The Board's promised him all kinds of development money for next season."

"I think that's wonderful."

"So do I."

"Then there were no waves at all from Pablo about Murf?"

"As long as hanky-panky is kept out of the headlines," Blixen said, "Pablo can pretend it doesn't exist."

"I see. Well, that's very American."

"Isn't it."

Hesitating, Irene said: "And—what will happen to Robert and Gail now?"

"I don't know," Blixen said slowly. "They've apologized—and separated. Robert needs a new life style, and Gail needs time to get to know herself."

"Is there time enough in the world for that? For any human being?"

"I wonder."

"What about the others?"

"Ken and Jennifer will grow up. Emmett and Wanda will marry."

"And live happily ever after?"

"I hope so."

"Yes . . ." She shivered, watching the sky.

Solicitously Blixen said: "Are you cold? Shall we go inside?"

"Yes . . ." She stood, took his hand. "By the way," she added, "I've decided to divorce Curtis."

Smiling, silent, Blixen nodded.

On their way to the house, Irene said: "I have another 'by the way.' We still haven't settled Murf's contract. Do you realize that?"

"There's nothing to settle," Blixen replied. "It's eminently fair as it is."

"Oh no, it isn't."

"Oh yes, it is."

"Oh no, it isn't."

The Dutch doors closed behind them.

Somewhere a nightingale started to sing.